Daughters of Green Mountain Gap

Daughters of Green Mountain Gap

A NOVEL

TERI M. BROWN

atmosphere press

This novel is dedicated to my husband, Bruce,
who is fighting a personal medical battle.
Glioblastoma is a disease that continues to baffle
everyone from local healers to the most learned
physicians. Despite his daily struggles, he never fails
to love and support me in my journey as an author.
I will be forever grateful that we found one another.

~

Prologue

Maggie
- January 21, 1894 -

During the daylight hours, she kept herself busy cooking, cleaning, feeding the animals, and chopping firewood. She had even taken to going far up the side of the mountain to hunt for large hardwood limbs to drag back to the homestead. Anything to make her tired enough to sleep.

But when the night came, she would lie awake, visions passing before her eyes like ghosts. Esther holding baby Malcolm. Her beloved Henry with his shirt tied around his waist as he drove in the nails that built their first home. The beautiful, silent face of her stillborn son.

Then would come her daughter, jabbing her finger, flecks of spittle flying from her mouth as she would scream, "You, mother, you killed him."

Sleeping, when she finally succumbed, only led to dreams. Esther begging, "No, please, Maggie. Don't do this. I don't want to die." And then she'd wake in a sweat.

Maggie pulled the door shut to the storeroom with her medicines, knowing she would never practice healing again. Instead, she carved two more notches on her walking stick. She rubbed her thumb across all seventeen indentations, remembering, in vivid detail, her role in each death.

The number was not insignificant. Though her Italian heritage was slim, she remembered the warning. "Seventeen is the number of death. Don't write it down, Maggie. Don't even think it. If'n you do, you're saying your life is over!"

Maggie never really believed it – until now. Now, seventeen people declared in her dreams, "I'm dead. My life is over." Seventeen deaths, she realized, were a direct result of her inadequacies and incompetence. No, she would never again be the granny woman. In fact, she should have never done so to begin with. Her daughter, Carrie Ann, had been right all along.

As if to make her isolation complete, a blizzard, the likes of which Maggie had never experienced, rolled in. She screwed her face into a mocking smile. "Very fitting, Mother Nature."

The sheer immenseness of the snow kept her homebound, leaving Maggie with plenty of time to wrestle with her thoughts. In addition to the specters of those who died because of her, she fought her conscience. How could she make amends when she couldn't bring the dead back to life? How could she ever move forward knowing her hands, the hands tasked to heal, did just the opposite? Then she remembered the utlinowa.

Many years ago, a Cherokee medicine man, Oukonunaka, warned her to be wary of a man exiled from the tribe.

"Waya killed his wife, Awinita, in a fit of anger. Our council considered the best punishment, realizing he was like the utlinowa, the soft-shelled turtle who is too aggressive to live among others of his kind.

"The tribe banished Waya, taking from him his name, his status, his village, his language – everything that made him Cherokee. You may spot him, Maggie, from time to time. He lives alone, no longer speaking. He creeps along the edges of humanity, wishing he had been less like the utlinowa. Beware of him. Do not give him food or shelter."

It was with this memory, she knew what she had to do. Waya's crime was murder – as was hers. But her victims had no voice and no way to demand retribution. So, she would take it upon herself to carry out justice.

"I am no better than Waya. In fact, I am worse. He killed in anger. I, on the other hand, did the opposite of what I was sent to this earth to do. Not in anger, but in carelessness. In foolishness. In incompetence."

Now, when the ghosts of Esther came to her, she begged forgiveness, telling her she would never hurt another.

"I have become an utlinowa. From this day forward, I will live alone. My hands will never touch another. My thoughts will never turn into words for another to hear. My actions will never again cause pain or suffering or death. I cannot bring you back, my dear friend, but I assure you I will never harm another."

By the time the snow began to melt, Maggie knew what she had to do. She packed some of her belongings, just those that would help her eke out the barest exis-tence, and loaded them into the wagon. Then she headed for the tiny cabin built by Henry all those years ago.

The small one-room building stood empty except for the animals who found refuge from the weather. Maggie pushed open the door, hauling in the blankets, one large stockpot, a cast iron pan, and an assortment of other necessities. Then, she made her way to the barn, which was more akin to a lean-to. The years of neglect caused the south wall to collapse.

"It will do," she thought as she led the mule into the space.

Though not banished in the same way as Waya, hav-ing to live among the trees on the edge of civilization, Maggie determined to live out her days in the small cabin. She did not want room and ease and a large garden. She did not want a front porch for sipping lemonade or a kitchen table large enough for guests. She didn't want to be reminded of her family or the storeroom of herbs. She simply wanted to be left alone to atone for her sins.

Chapter 1

Maggie
- October 7, 1892 -

Maggie concentrated on her steps as she hurried through the darkened town, intent on reaching the Stallard place before it was too late – if it wasn't already too late. Her breath came out in puffs, translucent wisps floating in the moonlight, the early freeze suggesting another harsh winter.

She lamented, as she often did, on the entirety of the human race and their inability to use the seasons to their advantage. Cows, horses, pigs, birds – they all gave birth in the spring, so their precious young had the best chance of staying alive. Not so with people. Babies came into the world despite severe winters, influenza outbreaks, and the lack of necessities.

This was Esther's seventh, though only two survived the delivery. Her hips were tiny, making the passageway narrow and unforgiving. Esther's continued survival was miraculous, but Maggie, understanding a woman could only count on so many miracles, quickened her pace.

Maggie didn't fault Esther for seeking out the new doctor in town. Dr. Daniel McKeithen hung his shingle a year earlier, and a good deal of her clients began to frequent his office for their ailments.

The shiny tools and bottled medicines lulled the towns-folk into false security, as though brain fever or consumption wouldn't find them sitting in his showy examination room. Unfortunately, as far as Maggie could tell, his success rate had been no better than her own.

Although Esther followed the doctor's instructions, eating specific foods, avoiding others, resting more than was necessary in Maggie's opinion, and taking a daily tonic, the labor did not progress. Now, twenty-eight hours in, Esther's husband, John, had reached out to Maggie, frantic to save his wife – no longer worried about the baby, who, he felt confident, had succumbed like so many of those who preceded it.

Maggie lived five miles from town in a tiny holler along Ray's Creek in the shadow of Green Mountain Gap. Her family had owned this land as far back as records were kept. Maggie, now in her fifties, intended to live on this homestead until she drew her last breath, much to her daughter's displeasure.

The thought of Carrie Ann caused her to misstep, almost stumble. She found her footing and set off again, pushing toward Esther, though her mind returned to her daughter.

Carrie Ann had been raised in the small valley, in the same home as Maggie, and Maggie's mother, and Maggie's grandmother. Despite this, Carrie Ann was nothing like her progenitors.

She rebelled against tradition and fought to create her own place in the world, rejecting anything that spoke of the past. "Why do you do it like that?" had been a constant refrain as she grew, and the answer, "We've always done it this way," only caused consternation expressed early on with balled-up fists and stamping feet, and in her teen years with glowering eyes and a dismissive about-face.

Carrie Ann moved from the holler into Burnsville at sixteen, getting a job at the general store. Not long after, she married a boy she met from Asheville, who whisked her away, promising her a modern city life full of glamor and sophistication. Nine months later, almost to the day, Josephine Mae Killian arrived.

Although Carrie Ann loved her daughter with a fierceness that surprised her, she did not have the same affinity toward her husband. Tavish was a scoundrel, gambling away his money, drinking, and finding comfort in other women's beds. When the plague ravaged the area and took his life, Carrie Ann moved back home with the toddler.

Maggie loved watching Carrie Ann care for Josie Mae, using a tenderness often missing in their own interactions.

"Come here, you silly little button," she heard Carrie Ann say. "Let Mama show you how."

Then, with loving affection, Carrie Ann helped the child manipulate the knitting needles almost as long as her tiny arms. Of course, Josie Mae was too young to knit, but the joy at being allowed to work with the women was evident in the child's eyes.

Despite her strong connection with Josephine, Carrie Ann yearned for more than the holler had to offer. With nagging and persistence, she convinced Maggie to care for the child while she went to Boston to become a nurse. The stories of Florence Nightingale managed to find a way into the mountains of North Carolina, and Carrie Ann, who craved the new and shoved anything old to the side, intended to bring modern medicine to the area – whether the locals wanted it or not.

Maggie wondered who would greet her at the Stallards'.

Would it be Dr. McKeithen or his assistant – her daughter? Which of the two would be more concerned with her lack of formal education and the herbal blends she concocted than the poor woman who had been laboring, likely in vain, for hours? Regardless, she was going to do what she could to save Esther's life.

* * *

Maggie's shoulders hunched forward over the wooden railing of the back porch. The sunlight filtered through the thick stand of pines, melting the ice frozen in the wagon wheel ruts. She drew a deep breath, blowing it out through pursed lips as the child's wail pierced the air.

She had no idea who would take credit for the infant's survival as both she and the doctor worked together to bring the babe into the world. When Maggie arrived, Dr. McKeithen had a grasp on a tiny foot. "Stop," she yelled, startling him and Carrie Ann, who was ready to push on Esther's protruding belly on the count of three. "Do you want to kill her?"

"Mama! Step out of the way. This baby is breech. If we don't help Esther now, she and her child will die. We know what we are doing."

Maggie spoke to John in a stern voice. "John. You called me to come because you were afraid for Esther's life. I'm here now, but I won't fight the doctor. It's up to you. Do you want Dr. McKeithen to continue, or do you want me?"

John's mouth opened and closed, his eyes wide, his hands trembling. Quieter now, Maggie said, "John, whatever you choose. It's up to you. But you need to decide. The baby isn't going to last this way, and Esther is in trouble."

John looked from Dr. McKeithen to Maggie and back again before saying in a whisper, so hushed Maggie had to lean in to catch his words, "Save her, Maggie. Oh, please save my Esther." Then he covered his face with his meaty palms, inhaling gulps of air as tears streamed down his face.

Maggie wasted no time and turned to wash her hands as Dr. McKeithen stepped away from the bed. Carrie Ann, not one to give in so easily, complained in a harsh, authoritative voice. "You are not a doctor, Mama. You have no formal training. You haven't read the textbooks. I can't believe you are going to shove aside a professional."

But Maggie was not listening. Instead, she whispered gently to Esther.

"Esther, it's going to be fine. I just need you to breathe in and out, nice and easy. I'm going to push the baby's foot back inside and try to assess how it is positioned. Okay? It's going to hurt, and I'm sorry, but I have to figure out how the baby is lying, or it is not going to make it – or you, either. Deep breath, now, ready?"

She pushed the little limb back toward the womb as she reached her hand into the birth canal. Esther's agony filled the room as she clutched at Maggie's arm. "Stop, Maggie, oh god, stop! Just let me die. Please, just let me die."

Her wails transformed into moans as Maggie sat back. "The baby's hips and left leg are still above the pelvic bone." She turned to the doctor. "Pulling on the leg is not the way to deliver this baby. I know what must be done, but I'm going to need help."

Her pleading eyes bore into the eyes of the man who had spent years learning to be a physician. He hesitated momentarily, assessing the woman in her muddy boots and faded blue dress while Carrie Ann continued to plead her case to the doctor.

"She has no medical training. Everything she does is contrary to what we learned. Before I came back from Boston, she never even washed her hands. Nothing she does is based on science. Instead, she gets her information from old ladies telling their stories from one generation to the next."

However, when he stated, "Tell me what I have to do," Carrie Ann fell silent. Within moments, Dr. McKeithen and Maggie were working as a team. Maggie's small hands guided the infant back toward the womb. The doctor applied pressure from the outside, pushing his large palms against the bump that was the baby. Both ignored Esther's screams.

Once satisfied the child was in the proper position, Maggie began a gentle chant, a cross between a song and a prayer. The Cherokee words were those gleaned from a healer she worked with for many years. Carrie Ann could not tolerate her mother's interference and what she saw as incompetence. Now, instead of trying to convince the doctor, she turned her words to her mother. "This is ridiculous. Can't you see that you've reversed all the hard work Esther did over the last hours? And how do you think mumbling Indian nonsense will help?" She pivoted on one heel to face Dr. McKeithen. "Are you just going to stand there and allow her to do this? This is the kind of thing I've been trying to tell you about. It isn't medicine at all. It's just tomfoolery, and unfortunately, those who believe it are more apt to die than get well."

Dr. McKeithen held up his hand to stop the flow of words and turned back, intent on Esther's transformation. The woman, who had done nothing but wail and writhe in pain for hours, began to take deep, steady breaths as she let her arms fall loose at her sides. Maggie's chanting continued, changing rhythm during contractions. She moved her hands counterclockwise on Esther's abdomen, pressing and releasing to the melody and Esther's breathing.

Without warning, Esther's belly swelled, then lurched, causing the woman to throw open her eyes before gently closing them again with a soft smile. "The baby has turned," Maggie stated to the doctor. And to no one in particular, "Now, the hard work begins."

For the next six hours, Esther labored, slowly pushing the baby out into the world. The child, a boy, was born blue and silent, but Maggie had seen bluer. She cleared the mucus from the baby's mouth and, while crooning encouragements, massaged his arms and legs using enough pressure to create friction between her hand and the infant's skin. One minute passed in silence. Then two. Esther turned toward the wall, unable to bear yet another loss. Still, Maggie crooned and rubbed until Esther's son let out a wail, sending his mother and father to tears. Even stoic Carrie Ann had to turn away and began straightening things that needed no straightening to hide her emotions.

Esther would survive. That's all she knew to do. Her son, Malcolm, named after his great-grandfather, had a fighting chance. Maggie drew another deep breath, trying to summon the energy to walk the five miles back home.

Chapter 2

Carrie Ann
- October 10, 1892 -

Carrie Ann strode down the street, arms swinging in rhythm with the thoughts swirling in her head. She finished visiting Esther and little Malcolm, both of whom were doing well.

"The baby is nursing well," smiled Esther, still weak from the delivery. "My milk came in this morning, nearly drowned the poor dear," she chuckled.

Carrie Ann found nothing amiss with either, and other than giving a few tips for eating properly and getting enough rest, she determined her services were not needed. She excused herself with an air of importance, stating she had other patients who required her assistance.

The white lie hung on her lips as she strode toward home. Dr. McKeithen's office was closed for the afternoon, so Daniel could take advantage of the trout feeding frenzy on the Cane River. Carrie Ann shook her head in disgust.

She met Dr. McKeithen while attending the Boston Training School at Massachusetts General Hospital. Daniel had been two months shy of finishing his degree at Harvard. He spent time every week working under various doctors to receive his clinical hours. This relatively new and somewhat experimental innovation replaced the apprenticeship model.

She was taking her lunch outside when he came bounding across the expansive lawn with another medical student. His loud, breathless words carried easily to Carrie Ann's ears.

"Dr. Fitz is a genius." He shook his head and held up his hand as his companion guffawed. "No, really. He is a genius. You should hear him discuss his understanding of the body and how it functions. He makes sense of the appendix and what happens when it ruptures. And the gallbladder, too. So much wisdom..."

His excited chatter faded as the pair passed, leaving Carrie Ann intrigued. Although she had little knowledge of the appendix, she had overheard the reverent whispers about Dr. Reginald Fitz. This enthusiastic doctor was not the only person raving about Fitz and what he knew.

The next day, as she ate her lunch, the same young man walked by again, this time alone. Though normally aloof, Carrie Ann was too curious about Dr. Fitz to remain quiet. "Hello," she called. Lost in thought, he looked up, swinging his head to find the source of the greeting.

Carrie Ann stood. "I'm Carrie Ann. I'm going to school here to learn to be a nurse. You were talking about Dr. Fitz yesterday." She shrugged lightly. "You were rather excited."

Daniel grinned. "That I was. And am. My name is Daniel McKeithen. I'm studying over at Harvard to become a doctor."

And that's how their friendship started. Although most of their conversations revolved around the medical practices each was learning, they soon discovered a bit about one another's backgrounds. Daniel grew up not far from the university and, from what Carrie Ann could gather, had no experience with the granny woman folk-lore her mother practiced. It was this, in particular, that drew her to him. He was a man of science.

The two finished their schooling within weeks of one another, and Carrie Ann hated for their association to end. However, staying in Boston was not in the plan. She had a child waiting in North Carolina, and her desire had always been to bring modern medicine to her community of Burnsville. Nonetheless, after living in a big city, the mountains seemed particularly uncivilized.

The night before she was to head home, they cele-brated their respective graduations at Atwood and Bacon, a well-known oyster restaurant in town. Although she would never have admitted it for fear of sounding unso-phisticated, she had never tried oysters before coming to Boston. This was only one of many things she would miss when she returned home to Burnsville.

Although she rarely spoke of home, other than to regale Daniel with the most recent achievements of her precocious daughter, her mood, aided by the beer on tap, loosened her tongue on their last night together.

"If I didn't have a daughter back home, I'd stay right here. Everyone seems to realize exactly what they want and exactly how to achieve it. They move with purpose and expectation. Back home?" She shrugged.

Daniel sat back, looking at her thoughtfully. "You've hinted before that Burnsville is different. But, honestly, how different can it be?"

"Not even close." She sighed. "There are more trees than people. There are probably more fish than people, too. Every last person raises their own animals and uses words you've never heard of."

Now Daniel laughed. "That's unlikely. I'm very well-read and have an extensive vocabulary."

Carrie Ann rose to the challenge. "Alright, then tell me what a poke is, but as a noun and not a verb."

Daniel drew his brows together. "If it doesn't mean sticking someone in the side with your finger" – he shrugged his shoulders – "I have no idea."

With glee in her eyes, she stated matter-of-factly, "It means bag. What about bald, and I don't mean hair loss? Or boomer? Or gaum?"

Daniel shook his head.

"Part of the mountain with no trees, red squirrel, and a mess."

As Carrie Ann took a deep breath to offer up another round of words, Daniel held up both hands, a handsome smile creasing his face. "I give up. You win."

Carrie Ann deflated despite the victory. "The people in my town and around it? They've never seen buildings like this." She gestured with her hand in the direction of the city. "They've never heard an orchestra play. Many have never been to school. And unless they've traveled to Asheville, almost forty miles away, they've never been to a real doctor."

Now she looked him in the eyes. "I'm lying to myself when I blame going back home on Josephine. It's more than that. Oh, I love it here. I can imagine myself living here happily for the rest of my life. But Boston doesn't need me. Here, I would be just another nurse. But in Burnsville? There, I could make a real difference. What I've learned here could be the difference between a young mother surviving childbirth and dying."

Daniel nodded, encouraging her to continue. "I haven't told you much about my mama. She's what they call a healer. Like a doctor but without the schooling. She relies on what she knows about plants and roots. She even has crazy ideas that are more like magic than medicine. But she, and the women in my family before her, are all that Burnsville has. I can bring them something better."

Carrie Ann lowered her eyes, feeling foolish. What must Daniel think? She was nothing but a nurse and thought she could save an entire town. She started apologizing, but Daniel reached out his hand, pulling up her chin. "No. Don't. You have nothing to be sorry for. I wish I had your passion, Carrie Ann. You came hundreds of miles and left your child so you could become something useful to those you love. I became a doctor because my parents expected it of me."

He shook his head to stop her from protesting. "No. It's true. Sure, I'm good at what I do. And I've come to enjoy my work, but you? You have this eagerness."

Then, before Carrie Ann comprehended what was happening, he bent his head toward her and kissed her lightly on the lips. She pulled back, shocked, utterly unaware that Daniel saw her as anything more than a colleague.

"I'm sorry," he murmured. "I should probably walk you home. It's getting late, and you have an early train."

Despite a long day ahead, Carrie Ann could not sleep. Her marriage to Tavish was not what she had hoped it would be. The only good thing that came of it was her daughter, and when she moved back home, she did so understanding she would likely remain a widow. When she met Daniel, she believed she had found someone to share her common interest in medicine. Had she missed his signals that he wanted something more? More importantly, did she want something more?

She couldn't decide what to think about the kiss or the apology. Was he sorry that he kissed her suddenly, or simply sorry that he kissed her at all? And what of her? Was she sorry?

Shortly after the sun came up, Daniel knocked on the door of her boarding house. As promised, he was there to take her to the railroad station. Despite his smile and easy conversation, the kiss stood awkwardly between them. Carrie Ann avoided looking into his eyes and answered his questions in monosyllables. Yes. No. Maybe.

As the time neared to board the train, he reached for her hand. "You'll write?" he asked. Carrie Ann nodded. "Good." He squeezed her fingers, and then, without any fanfare, she boarded the train that would take her most of the way home.

Once settled back home with her mama, Carrie Ann realized using her nursing skills while living with a granny woman would be nearly impossible. Folks round about looked to her mama when they were ailing, and they had no reason to do otherwise. What was needed was a local doctor. If there was a doctor's office in town, then surely she would succeed at bringing real medicine to her community.

Hesitating long enough to push the kiss from her memory, Carrie Ann wrote a letter to the only doctor she knew well enough to bring to Burnsville. She hoped the letter reached him before he found suitable employment in Boston and that her praise of his skills, along with the great need in the area, would be enough to tempt him to make a significant move to a small town in the North Carolina mountains.

She wondered if her motive was solely medical. Yes, she wanted to bring modern medicine to the area. Yes, she wanted to be a practicing nurse. But... she reached up and touched one finger to her lips... perhaps she wanted to see Daniel again?

After a short series of letters, Dr. McKeithen moved to Burnsville to open a practice. That had been almost two years earlier.

When he first arrived, Carrie Ann assumed modern medicine would finally push her mother's version of healing to the distant past. But, instead of Dr. McKeithen helping the townsfolk become more progressive, she noted with a raised eyebrow, it was he who was becoming more like the locals.

He regularly left the office to fish or go hunting with the men. He spent hours rocking on the porch of the Wray Hotel, chatting with farmers about the corn crop and moonshiners about corn liquor. And what about what happened the other night with Esther? Rather than demand her mother step aside, he is the one who stood back and observed.

Despite her annoyance at the doctor's fishing expedition, she was secretly happy he was not around. She didn't think she could take another minute of his incessant chatter about Maggie.

"Did you see how she got Esther to calm down? I've never seen anything like it. Honestly, I would have never considered trying to turn the baby at such a late stage of delivery." When he asked, "Do you think Maggie would come to town and teach me the song she sings to quiet her patients?" Carrie Ann exploded.

"Are you mad? Have you lost your mind? You are a university-trained doctor, and nowhere in all your training did they find it necessary to instruct you how to chant in Cherokee. Science classes. Yes. Laboratory experience. Yes. Mountain magic? No. Why is that, do you think?"

She stalked out of the office toward her home, muttering to herself about her mother's ability to fool even the most intelligent men. That had been Saturday afternoon. With the Sabbath and now the fishing trip, she hadn't seen Daniel since her outburst. She hoped he would no longer be under Maggie's spell when they began seeing patients in the morning.

With nothing else to do and hours before the sun sank below the horizon, she decided to put up some applesauce from the last of the apples picked on the farm. Josephine had been by a few days prior to the fiasco with Esther and her baby. She pulled a cart with three bushels of fruit from the far orchard.

"Hey, Mama! Granny asked me to bring you these here apples. Said you'd likely wanna make some sauce or butter with 'em." Carrie Ann shook her head at her daughter's language. She wanted to enroll her in school, but the nearest was in Bald Creek, seven miles away – and that was if she could persuade Josephine to live in Burnsville instead of with her grandmother in the Green Mountain Gap holler.

Now that she lived in town and had a steady job, she was ready to, once again, care for Josephine. But those early years spent on the farm with Maggie shaped the child.

Though Josephine loved and respected her mother, she wasn't comfortable living in a place surrounded by people, buildings, and the comings and goings of town life. She'd rather do her schooling from the Good Book under Maggie's tutelage and spend the day learning the ways of the land. Nothing about life in Burnsville interested her.

Carrie Ann didn't understand her daughter, and Josephine didn't understand her mother.

"I would prefer you didn't call her Granny. She is your grandmother. And I'll never 'likely wanna' do anything."

Josephine rolled her eyes and sighed, repeating her sentence with a dramatic flair that almost made Carrie Ann laugh, except she would never show amusement at such impertinent behavior. "Good morning, Mother. Grand-ma-ma requested me to bring these apples to your fine doorstep. She believed you might wish to make applesauce or apple butter. May I tell her you approve?"

Hiding her amusement, Carrie Ann put her hands on her hips and tapped the toe of her left shoe. "Do not speak to me that way, young lady. You might be living with your grandmother, but you are my daughter. I'll move you to town this very day and show you who is boss."

The threat, though empty, did what it was meant to do. Josephine apologized for being disrespectful, Carrie Ann accepted, and both stood awkwardly, trying to figure out what to say or do next.

Finally, Josephine said, "Well, I need to head to the store. Granny – I mean, errr... – Grandmother needs a few things." They embraced, releasing one another just as they came together, and the girl walked on down the road with the cart. Carrie Ann wondered how long it would be before Josephine realized her mother had no control and Maggie was firmly in charge.

Due to her work and the late night spent with Esther, the apples still sat on the porch, and if Carrie Ann didn't do something with them soon, they would spoil.

She got out her largest pan, filled it halfway, and set it on the stove to boil. Next, she cut the fruit into quarters, throwing the pieces into the bubbling water – skins, seeds, and all. When the pot was full, she pulled out the straining sieve and pestle, wiping out the spiderwebs formed after a year without use.

The steam swirled away from the stovetop, bringing with it the sweet aroma of autumn in the mountains. Once, while still living in Asheville, she tasted some applesauce from Max Ams, a company based in New York. Although jarred fruits and vegetables from a manufacturer were the latest innovation coming to stores across America, Carrie Ann found the concoction to be watery, thin, and taste-less. She would never admit it to her mother, but some things were better the mountain way, and applesauce was one of them.

After the apples cooked down to mush, Carrie Ann pushed the mixture through the sieve into a fresh bowl, careful not to let the steaming sauce burn her hands. She saved the apple mash for her mother's pigs, then carefully put the fruit into bottles. Once full, she set on the lids, screwed down the caps, and placed the jars into a bath of hot water until the seals began to ping. By nightfall, Carrie Ann had sixteen quarts of applesauce and one less bushel of apples sitting on the porch, and an uncomfort-able notion she was more like her mother than she cared to admit.

* * *

Tuesday morning was busier than expected at the little clinic. Dr. McKeithen, aided by Carrie Ann, attended to several patients with chest colds, a baby with croup, two pregnant women, and an elderly man complaining of pains near his heart when he climbed the stairs. The two worked together seamlessly, as though no harsh words had been uttered between them.

The sun began its slow descent, casting long shadows before there was a lull. It was then that Daniel seemingly started where he left off. "I still can't believe your mother, Carrie Ann. She has an amazing ability I wish I possessed."

Carrie Ann's back straightened, her hands automatically moving to her hips as her mouth pulled back at the corners. "Not nonsense about Mother again, Doctor."

He interrupted her exasperation. "It's true, Carrie Ann. And please, I've asked you many times. Don't call me Doctor. My name is Daniel." This was an ongoing argument between them. Carrie Ann worked diligently to keep everything between them professional. She was unwilling to believe this man, this doctor, came to Burnsville for any reason other than to practice medicine. For almost two years now, she had strictly been his nurse, stopping anything that seemed to get too personal.

With a tight voice, she declared, "Someone has to remember who you are and remind you. You are the doctor here in Burnsville. The first one we've ever had. I'm afraid you've forgotten you know more about medicine than everyone in this town combined.

"As for my mother? She's not a doctor or a nurse. She's just a local woman who spent too much time with her herbs and Cherokee friends. She's full of twaddle, and quite frankly, I cannot fathom why you would allow her to work alongside you, let alone prattle on about her foolish nonsense."

Daniel sat down, stretching out his long legs, unaffected by her tirade. "What is it about your mama that gets you so worked up? You were there, Carrie Ann. You were witness to the difficulty Esther experienced. Surely, you realize we would have lost the baby. There's a good chance Esther would have died as well."

He reached out his hand as if he were going to take hold of one of her own but dropped it as Carrie Ann took a step back. Sighing, he continued.

"But your mother knew just what to do. She was able to help Esther deliver a healthy boy despite the odds. You saw it. I saw it. Your mama may not be a doctor. Or university trained. But she has some kind of gift. I would give away every bit of schooling to have her instinct. All of it."

He put his hands behind his head, flaring his elbows out to the side, and closed his eyes before continuing. "Book learning is valuable. No doubt. But what your mama has? It's invaluable." Carrie Ann turned on her heel, missing his flinch when the door banged shut at her departure.

Carrie Ann strode along the road, dodging townsfolk, horses, and carts, inwardly seething. "He wants what Mama has? The ability to fool folks into thinking she knows something she doesn't?"

It made no sense to her. She worked so hard to move beyond the traditions and lore and focus on science. She thought she had yoked herself to another professional, but it appeared the holler was working its spell.

She ruefully wondered how long it would be before he chanted and danced for his patients and offered them ground-up leaves and roots. Snorting at the thought, she pushed into her tiny home and scattered the applesauce sieve, pot, and spoons from yesterday's foray into tradition. Not able to waste the apples, but knowing she wouldn't spend another minute canning, she determined to take them to Esther's family in the morning. She was finished with mountain traditions.

Chapter 3

Josie Mae
- October 12, 1892 -

Josie Mae stretched out in the sunshine, soaking in the buttery glow as if she could save the warmth for the dark months ahead. She marveled that even with her eyes closed, the light made red and orange patterns on the inside of her eyelids, and she could detect the insects moving about in the late autumn blossoms.

She was supposed to be gathering roots for her grandmother. Once the hard frost came, Granny would rely on dried herbs to help her patients. Nothing of value grew in the depths of winter, and even if it could, no one would find it beneath the layers of ice and snow.

Although this was an important job, it was not one she enjoyed. Sure, she loved to walk along the holler, taking in the greens, reds, and golds, the musty smell of rotting leaves mixed with the henbit's slightly minty aroma blowing in the breeze. But gathering the plants needed to heal folks was work, and her granny was particular.

She recalled in vivid detail the day she brought home a basket of bloodroot stems. "Look, Granny! I found a passel o' bloodroot for you, just like you asked." Except, what she collected was useless.

"Child, how many times do I have to tell you to listen

to me the whole time I'm speaking? I don't just spout off words to hear myself talk. These stems? Where did you find them?" Josie Mae pointed in the direction of trees, but Granny just shook her head and kept on lecturing. "I don't mean where you picked the plants, Josie Mae. The stem itself. Where was it?"

Josie Mae, though perplexed by the question, answered in an uncertain voice. "They was right under the leaves, Granny. Just where I expected them to be."

Granny snorted. "And that, child, is your problem. You think you understand things you know nothing about. How long have you been picking bloodroot? Drying it? Using it to help folks with the fever?"

Josie Mae looked down at the floor. "Exactly. So, when I told you to pick bloodroot stems, you should have listened to everything I said and not just where I started." She went on to explain how these particular plants have stalks that grow under the ground before finally coming to the root. It was the buried part she used for medicine. The parts Josie picked, those splashed with sunlight, were useless.

Had the bloodroot failure been the only mistake, she might have enjoyed the process. However, she often found her choice of stems over leaves or berries over roots had been the wrong one.

Now, with a cloudless afternoon ahead of her, it was difficult to imagine sitting beneath the trees, hunting for fairy wand roots. But she also knew from experience her Granny's wrath, so she reluctantly rose and headed to the canopy of shade on the edge of the field.

Patches of fairy wand were easy to find. Their long shoots, many longer than Josie Mae's arm, hung heavy with seeds. She knelt in the dirt, pulling out a small digging fork. Granny said to use this particular tool rather than the shovel because the roots were tiny and delicate. The wrong one would easily cut them in half.

She dug with care around the first stem, plucking the roots free. She gently shook the root but had been taught not to remove all the soil. Her first batch of fairy wand, clean and bare, dried out before she got it back to Granny. Yet another one of her mistakes. That's why she left enough earth to keep the roots damp, layering fairy wand with layers of wet leaves.

With a full basket, she hurried to the cabin. Because of her many earlier mishaps, she chose not to announce her arrival with a proclamation of accomplishments. Instead, she held her offering out with downcast eyes, hoping Granny would be satisfied with her efforts.

Maggie looked into the hamper, a slight smile crossing her face. As she pulled off the first layer of damp leaves, she inspected the roots.

"Very nice, Josie Mae. Very nice. You see here?" She pointed to the tiny, feathered root tips. "You used the fork, didn't you?"

Josie Mae nodded. "And because you did, you got the entire root, even these fuzzy ends. And," she said with pride, "you layered them with such care." With a satisfactory nod, she said, "I can leave them in this basket until I'm ready to dry them."

Maggie took her granddaughter's contribution to the storeroom, where she kept her medicines. She looked over her shoulder, saying, "Do you know why I store the herbs here instead of the in main room?"

Josie Mae cocked her head a tad to one side. A reason? She assumed Granny used the small, dark room at the back of the house because drying plants in the living area would be messy and give the room a musty odor. She said as much, and Maggie laughed.

"You are probably right, child. But it isn't just about aesthetics." Josie Mae looked at Maggie, a question forming on her face. "Aesthetics?"

"Ah, yes. A fancy way of saying 'how things look.' Your mama loved that word. Said it so often it worked its way into my own ramblings. Anyway, storing the roots, stems, and leaves back here means they are far away from the fire. Although I want to remove the moisture from the herbs, I need to do it slow and easy. If'n I had them in the front room with the blazing logs, I wouldn't have what the folks in town needed when they got sick."

Josie Mae considered her explanation. "There's lots you do to get the medicines right, isn't there? You gotta pick it right. And dry it right. And keep it right. And give it right. Or else, it don't help at all."

"Exactly, Josie Mae. But here is something I want you to understand. Doing the job right is important, but not just in my work as a granny woman. Every single thing you do. There is a right way and a wrong way.

"Look at canning apples, for instance. If you don't heat them enough for the lids to ping, then the fruit goes bad, and you don't have food for the winter. Or what about feeding the chickens? If you feed them foods they can't eat, like rhubarb, they'll become sick and die. Then you won't have any eggs or fresh meat. Do you understand what I'm saying?"

Josie Mae nodded, a slow, thoughtful movement, thinking about this idea. She had always assumed adults were picky because they were older and young'uns had to respect 'em. She never considered there was more to it. But

Granny said everything had a right way and a wrong way.

"That makes sense, Granny, when talking about drying herbs, and applesauce, and chickens. But what about healin'? Mama says the best way to cure the cholera is with opium and maybe bleeding 'em a bit. But you use copper from the rocks and white hellebore. If'n there is a right way and a wrong way, then which of you is right — and which of you is wrong?"

Josie Mae wasn't trying to find a loophole around doing things the way she'd been told. She honestly wanted to understand the tension between her mother and her granny.

"I'm impressed you can recite the medicines needed for cholera. Makes me wonder if you have the makings of a healer. I'm also impressed with your question, Josie Mae. Unfortunately, it ain't easy to answer. It depends on who's askin' and who's tellin'."

Chapter 4

Maggie
- November 1, 1892 -

Maggie's boots crunched the brittle grass, the season's first hard frost demanding more time before disappearing in the anemic sun. She recited her shopping list, not wanting to forget anything important because, soon, coming to town would be far less frequent. Yes, she would always come if someone needed the granny woman, but those in Burnsville were more likely to rely on the doctor when the snows came.

Maggie understood completely. To fetch Maggie, a person would have to slog for several miles through the bitter cold and hope she was home to receive them. Then, they would have to make the trek back — all while their loved one suffered. For many, it was simpler to call on Dr. McKeithen.

Maggie liked him. He was soft-spoken and interested in his patients. He worked diligently to connect with the locals, learn about their lives, and help them the best he could. Maggie also was pleased that, despite her daughter's disdain, he insisted Maggie use his given name and treated her as an equal rather than an uneducated woman with potions hidden in her bag.

That is what her daughter called her healing methods. Or worse. Magic. Unscientific nonsense. Quackery. Foolishness. Carrie Ann often suggested she only had fake remedies and false hope in her medicine bag. Of course, Carrie Ann was not completely wrong.

On occasion, all she had to offer was her calm assurance that everything was going to be fine, when she had no idea if this was true. She relied on local herbs when others from far-off places might do a better job.

And, like with any healer, there were times when, despite all she did, her patient died. Young. Old. White. Negro. Cherokee. Rich. Poor. It didn't matter. Sometimes, she was unable to do anything more than watch them slip away.

What frustrated her was Carrie Ann's modern medicine, though different, had outcomes that were not superior. When her daughter and the doctor visited their sickest patients, they, too, had some who lived while others did not – something Carrie Ann didn't take note of.

Maggie was also not impressed with how Carrie Ann treated those under her care. However, her actions were not a surprise. She had the same mannerisms toward those who sought her help as she did her family. Carrie Ann always possessed the final answer. If one disagreed or even questioned her, they were on the receiving end of her temper.

For instance, recently, Carrie Ann was instructing Esther on breastfeeding. Maggie had come in to check on the family in time to witness the exchange.

"Here, Esther. Pull him close and tight and make sure his head is held up higher." She prodded the child into the correct position only to have Malcolm begin to wail. Using her mother's intuition, Esther lowered the baby and loosened her grip. As soon as she did, the infant began suckling again.

"It's the darnedest thing, Carrie Ann. This little one doesn't like swaddlin' the way the others did. Seems the closer I hold 'im, the more cantankerous he gets. If'n I jes let him loose a bit, he's a happy little feller."

Carrie Ann glowered, her eyes narrowing and her voice turning somewhat steely. "Fine, Esther. Do it your way. But don't come running to me when he develops colic or worse, chokes to death on your milk." Without saying another word, she turned from the woman's bed and strode out of the room.

Maggie began speaking, hoping to smooth the rough edges left by her daughter. "Babies are amazin', aren't they? Comin' to us with their own minds made up, not carin' one smidgen what we think!" Esther's shoulders relaxed as she nodded in agreement.

Despite all her fancy learning, Carrie Ann could benefit from a lesson or two in the ancient art of healing. Something Maggie understood meant far more than offering the right medicine at the right time.

Yes, as a granny woman, Maggie measured pinches and smidgeons of ingredients. She heated the concoctions until a sufficient amount of water boiled away. She used her knowledge to determine when to use the leaves of a plant for one illness and its roots for another while avoiding it entirely at certain points in its growth cycle.

But being a healer required more than medicinal knowledge. It also called for connecting, understanding, listening, grieving, celebrating, serving.

Her first experience with healing came when she was

a small child. She didn't rightly recall how old she was but, looking back, figured she was four or five. She'd been helping her ma in the kitchen, and then the pain and the noise. All she could remember was the immense, burning sensation, her ma and pa shouting, and the baby fussing.

To this day, she isn't sure how it happened, but the pot of water meant for the supper taters upended. The boiling liquid landed on Maggie, soaking her dress and flowing down to her shoes. But it was the soft flesh of her arm that sustained the most damage.

The memory was hazy. She remembered crying and Ma pulling her clothes off over her head. Then, as if out of thin air, Nanna appeared.

Before Maggie knew what was happening, Nanna was rubbing under and around the painful sores, careful not to touch the scalded tissue, massaging her fingers, and easing the tension in her shoulder. She rubbed while crooning words that made no sense coupled with those she recognized.

Maggie remembered Nanna telling the burn it needed to leave and take the pain with it. She pointed with one hand, showing the burn where she expected it to go. Then, as quickly as the throbbing, stinging sensation appeared, it eased.

Now, she pulled up the sleeve of her dress, letting her gaze roam from the wrist to the elbow. The story was true, and except for a slight discoloration about the size of a blueberry, no evidence remained.

Nanna had been a genuine healer, but what of Carrie Ann? She wondered how Daniel put up with her.

The general store came into view, but Maggie decided to stop in at Esther's before tackling her shopping list. She hadn't seen her friend for a couple of weeks. The baby was almost a month now, and she wanted to check how they were getting on.

White puffs of smoke rose one after another from the chimney, and the wind pulled along the scent of frying bacon. It seemed Maggie might be in time for a hearty breakfast, a welcome treat after her long walk.

"Hello!" she called out as she approached the front porch. The door opened and out stepped John, a broad smile on his lean, whiskered face. "Maggie! Hello! What a fine surprise! Why, you are just in time for some of Mama's eggs plus a little leftover bread and honey from last night's dinner. You'll stay for a bite now, won't you?"

Maggie returned his smile. "If'n you're offerin', John, I'm acceptin'. The trek from my house to town gets farther and more difficult each time I make it!"

John ushered her into the cabin, guiding her toward the stove in the center of the room. "Jes' stand right here, Maggie. Warm up a bit. I'll fetch Esther. She's gone in to feed the babe."

He turned to his eldest daughter, eight-year-old Maribelle. "Keep stirring them eggs. Don't let 'em turn brown, now, hear?"

Maggie followed the child's arm making circles in the pot, intent on her job. Lloyd sat on the floor at her feet, stacking some blocks into a tower. Maggie squatted down despite the protest in her knees. "Good morning, Lloyd. Whatcha doin'?"

The child continued playing with his toys as if she had not spoken. She tried again. "Lloyd, can I have a block? Can I help you make a building?" Still, the boy said nothing.

He didn't have any hearing problems. She tested him several times. He flinched, pulling in his arms and covering his ears, when she dropped a pan. He even turned his head when she whispered, as long as the whisper concerned food. But when it came to everyday conversations, he was mute.

Maggie pulled herself upright, wondering what would become of this little boy. Although a three-year-old who didn't talk was unusual, it wasn't something the town folk talked much about. When they did mention it, they'd say things like, "He'll come into his own soon 'nuff. You jes' wait. When he has sumpin' to say, his mama won't be able to get him quiet again."

But Maggie had reservations. Lloyd's birth had been a difficult one. No worse than Malcolm's, of course, but bad in its own right. She wondered if all those hours of labor had left him damaged, and it worried her. His mama didn't need more woes. She'd already lost most of her babies, and folks weren't too keen on defective ones.

While she mused, Esther came into the room carrying a squirming, plump baby. He looked up at his mama, and a smile broke his face in half. Esther grinned back. "He started doing it – jes' for me – yesterday. He ain't smilin' for his pa, but he's got eyes for his mama, that's fer sure."

All thoughts of imperfect children fled as Maggie regarded Malcolm. He was healthy, happy, and brought his mama and pa great joy. Maggie reached out her arms, hefting the child up to her shoulder. "He mostly likes to be held outward," Esther stated. "Seems he wants to see what everyone is doin'. Doesn't want to miss a thing."

Maggie gently flipped the boy to face forward, her arm holding around his waist. He pulled his fist into his mouth, contented.

Esther patted Maribelle's straight, dirty blond hair. "Why, Maribelle! Look at them eggs! You done a fine job. A fine job, indeed. Why, I believe these may be the best I've ever seen." Maribelle's eyes lit up, and faint red dots highlighted her cheekbones at the compliment. "Thank ya, Mama."

Esther turned to Maggie. "She's been such a big help since Malcolm arrived. I don't know what I'd do without her." The girl continued to blush, looking at the ground.

Maggie faced the child, tipping her face up so their eyes met. "Thank you, Maribelle. Because you've been an excellent helper, your mama is getting stronger every day. You are making my job so much easier by being an excellent nurse."

Maribelle sucked in deeply and glanced toward her mother. "Did ya hear that, Mama? A nurse!" She faced Maggie again. "I want to be one someday. A nurse. Like Carrie Ann. Do you think I can? Mama says so, if'n I try my best at school and do my figgers and practice readin' out of the Bible."

Maggie nodded, holding the child's gaze with her own. "Yes, Maribelle. You've got a knack for it. Study hard, and I'm certain you can be a nurse." The child beamed.

"Like Carrie Ann? And working with a real doctor in the city?" The words 'real doctor' stung a bit, but Esther cut in before Maribelle could continue. "Go ahead and call your pa. Let's put these eggs on the table, or they're gonna get cold."

As Maribelle left the room, Esther said, "She didn't mean nuthin' by her chatter, Maggie. She's just wantin' to be like Florence Nightingale. She got a book from school, and now it's all she ever talks about."

Maggie smiled. "It's fine, Esther. She's right, ya know. I ain't a real doctor."

Esther shrugged. "You're better than one, as far as I'm concerned, Maggie. You saved my life. You saved Malcolm's life. I'll always be callin' on the granny woman, even if'n Maribelle does become a nurse!"

Chapter 5

Carrie Ann
- December 12, 1892 -

Carrie Ann sat, her back erect and her arms stiff at her sides, in a wooden chair in the small reception area of Dr. McKeithen's office. The two of them had worked without a break during the morning, the last patient coming in for the third time in as many weeks. Carrie Ann greeted her coolly.

"Sadie. What brings you back to the doctor again?"

The young woman flushed crimson. "It's the same issue, Carrie Ann." She looked around to determine if anyone was within earshot. "Just like what I told you about last time. My womanly. It won't go away. I been bleedin' now goin' on more than two months. Something just ain't right."

Carrie Ann bristled. "Still? Every day? Did it stop and start again? You can't mean you've been bleeding for a solid month."

Sadie nodded. "I have, Carrie Ann. Every single day. Some of 'em is pretty bad, too."

Despite knowing everything about Sadie's previous visits, Carrie Ann pulled open a file. In her careful handwriting were the notes.

Nov 27, 1892 – Sadie Flynn – young woman of twenty-one – married – no children – complaining her menses has lasted over two weeks – some cramping – bleeding heavy at times – recommend a vigorous walk each evening to rid the body of excess blood.

Dec 4, 1892 – Still menstruating – increased cramping – heavy bleeding often – recommend continued exercise and Dr. Jackson's English Tablets to help cure female issues.

After skimming through the notes, she said, "And you are walking at a fast pace before bed?" Sadie nodded. "And you've been taking the pills as directed?" Sadie looked down. "No, ma'am. I did. For a couple o' days. But I couldn't think. Everything seemed blurry. And the flow was just as bad as ever."

Carrie Ann slapped the chart on the table. "It's no wonder you haven't gotten better. You aren't listening to the doctor. And now, you come back here for what? So he can tell you what you need to do, and you can ignore it again?" Her words got louder and harsher as she spoke, bringing Dr. McKeithen to the door.

"What is going on here, Carrie Ann?" He looked from one woman to the next. Sadie stammered, "Nothing, Dr. McKeithen. I didn't listen to what you had to say the last time. It's my own fault. I'll go." And she left the office, almost running toward the edge of town.

"What was that about? Why were you yelling at a patient?" he demanded.

"She came in here for the third time for the same thing but isn't doing what she was told. It makes no sense to keep bothering you if she doesn't plan to heed what you say," Carrie Ann declared, her hands placed on her hips in a way that indicated she was correct. "You aren't some uneducated mountain healer like my mother, and these people should respect what you do and what you say."

Daniel became still. The only movement was a slight twitch in his right cheek. He breathed in, a slow inhale through his nostrils, and with the same care, blew out the air before speaking in measured tones.

"Nurse. That is your title. Not doctor. As you said, I am the doctor here, not you. If Sadie didn't follow my instructions, she likely had a legitimate reason. Perhaps she didn't understand them."

At that, Carrie Ann started to speak, to clarify Sadie's why, but Dr. McKeithen held up his hand. "No. You listen to me. She may not have understood the directions. Or what I suggested may not have been working for her. Or maybe her symptoms had changed in some way. But now, I'll never determine the true cause because you chastised and embarrassed her. Because of your lack of empathy and compassion, I've lost a patient. What's more, I have most certainly lost a piece of my reputation."

He spun on his heel, reaching for the door. "I'm going to make a house call and figure out what I can do to help that poor girl. In the meantime, please tell any patients I'll be back late this afternoon. Say nothing to them about their condition or complaint. In fact, say nothing except 'Dr. McKeithen had to step away on an emergency. He will be back late this afternoon.' Nothing else. Do you understand me?"

Heat flushed her face from the reprimand. Sadie refused to follow his instructions because she was willful. Certainly, he'd see that when he caught up with her.

As instructed, she told those who came to see the doctor that he was attending an emergency. Each time she uttered those phrases, her humiliation renewed, but thankfully, no one seemed to notice, being more concerned with their own issues than hers. That had been over two hours earlier. She now sat in the chair waiting for his return, becoming less sure of her actions toward Sadie.

His words echoed those often spoken by her mother. "Think before you speak, child," she would say when Carrie Ann was younger. "And watch your tone with me," was a refrain as she grew.

Carrie Ann shook her head. She did not intend to be rude and unkind. She didn't. She was being honest. Sadie had come back expecting the doctor to give her new instructions when she was unwilling to follow his recommendations the first time. That was a true statement. How could pointing out a fact be improper?

Immediately, she heard her mother's voice in her head. "Carrie Ann, there is nothing wrong with the truth. It's in the telling you have a problem."

Carrie Ann broke from her reverie when footsteps sounded on the porch. It was Dr. McKeithen, face drawn, eyes downcast, tired, and spent. He pushed open the door, stopping when Carrie Ann, sitting straight-backed and rigid, came into view. He sighed and ran his hand through his hair.

"I couldn't find her. Not right away. Without too much thought, I realized where she would be. I trekked out to Maggie's and found her listening to everything Sadie had to say. I apologized to her – for you."

Carrie Ann's eyes flashed. Her mother would, no doubt, use this against her at some later date. She wanted to tell him he had no business involving her mother, but before she could speak, he shook his head in her direction. "After apologizing for you, I asked her to forgive me for not attending to her complaints or taking them seriously enough."

He sat down, heavy with weariness. "I figured it was a lady problem. It would clear up. It was no big deal. Sadie was probably exaggerating. I realized my attitude toward Sadie is what gave you the belief you could talk to her the way you did. So, I did the only thing I could do. I told her how sorry I was. Then, I asked Sadie if I could listen to Maggie's advice and try to learn something."

Carrie Ann's eyes grew enormous. Not again. How was it her mother kept interfering, and Dr. McKeithen not only let her but invited her to do so?

"Don't look so surprised, Carrie Ann. I may have gone to school, but your mother has been helping folks around these parts since before I was born. But it isn't about time. She never fails to use empathy, something you and I both neglected. And something that I will work fervently to never neglect again."

He turned in his chair toward Carrie Ann. "I owe you an apology, too, Carrie Ann. I expected you to be something I wasn't willing to be myself. And then I got angry when you merely reflected what you'd seen in me." He put his head in his hands. "My goal has always been to care for my patients – not only their bodies, but their minds, their emotions, everything. I failed with Sadie."

He rose slowly, head hung low. "I'll see you in the morning, Carrie Ann."

As she locked up and headed home, she didn't comprehend all her feelings. He apologized, but not because he realized she was right. Rather, it was because he believed he encouraged her to do wrong. And, once again, he was convinced her mother had something of value to add to the science of medicine.

She let herself into the house but didn't burn the lantern. Instead, she sat in the dark, trying to understand the lesson she was certain she was supposed to be learning.

Chapter 6

Josie Mae
- January 5, 1893 -

Josie Mae bustled around the kitchen, helping her granny and her mama – who was joining them for the celebration of Old Christmas – ready the house for the guests who were sure to start arriving at first light the next morning. Although Josie Mae had celebrated Christmas on December 25th with her granny, the townsfolk still clung to the tradition of the Old Country, celebrating Christ's birth on January 6th.

Josie Mae had asked her granny about it while they exchanged small gifts – a sweater knit by her grandmother and a scarf homemade by Josie Mae. "Granny, why are there two Christmases?"

"Well, Josie Mae, there aren't. Not really. Some people celebrate on January 6th because, long ago, the calendars were different. When they adjusted the dates, some people stuck with the original celebration, and others changed to the new one. Around here? Well, folks don't do much in the way of changin' lessin' they have to."

Josie Mae nodded. That was true. She and Granny had a small Christmas tree in their house decorated with little candles and dried flowers. But many people in the area wouldn't consider it. "That's a Pagan tradition," they declared. Despite this belief, some of the churches had a tree, while other congregations did not. She and Granny removed theirs long before Old Christmas. There was no need to upset the folks who liked the old traditions.

She realized Christmas customs weren't the only things slow to change. Her mama was always going on about people and their beliefs about medicine.

"Childbed fever used to be a real problem. Women would get mighty sick after delivering a baby. They'd come down with a fever and experience lots of pain. Most who caught it died. Finally, doctors figured out all they had to do was wash their hands and their tools. As soon as they did, childbed fever became quite rare.

"But we still have folks out here in the mountains who just won't do it. They look at their hands and don't see anything out of the ordinary. So, they refuse to believe something invisible, some germ, is sitting there waiting to make someone sick. It's been thirty years since Louis Pasteur discovered germs cause diseases. That's as long as I've been alive. And still, we have people who won't accept it."

But Granny had no fear when it came to change, noted Josie Mae. They decorated a Christmas tree, Granny washed her hands before treating people, and she often brought back new information after visiting the Cherokee village. Josie Mae had never been on one of the journeys to visit with the didanawisgi or medicine man. But Granny promised this spring, when the snows melted away, she would take her.

"It's a hard journey, Josie Mae. We can't take the wagon, which means we have to use the pack mules. If the weather is jes' right and the creeks aren't too high, it'll take five days. Once, it took me eight. We'll be gone about two weeks, and most of it is travelin'. You sure you wanna go? It's not like a Sunday outin' for a picnic."

Josie Mae's eyes had glowed with excitement. She hadn't been anywhere except Burnsville. And Asheville, where she was born, but she had no recollection of her time in the city. And the Cherokee? To learn about healing? It was like a dream come true. Of course, her mama did not approve.

At first, she forbade Granny to take her. Then, when Granny didn't budge, she pleaded. When pleading had no effect, she started calling her names and telling her just what she thought of Cherokee medicine.

"Why do you even want to go? They are living in the past, Mama! Everything they do is exactly what they've been doing for centuries. You are crazy to bring back their uncivilized superstitions when you have access to a real doctor right in town. And people already talk about you behind your back. Some say you are carryin' on with an Indian lover." She flung the last words at her mother like a dart.

Without raising her voice, Granny said, "I ain't too worried about local gossip, but I do care about learning. The Cherokee use herbs and plants they've been using for generations because they have discovered remedies that work – and work well. I bring back those things that allow me to help folks when they're ailin'. It was the Cherokee who taught me about nettles, and it was this remedy that finally got Sadie to stop bleeding." She looked pointedly at Carrie Ann.

Josie Mae did not understand what her mama meant about lovers and bleedin', but she did figure out when her mother left without another word that Granny won the argument. She would be allowed to go to the Cherokee village this spring.

No, Granny wasn't afraid of change. But she also would not push people to do things a different way if they didn't want to.

That's why they celebrated twice. The first time was something between the two of them with their own traditions. The second time was so they could include everyone – her mama, the doctor, Esther and her family, the blacksmith, the grocer – anyone who wanted to experience the Old Christmas spirit.

The sweet aroma of apple stack cakes, fried apples, pumpkin and mince pies, popcorn balls, and chocolate fudge filled the cabin. Granny finished dressing two chickens, plopping them into the roasting pan, and covering the lid with coals. "There. That'll do. If we're a gonna make the Christmas Eve service, we best be leavin'."

Josie Mae pulled on her woolen coat, stocking cap, and mittens before fitting her feet into the boots warming by the fire. Granny and her mama bundled up, too, and the three of them hitched up the sleigh and headed into town.

Although it was cold, Josie felt cozy, snuggled between the two women she loved more than anybody in the world. She cherished this holiday season because her mama and granny worked together in the kitchen and acted like old friends. Josie Mae held onto these moments all year, especially when Granny and her mama fought – usually over her or medicine – sometimes both at once.

The church, lit with candles, was bright and cheery. Mrs. Robertson played beautiful carols as the townsfolk came in and took their seats. When everyone arrived, they all sang "Oh Come All Ye Faithful," and then the young children did a reenactment of the first Christmas. Josie Mae remembered the time she got to be a sheep. Another year, she was a shepherd. She never wanted to be Mary like the other girls. Mary had to be too quiet. Josie preferred bleating. They ended the service with "Silent Night" while exiting the church to find snow falling softly in the moonlight.

Despite having exchanged gifts on December 25th, Josie Mae and Granny hung their stockings next to Carrie Ann's. Josie Mae was aware her mother filled the socks, but she insisted it was Father Christmas.

Every year, she would discover walnuts, hickory nuts, and hazelnuts in the toe, some penny candy and peppermint sticks, and a piece of fruit. When she was younger, Josie Mae would be given a doll or jack straws. Now, she usually received a new hat and mittens.

"Alright, Josephine. Climb into bed, or Father Christmas won't arrive." Josie Mae rolled her eyes but climbed into the soft mattress with the warm stone at her feet. It had been a long day, and tomorrow would be longer still. She wasn't going to fight her mama about bedtime even though Father Christmas had nothing to do with it.

When she awoke, the sun was beginning to peek through the trees. Granny already had coffee on to brew, and her mama was stirring the pancake batter. "It's about time you woke up, sleepyhead! You better put on some clothes before the guests start arriving."

Josie Mae hurried to do as she was told. Her mama was right. Everyone would begin descending upon the house soon, and the entire day would be spent receiving friends, feeding them, and sending them on to the next stop.

It was tradition to visit the neighbors, and some folks believed getting twelve visitors meant you'd have good luck the rest of the year. Granny said they were bound to have lots of blessings because they always had more than twelve.

No sooner had Josie Mae pulled her dress over her head than laughter erupted in the yard. She opened the front door and ushered in Esther, John, Maribelle, Lloyd, and baby Malcolm. "Merry Christmas!" chorused from one to the other as boots, mittens, and coats were heaped into a pile.

In no time, the whole family was sitting down to breakfast, as well as a stack cake or mince pie. Leaving without eating one or the other was bad luck – and no one wanted to start out the year with bad luck. Before Esther's brood was out the door, in came another crowd, and another. And, as Granny predicted, they had more friends stop by than they needed.

Despite everyone devouring every last crumb prepared, Granny ended up with almost more food than she started with. Visitors who came through the door did so bearing breads, cakes, and pies, sacks of nuts, honey, peanut brittle, or maple sugar candy.

Mama had gone back into town, and Josie Mae and Granny washed the dishes, chatting about the wonderful day spent with friends.

"I can't believe all the sweets, Granny! We'll be feasting on them all winter long."

Granny laughed. "We most certainly will, but I can't imagine we need all this. What would you think if I packed up some of the treats and took them to John and Esther? I'm sure the kids would love to have some of the candy."

Granny had a special friendship with Esther, though Josie Mae didn't understand why. Esther was closer in age to her mama. As Josie considered which goodies to give away to the children, she realized something. "Granny, when Esther came today with her family, they didn't bring us a gift like everyone else, did they?"

"No, child, they didn't. Esther would have if she could have, but it's been tough. I think the only gifts they got this year was what they got going from house to house."

"You mean Father Christmas didn't deliver gifts to Maribelle, Lloyd, and Malcolm?"

"I doubt it, Josie Mae. Certainly, nothing like you and me got in our stockings from your mama."

Josie Mae suddenly had an idea. "Granny. Let's gather the food and go into town." As Granny started to protest, she rushed on. "No, right now. With the treats. And I've got a top for Lloyd and a baby for Maribelle. Mama made me new mittens and a hat, so I could give Esther my old set. Oh, but what do we have for John and little Malcolm?"

She searched in vain for something when Granny said, "I've got a clay pipe from the last time I visited the medicine man. It would be perfect for John." She opened a drawer to show Josie Mae and received enthusiastic nods. "And what about this bear for Malcolm?" asked Josie Mae as she pulled the tiny toy from under her bed.

With a gift for everyone, they made their way into town for the second night in a row, but this time, Josie Mae was warm from the inside. It felt good to help Esther and her family.

Once they were within sight of the cabin, Granny turned the sleigh around. "Get out here and take the sack up the steps. Be quiet, but make sure they will see it when they open the door. Then I want you to knock real loud and run. Don't let 'em catch you. We want those young'uns to believe Father Christmas came even if he was running late."

Josie Mae slipped onto the porch, rapped her knuckles on the wooden door, and ran, pumping her arms and legs as fast as she could. As she climbed into the sleigh, light spilled out the door. Soon, five faces peered from the doorway, marveling at the presents. Before they figured out what was happening, Josie Mae and Granny were gone.

"Josie Mae, I'm proud of you. Givin' them gifts was a very kind thing." Josie Mae smiled, thinking she finally understood the true meaning of the holiday.

Chapter 7

Maggie
- February 27, 1893 -

The last time Maggie experienced a winter as cold as this one, Carrie Ann was hardly older than Josie Mae. She recalled Carrie Ann creating a fuss during a three-week stretch when it was too dangerous for them to venture to town.

"Mama!" she stormed, stamping her foot, eyes flashing fire. "I can't stand being in this cabin one more minute. I've had about all I can take with roots and twigs and dried flowers and the symptoms of smallpox and cholera. And if I hear one more thing about those Cherokee friends of yours..." She spat the word friends as though it had a bitter flavor. "Suffice it to say I would rather take my chances with the weather than spend one more second trapped here with you."

Sighing, Maggie realized Carrie Ann wasn't the only one who wanted a break in the winter storm. Her daughter may be tired of being stuck inside, but Maggie was tired of her daughter. She wondered what she had done in life to deserve such a bullheaded child.

Maggie was a fourth-generation granny woman. Her great-grandmother, Sophronia Jean Campbell, was born in 1775 on Old Christmas. Those who came to earth on

January 6, the Lord's own day, were considered magical, having the power for healing the sick. From the day of her birth until the day of her death, Sophronia, known to her family as Sophie Jean, was a healer.

When Sophie Jean married and had children, she naturally taught her skills to her eldest daughter, Emma Louise, who taught it to her eldest, Eloise Rose, who taught it to her, Margaret Louise. Maggie didn't believe her great-grandmother had supernatural powers because of her birthdate, any more than she really believed her great-grandfather's fear of the number seventeen.

"It's a dreadful number, Maggie Lou. You gotta avoid it, 'specially if'n it's a day fallin' on a Friday. Certain to bring bad luck." She didn't cotton much to superstitions and old wives' tales, though they did rattle around in her head, intent on making mischief.

Despite the family lore, Maggie presumed her great-grandma learned the healing arts in the very same way she had and in the way she hoped to teach her daughter.

Carrie Ann kept bemoaning her fate. "I don't understand why I can't go visit Missy and Caroline. You are the one who insists we live out in the woods in the middle of nowhere, away from people. Away from stores. Away from parties." Although Carrie Ann's list continued, Maggie tuned out the noise.

Maggie had inherited her daddy and mama's property when Carrie Ann was barely old enough to walk. Regardless of the place always being her home, Carrie Ann seemed to want nothing to do with it. Or becoming a granny woman. Or family. Or anything that wasn't new and fancy.

But this winter with Josie Mae was as different as the

two girls. Even though it was colder than 1877, with temperatures dipping to twenty below, and despite the cold snap lasting well over thirty days, Josie Mae was content. She spent her time knitting, drying herbs, grinding roots, making tinctures, and reading from the Bible.

And the two of them talked for hours. A majority of their conversations revolved around healing, but many also included the Cherokee.

"You're still taking me with you to the Cherokee village this spring, ain't ya?" Josie Mae asked one evening. At her grandmother's nod, Josie asked, "How long have you been going to visit them, Granny?"

Every March, Maggie made the trek west while Josie Mae stayed in town with her mother. When Maggie returned, she brought pottery, baskets, and jewelry to sell to the general store, burlap bundles of roots and herbs for medicinal use, trinkets for her granddaughter, and stories of bears and singing and drawn-out nights in front of the fire.

Maggie said, "I've been going ever since your mama was a bitty girl. So, what's that now? Nearly thirty years."

But Maggie's answer did not leave Josie Mae contented. "But why, Granny? Why do you go every year?"

Maggie sat back in her chair, taking a slow rock back before reversing course and coming forward. Josie Mae was twelve, almost thirteen. She was old enough to take the trek with her this spring. Perhaps she had the maturity to understand why it was important.

"It's a long story, child. A very long story. Why don't we make us some tea and biscuits and make ourselves all cozy in front of the fire? Then, I'll tell you my tale."

Maggie and Josie Mae pulled their chairs closer to the

warmth of the hearth, a plate of biscuits and jelly between them. Josie Mae had gotten her ball of wool and needles.

"If'n it's goin' to be a long story, I figured I'd knit while I listened." Maggie smiled. Josie Mae was making mittens for Esther's children – already thinking of Christmas the following year. "I don't ever want them missing Father Christmas again, Granny."

Once they were settled, Maggie started. "You know how Esther has babies, but they don't live?" Josie Mae nodded, wondering what Esther's babies had to do with the Cherokee. "Esther isn't the only one who has problems with those issues." Josie Mae looked up, staring into her Granny's eyes with the earnestness of innocence. "You, Granny?"

Maggie dipped her head. "Before your mama came, I lost several babies 'afore they was ready to be born. When they come way too soon, it's called a miscarriage. I tried everything to keep them babies inside me, but nothing worked.

"Finally, I had a baby grow in me for the full nine months. My mama was with me when I labored, but even with all her skill, the little boy died minutes after he arrived."

Maggie stopped speaking, the three-decades-old grief bubbling to the surface. "We named him Henry after his daddy. He's buried out by his daddy's resting place."

Josie Mae screwed up her face, trying to remember a burial spot for a baby. Granny's parents had stones, as did her grandfather, but she never saw a stone for another Henry. "I ain't never seen no baby grave, Granny."

"It's because you wasn't lookin' for it. There is a small white stone to the right of your granddaddy. It is just a marker. No dates. No words. He was here and gone so fast..." She let her voice trail off.

"Anyway, I lost little Henry before I even got to know him. After Henry, I miscarried twice more. Your granddaddy and I didn't think we was ever gonna bring a baby into the world. And then I met Degataga."

Chapter 8

Maggie
- Spring 1862 -

Degataga was a Oconaluftee trader. Unlike some Cherokees who were forced to leave North Carolina and the surrounding hills back when Maggie was a child, the Oconaluftee were granted permission to stay in the area. Degataga traded Cherokee baskets, pottery, and jewelry along with pelts with white settlers throughout the region.

Maggie and Henry were trying to make a homestead a small distance to the south of the cabin where Maggie was born, and her parents still lived. The patch of land was given to them by her pa on their wedding day. "It's yours, if'n you want it," he had said to Henry, and the two had immediately begun to build their life.

The house was a tiny affair, with one square room serving as a kitchen, main room, and bedroom, depending on what a person was using it for. One evening, getting close to dark, Degataga came into the little clearing with several pack mules.

Henry, though not afraid, did ease his gun onto his lap. As Degataga approached, he called out a greeting in English. "Hello! I'm heading to Burnsville to trade. It's late in the day. My animals are tired and need water. I was hoping you might let me use your well. Perhaps rest for the night before making it into town tomorrow?"

Henry took an immediate liking to the young man, and in no time, Degataga was sitting on the front porch and sharing their meal. They talked long into the evening, and the young couple learned he was the son of a medicine man. "We have something in common," Maggie murmured. "I am the daughter of a healer – a granny woman." Henry puffed out his chest. "She's more than that. She's a granny woman herself."

Maggie shook her head, smiling. "No, no. It's my mama. I ain't nothin' but her apprentice. But," she said with a slight, bashful smile, "I do hope to one day be a granny woman in my own right."

Degataga nodded. "My brother has the healing gift. He will one day be the didanawisgi – medicine man. I have the gift of language. I read and write Tsalagi Gawonihisdi, what you call Cherokee, as well as English. I have a tutor during the winter months who is teaching me French."

Maggie's mouth dropped open. She had enough trouble with English, but to be learning a third? "Why French, Degataga?"

He started to laugh. "A schoolteacher for English children lives not far from my village. He needed my father's services and had nothing to trade but his ability to speak French. So, I will learn it, though I don't believe I will ever use it except to gossip with Monsieur Garnier."

Degataga pulled a clay pipe from his pocket and filled it with dried, brown tobacco, tamping down the leaves before lighting the bowl. He offered it to Henry, who took a puff and passed it to Maggie.

Maggie had never smoked. Her mama didn't cotton to it. "There ain't no need for a lady to go about breathing smoke. Save that for the men." Despite hearing this her whole life, Maggie was curious. So, she took the pipe and sucked on the end as she had seen Henry do.

Hot, burning fire filled her lungs. Her cheeks turned red. Tears streamed down her face. Finally, Maggie began coughing and gasping for breath. Both men started to laugh, and when she could breathe again, she laughed, too. "Well, I think I'll leave the smokin' to you." It rankled her a bit for her mama to be right again, but this time, she determined to give in without a fuss.

Degataga stayed the night on the front porch, insisting on his preference for remaining outdoors. When Maggie and Henry rose the next morning, Degataga was gone. In his place was a small bundle containing a clay pipe for Henry and several dried herbs for Maggie, some of which she recognized and some of which she did not.

Degataga stopped by to visit throughout the spring as he traded goods with the English. Every time, he brought tobacco and dried herbs, teaching Maggie the uses of each – boneset tea as a remedy for colds, wild cherry bark for coughs and diarrhea, and blue cohosh root to ease the pain during childbirth and speed up delivery.

At first, Maggie ran to her mother with the new remedies, but her mother wanted nothing from the Cherokee. "Their ways are not our ways," she said and flatly refused to listen.

"But, Mama!" she had insisted. "These here are roots and herbs found right in our own holler. They was used by those who lived here before we got here. It makes no sense to throw away their ideas simply because they ain't white."

Her mama flushed red. "It ain't about their color, Maggie Lou. They don't believe what we believe. Great Spirits and talking trees. No use for the Lord, Our Savior. They are savages, and we ain't usin' any savage medicine."

It was the first time Maggie truly experienced bigotry firsthand. She was aware, of course, that the Cherokee stayed in their own part of the mountains, and they had been forced to move. But she had never seen anyone mistreat them or so blatantly disregard something that could be so helpful simply because of its origins.

She wondered if her mama understood Granny and Great-granny had likely learned things from the native people in the area. Still, she knew better than to speak of it again. Instead, Maggie hoarded the new knowledge, believing someday, she would begin adding these remedies to help the folks living around Green Mountain Gap.

Early in June, the fever struck. Maggie's mama and pa got sick on the same day it hit Maggie and Henry. Her mama, too weak to climb out of bed, sent Maggie's pa to fetch the girl. He called from the yard, sick with fever, knowing he could spread the bad air.

"Maggie! Your mama's taken ill. Me, too. She wants you to go to town. Seems several people is ailin'." The walk and the hollering took the last of his strength, and he sat down hard in the dirt.

Maggie, drenched with sweat, eyes glazed, pushed open the door. "I can't, Pa. I got it. Henry's got it. Them folks is jus' gonna have to do without the granny woman or her apprentice. Now, go on home, Pa. You gotta get in bed. Make sure you and Mama drink water out of the rain barrel. Lots of water, hear?" With his nod, she closed the door.

Maggie dreamed of babies. They would be in her arms, suckling her milk. When they would smile and start to coo, fire would spew from their mouth, burning Maggie's face and chest.

As she thrashed and cried out, someone would spoon water into her mouth or put a rag on her head. "Henry," she would remember. "Henry is here. He will help me."

Then, she would begin to shake, the chill making her bones ache. Each time, piles of heavy blankets would appear, helping to fend off the shivering. The cycles of fiery heat and icy cold continued for hours on end, with Maggie only mildly aware of anyone tending to her.

When she woke days later, exhausted and weak, she realized Henry was lying on a pallet next to the fire. His pale skin glistened with sweat.

"Henry!" she croaked, nothing more than a hoarse whisper escaping her lips. She tried to push up, to go to his side, but firm hands guided her back toward the mattress. "He's doing better, Maggie. He's going to make it. It was you we were worried about."

"You?" Maggie whispered. "You been here this whole time? It was you givin' me water and blankets?"

Degataga nodded. "I came by to visit and found you and Henry sick. Really sick. You had the fever. I've seen it before. Ain't much to do but cool off the body when it's hot and warm it when it's cold. If the body is strong, it will survive. If not?" He shrugged his shoulders. "But you and Henry are strong. You will survive."

Maggie remembered her pa coming by. "My mama and pa. They got it, too. And lots of the townsfolk. I gotta check on 'em." She tried again to rise from the mattress, only to realize she didn't have the strength.

"Be still now. There isn't anything you can do to help. There isn't any medicine to stop this fever. They will be strong, or they won't. You going to them won't change the outcome."

As they spoke, Henry began to shake, the icy cold winning over the heat. Degataga left Maggie's side, covering her husband in blankets before coming back to spoon some soup into her mouth. "Sip this, Maggie. We got to put some food into your belly."

"But Henry?" she protested.

"Henry is tough, Maggie. He's through the worst. I expect him to be sipping broth by morning. But it's up to him and the Great Spirit. I can do nothing more. But with you? I can make you drink."

Degataga's prediction held. By first light, Henry was weakly drinking clear soup, and by week's end, Maggie was strong enough, with Degataga's help, to take the wagon to her mama and pa.

The stench reached them before the sound of the flies. "No, Maggie. Wait here. You don't need to go any closer." He jumped out, strode to the front door, and pushed his way inside. Moments later, he came out again. "They're gone, Maggie. Probably been dead a week or more."

Maggie began to cry, sobs wracking her body. Degataga put his arm gently around her shoulder. "Let me drive you back to Henry. Once you are settled, I'll come back and bury them." Maggie pointed toward the burying place, where her granny and peepaw were laid to rest. "By the old oak, near her ma and pa."

Degataga not only buried her folks but cleaned the cabin, ridding it of the flies and stench of disease and death. "You won't be able to go inside for a time," he declared. "You want to be sure all the bad air is gone. And you won't want to be going to town any time soon. Lots of fever."

He looked away before adding, "I'll be leaving tomorrow. Can't stay here any longer."

Maggie, startled by his sudden proclamation, said, "Why so soon, Degataga? You've been an enormous help to me and to Henry. I doubt we would have survived without you caring for us."

Degataga glanced at Maggie and back toward the horizon. "People are talking. They think I brought the disease with me. They haven't figured out I'm staying here. They assume I'm camping somewhere in the forest, and I'm going to keep 'em believing it."

"What in tarnation do you mean? You didn't bring the fever. Mama, Pa, Henry, and I were sick before you came."

He shook his head. "It doesn't matter what the truth is. It just matters what they think. And they think the sickness is my fault. Some think I did it on purpose, as revenge for the English because of their treatment of my people. It won't do to put you in the middle. I'll leave at first light."

Maggie, despite her weakened state, stood up and stamped her foot. "This is ridiculous. Henry! Henry!"

Henry pulled open the door and shuffled outside, eyebrows raised. "Maggie! What has gotten into you? Why all the hollerin'?"

"The folks in town? They think Degataga is the cause of the fever. So, he's planning to head out in the morning."

Henry sat with effort on the edge of the porch, letting his feet dangle. "It's crazy, that's for sure. But once people get something in their head... What can we do about it, Maggie, other than help him sneak out of here without getting caught by 'em?"

Maggie's face flushed with anger, hot and cold washing over her body. "If Degataga isn't welcome here, I'm not welcome here. Pack your things, Henry. Nothing is holding us to this holler anymore with Mama and Pa gone."

Then, turning to Degataga, she said, "We'll be ready at first light."

Chapter 9

Maggie
- Spring 1862 -

Although Henry argued that they weren't strong enough to travel, that it made no sense to leave their home, and that Degataga would be able to move faster without them, Maggie's mind was set.

"I'll not be stayin' in a place that acts this way toward a friend. I've been taught from infancy about healin' people. What they need to make them well. But this community ain't well, Henry. It's full of disease far worse than fever, and it's an illness I got no cure for. Mama had it. Pa, too. I just can't imagine me livin' here helping such folks."

In the end, Maggie won. Because the route was over mountains and across streams, the wagon was useless. Instead, they loaded up the horse and two mules with supplies. Degataga would introduce them to his father, and she and Henry would settle in the little town at the edge of the Cherokee village. Here, she was certain, she would find people who respected what the Cherokee had to offer.

The ride was challenging despite the fine weather. Maggie and Henry were still weak from the fever, which slowed down their progress. Nevertheless, Degataga was an experienced traveler and made their burdens as light as possible.

The only difficulty happened within hours of leaving their home. A stranger on a horse drew up, aiming his gun at Degataga. "What you doin' with these here white folk?" His glassy eyes suggested he'd been drinking. Whether still drunk from the night before or starting afresh that morning was anybody's guess.

As Degataga began to explain, the man pulled back the hammer. "I don't think you're telling me the truth, Injun. No respectable white woman would be out in the woods with you, less'n you done stole them. Now, climb off that horse of yours and lie down on the ground."

Though still weak from the fever, Henry spoke with force. "That's enough. My name is Henry, this is my wife Maggie, and this is our friend Degataga."

The stranger kept the weapon trained on the man but glanced toward Henry and Maggie. "You with this dirty Injun?"

Maggie, furious, stormed, "We are with Degataga. He is a fine man and a fine friend. Now, put that gun away."

"Degataga. What kind of name is Degataga? Me? They call me Jones. And here we got Henry and Maggie. Normal, respectable names. Nope. I don't rightly think these folks are with you on purpose, not even if they say so."

Without warning, Jones pulled the trigger. The explosion split the tree behind Degataga, sending slivers of wood into the air. Maggie began to scream. Degataga, unhurt due to the drunk man's poor aim, dove down, using the horse as cover. Henry grabbed a rifle from the bundle on his saddle.

"That's about enough of that," he stated. "I reckon you better put your gun back where it belongs and head on to wherever you are going. We told you we were with

Degataga, and we ain't planning to tell you again."

When Jones didn't move, Henry shot at a branch to the man's left. Jones dropped his pistol and, with a wild look in his eyes, galloped away.

Degataga hefted the abandoned weapon into the thick brush. "He'll be back. He'll likely bring friends. We need to set off before that happens." Although the threesome worried about further trouble, none materialized. One week after they began, they arrived in Degataga's village.

He made a camp for them on the outskirts, setting up a tent with their bedrolls and bringing in enough wood for a fire. "I'll go and visit my father this evening. Tomorrow, I'll introduce you to him."

The next morning, Degataga rode into the tiny encampment. "My father, Oukonunaka, is preparing a feast in your honor." He looked at Maggie as he spoke. "He asked me to tell you it will be his pleasure to meet with the healer woman of the English people. After the celebration, you and your husband will be his guests in the village. He hopes to talk to you about your healing ways. He also wishes to thank both of you," his gaze now included Henry, "for bringing me here safely from the hands of those who wished to harm me. He is in your debt."

Henry began to protest, but Degataga held up his hand. "My father understands you left your home because of our friendship and defended me against one of your own. Such allegiance is rare. The ceremony this evening will honor our friendship and the cooperation it will bring between our families.

"As it happens, your arrival coincides with nvda atsilusgi, the flower moon ritual. My people celebrate the plants coming to life and blooming again, renewing the Earth.

We thank the Great Spirit, Unetlanvhi, for bringing us the herbs and medicines which taught us how to defend ourselves against sickness. And, we thank Yvwi Gvnahita, Long Man, for bringing us the life in streams and rivers. But tonight will be special because we will also be thankful for oginalii, friends."

As evening approached, Degataga led Maggie and Henry, adorned with gifted beads and feathers, to the ceremonial grounds where the sacred fire created with oak branches burned bright. They were formally introduced to Oukonunaka and given seats of honor next to the medicine man.

Ornate women brought food on slabs of bark. Wild trout, leeks, and fry bread. Sweet potatoes and sunflower seeds. Maggie and Henry ate until their bellies extended, and sleep threatened to overtake them. But they needn't have feared falling asleep.

At midnight, the first dance began. Men and women gathered near the glowing embers behind the one leading the singing. The dancers moved forward, alternating between walking and dancing in a stomping step to the music. The men answered the call-and-response of the leader, while the women created the rhythm with leg rattles made of terrapin shells secured around their calves. Even the children joined in the dance at the end of the line.

Maggie was transfixed by the scene. The women, wearing long skirts and dresses, had colorful yarn belts tied at the waist. The men had feathers and beadwork. The rhythmic movements flowed from one song to the next. As one set of dances finished, another would begin, this time with a different caller.

The dancing lasted until sunrise, at which time the ceremony officially ended. Maggie and Henry rose with their host and were ushered to a windowless log cabin where they slept upon mattresses of soft river reeds and blankets of fur. When they woke, the sun was high in the sky.

A woman escorted them to a fire circle where Degataga sat speaking with Oukonunaka. Both men stood. Oukonunaka raised his hand to them. "Welcome, my friends."

"Thank you for your hospitality," Maggie said, looking to Degataga to determine if his father understood more than a greeting.

Degataga nodded. "My father learned some basic English. He has asked me to remain as an interpreter if doing so is alright with his guests."

"Of course," said Maggie.

Before long, Maggie and Oukonunaka were deep in discussion about herbs, plants, and tinctures. Henry and Degataga sat listening, with Degataga helping the two communicate as needed. Henry was drifting, not paying much attention to the chatter, but his eyes flew open at the mention of childbirth.

"You are married for how long?" asked Oukonunaka.

"Almost three years," Maggie answered.

"No children to your womb?" He pointed to her midsection with a curious expression.

"Several children, but none have made it to the world alive." Maggie's eyes filled with tears, and her mouth set in a firm line to keep her chin from quivering.

"And you had the fever?" he asked.

"Yes. Both Henry and I had the fever, but your son nursed us back to health."

Oukonunaka shook his head. "No. There is nothing

to be done for the fever. One either survives or dies. The strong survive. You are strong. Your Henry is strong. Your womb can be strong. Here. Let me show you."

He led her to a small building. Inside, the shelves contained roots, dried leaves, stems, and oils. The room smelled of her mother, bringing tears to her eyes. She hadn't yet grieved the loss of the woman who brought her life and a passion for healing.

Oukonunaka was busy collecting medicines, unaware of her melancholy. "You take these every morning and evening as a tea."

She looked at each substance, recognizing black cohosh and false unicorn, though she had never used them to help with pregnancy. She held up the other ingredients one by one. Oukonunaka said, "Cherokee rosehip. Bee pollen. Sundrop oil. I will have Ayoka, my wife, show you how. Do this, and you will find your womb becomes strong like the body which beat the fever."

Chapter 10

Maggie
- Autumn 1862 -

Maggie and Henry lived in a small community along the Tuckasegee River beyond the border of Cherokee lands. Degataga introduced them to his French tutor, Lucien Garnier, who invited the couple to board with him. "I've got a spare room," he said, first looking at Maggie, "If you'll do the cookin' and cleanin'," and pivoting to Henry, "And you'll handle the rest of the chores?"

The pair wasn't sure how long they would stay in the area. However, Maggie enjoyed learning the healing arts from Oukonunaka, and with her mama gone, she had no one else to teach her. In turn, she taught Oukonunaka the things she learned from her mama, which had been passed down from traditions from the Old Country. The two didn't always agree and spent hours discussing their differences.

The biggest was about the fever. Oukonunaka believed the fever had no cure. One had to let it run its course. The strong would survive. Although Maggie agreed to a point, she thought healers had many remedies at their disposal that could improve the odds.

"You have medicines you use for fever, Oukonunaka. What of your teas made from dogwood, feverwort, and willow bark. Wouldn't adding this help?"

Oukonunaka shook his head. "Even with the drink, those who are weak, die. Even without, those who are strong live. As the healer, the herbs make you feel better for giving them, but it does nothing for those who suffer."

Throughout this time, Maggie drank her fertility tea morning and night. In early September, as she canned fruits and vegetables and smoked fish for the winter, she realized her monthly flow was overdue. She sat down the jar of applesauce and began to count back. It had been late July, during the Ripe Corn Moon celebration – six weeks earlier.

A rush of adrenaline heated her arms and legs. Could she be with child? More importantly, would she be able to hold onto this baby until birth? She didn't want to tell Henry until she was certain. On the other hand, she didn't want to keep the news to herself. So, she pulled off her apron, grabbed a basket, and headed toward the Cherokee village to chat with the medicine man.

She called out to Henry, "I'm going to visit Oukonunaka. I have a few herbs I need to collect." He nodded in her direction, used to her comings and goings. She suffered a little guilt for not telling Henry the reason she was going, but, on the other hand, if she were pregnant, she was sure to bring back some concoction, making what she said at least somewhat true.

As she approached Oukonunaka's cabin, he looked up and waved. "Good morning, Maggie. What brings you here today?" He began walking toward her and stopped suddenly, his smile broadening. "You are carrying a child!"

Maggie's mouth fell open, and her eyes widened in surprise. "I think I may be, but how did you know?" She ran her hands over her still-flat stomach and shrugged her shoulders.

"It's in your eyes," he said. "A mother always has a child in her eyes."

Maggie crossed the short distance between them and aired her fear. "I've carried babies before. Several. I lose them. Usually early, but one came all the way to term."

He nodded, tilting his head to one side. "The tea worked well for you. Now, we have to help you keep the baby inside the strong womb we've created. Come."

Once again, Oukonunaka took her into the medicine hut – and once again, he suggested herbs to make a tea she was to drink each morning and evening. "Red raspberry leaf will keep your womb strong and able to deliver a healthy baby. Dandelion and nettles help the baby become strong. Once you are closer to delivery, we will add sundrop oil to ready your womb."

A broad smile broke across his face, his eyes crinkling beneath his heavy brow. "Have you told Henry the happy news?"

She shook her head. "I was too afraid. I have lost so many."

He placed his hands on her shoulders. "You will keep this baby. It will grow big and strong and healthy." He turned her around. "Go, now. Go tell your husband and celebrate."

Maggie felt like a little girl with an enormous secret as she half walked, half skipped back to the cabin they shared with Lucien. As she neared the property, she found Henry splitting logs, the white innards shining against the dirt.

When she came into view, he stopped and smiled. She handed him her basket. "Look what Oukonunaka gave me." He peered inside, unsure what he was supposed to see. At his blank look, she said, "Herbs. For a tea. For *my* tea. Actually, for my *new* tea." She waited expectantly while he studied the contents. For a long moment, he said nothing, then his head jerked up, and he looked her in the eye.

"Your new tea? New for what? What happened to your old one?"

Maggie danced from foot to foot, a smile spreading across her face. "I don't need the old tea anymore. I need this one instead."

"Are you saying? Maggie? Are you... are we? Is it?" he stammered.

With laughter bubbling from her chest, she grabbed his hands. "Yes! I am. We are. It is! I am with child, and Oukonunaka says it will be a strong, healthy child." At this, she sobered. "I pray, Henry, it will be a strong, healthy child. Maybe Mama and Pa are looking over the baby and will help it arrive here safely."

Henry held her as she allowed tears to fall, allowing herself a moment to grieve for her parents. After a few moments, she rubbed the sleeve of her dress across her eyes. "Enough of that on such a day as this. Let me put up these herbs, and then I'll set about making a fine supper to celebrate."

She turned on her heel and strode toward the cabin, turning around before she entered the door. "Henry! We are going to have a strong, healthy baby – I'm sure of it!" With that, she disappeared into their home.

* * *

In addition to the daily tea, Oukonunaka had many suggestions to help the child inside of her grow healthy. In some cases, what he suggested seemed ridiculous.

"Henry, you are never going to believe what Oukonunaka told me today," she giggled, something she had to work hard not to do in front of the healer she respected. "I cannot eat speckled trout. Do you know why?"

Henry shrugged. "Indigestion?"

"Worse! The baby will have birthmarks! And no walnuts for me either."

"Walnuts? What could be wrong with walnuts?"

"The poor baby will end up with a big nose. We certainly don't need that." She began to laugh again but soon sobered. "I shouldn't make fun. Every culture has its own customs. I'm sure many of ours appear ridiculous to him, as well as the women.

"Did you know they believe that once pregnant, a Cherokee woman has enormous power? Spirits, good and bad, can use them as a conduit to send down blessings and cursings. The women have no control over which type of spirit uses their body, and that's why the women don't really participate in the daily life of the village. See, if a bad spirit has possession and the woman prepares meals, grows food, or goes fishing, she could be the source of sickness. She could end up causing great destruction to her people."

Henry tilted his head to one side before replying. "That's interesting, I guess. Very different from what we believe."

Maggie nodded in agreement. "Even the father of the baby has to be careful. As long as his wife is carrying a child in her womb, he cannot join in certain dances, dig a grave, or play stickball."

Maggie realized she had the option to ignore these suggestions because she was not Cherokee. However, when it came to the best way to keep her baby safe, she wasn't willing to risk the consequences. She would never forgive herself if she didn't do everything within her power to bring this baby into the world safe and healthy.

Because of this, Maggie steadfastly avoided raccoon and pheasant, both of which could make her baby sickly. She also stopped wearing anything around her neck because Oukonunaka believed this could cause the baby's cord to follow suit, causing strangulation.

But when Oukonunaka made one final suggestion, Maggie balked.

"You came to us, Maggie, during our celebration of Long Man. Do you remember?" She nodded, recalling the delicious food and dancing until dawn. "We also celebrated friendship between us – the healers of two peoples." She nodded again, thankful for their acquaintance and all it brought to her and Henry. "I have consulted the Great Earth, who says you need to honor Long Man, who will, in turn, honor the child growing inside you."

Maggie scrunched up her nose a bit, asking, "How would I honor Long Man?"

"Wash your face and feet in the river each morning and each evening while praying. In this way, Long Man will learn of your gratitude toward him."

Maggie thought about it. Was it possible for her to honor a Cherokee god and still honor her own?

"You must also begin praying by the water at each new moon. As the medicine man, I will wash your head, chest, and face and pray with you and the other women in your condition."

Maggie, who had been sitting outside Oukonunaka's hut, stood. "I'll think about what you've said, but I want to talk with Henry about it. You understand, don't you?"

The medicine man stood, too. "Yes, Maggie. You and I are the same, yet different. My beliefs are not yours. Yours are not mine. Speak with Henry, and then? Do what, in your opinion, is best for your child."

On her way back home, Maggie realized she was seriously considering Oukonunaka's proposal. When she arrived home, she didn't ask Henry. Instead, she told him about the rituals and her intent to give them a try. Henry's eyes grew wide with concern, and they began an earnest discussion, batting ideas and thoughts back and forth like a child's game of ball.

Eventually, Henry asked, "Maggie, what will God think of such things? Surely, He will be unhappy with your prayers to a heathen idol?"

She let out a deep breath. "Heathen? Is that what you think of Oukonunaka? You believe he's a heathen?" They had been discussing the rituals proposed by Oukonunaka for over an hour.

Henry rolled his eyes, matching Maggie's sigh with his own. "That is not what I mean. He and his people have been nothing but kind to us. Without Degataga, we would likely be dead. No, what I'm saying, Maggie, is our religion isn't theirs. It's not the same, and I fear by honoring their river god, you are trying to walk on both sides of the line."

Maggie pulled her chair to the table, resting her chin in her hand. "I don't believe the way they believe. I don't believe spirits can possess my body or that I can bring evil to our home. What I do believe, though, is the Cherokee understand how they are one with nature. They understand balance. They look to nature, just as my mama did, to find the answers to what ails man.

"When I go to the river to pray, Oukonunaka will say his prayers to his god. I can say mine to mine. Although he believes every aspect of nature has a different god, I understand there is one God over everything. He doesn't realize it, but when he is praying to Mother Earth or Long Man, he is really just praying to one part of our God."

Henry squirmed in the chair, uncomfortable with Maggie's line of reasoning.

"Don't you see? In reality, he is praying to our God and just doesn't realize it. But when I'm praying by the river with him, I'll understand. I can be grateful to the river for all it brings to me because I'm aware of the real source of the river."

Henry shrugged. "I just don't want you to be givin' up God because of fear." He stared into her eyes. "You are afraid. You've lost so many babies. Just so you understand it isn't God's doing, and the magical prayers of a medicine man won't make everything right. That's all I gotta know."

She nodded. "I just need peace, Henry. Standing by the water, saying a prayer, listening to Oukonunaka chant – these things calm me. They will help me feel grounded instead of terrified."

Henry moved behind Maggie's chair, wrapping his arms around her shoulders. "Then you have my blessing."

Chapter 11

Maggie
- Winter 1863 -

The mild winter allowed Maggie to spend time outside and meet with Oukonunaka to continue to learn from him. Because of her condition, she could no longer walk through the village. Though she had no fear of tainting their food, she knew better than to offend her friends. The two healers often met at the river, on the border of Cherokee land and the tiny settlement where she now made her home.

He came not only to visit with her but also to help those who were sick. Surprisingly, unlike in Burnsville, which was fraught with prejudice, everyone in this little community came to the medicine man for care. White, black, and Indian all had faith in him to do his best to cure them.

She supposed the difference was these people had no other choice. Either those living at the edge of civilization trusted Oukonunaka, or they figured out what to do on their own. The latter choice could easily result in death.

Maggie continued to study the various ways her mentor used herbs and roots. She began keeping a small notebook to help her remember what his herb choices were, as well as the different methods he used to prepare his remedies.

But Maggie was more interested in the reasons behind the Cherokee customs. Oukonunaka explained how everything in the environment – from people to squirrels to snakes to corn to herbs to rivers to mountains to fire – had a spirit. These spirits all had a role in the world and in the lives of his people.

"Man does not rule over the plants and trees. Or the animals. Nor do plants and animals rule over man. We are each trying to find our proper place. We are each just one small part of nature, and each part has a job to fulfill. If one part cannot find their place, the earth becomes sick."

To help her understand their beliefs further, he told her the story of how sickness and disease first came to earth. "Long ago, when the world first was, everyone had a voice. Animals and plants could talk, and all lived in harmony with humans.

"But the humans refused to find their place in nature and constantly pushed for more. More space, more food, more power. They began to spread over the earth, crowding out the animals and the plants, causing them to leave their homes. They hunted too many animals for food.

"The animal tribes – the deer, the bear, the moose, the elk, along with smaller animals such as the raccoon, the birds, the fish – called a council. They were angry about their treatment from the humans and declared war.

"Each animal tribe selected a disease to send to the humans. Some left them crippled. Some made them sick. Some killed them.

"The plant tribes, when they heard this, believed the animal tribes had gone too far. They called their own council and agreed to be the cures for the diseases sent by the animals. Every plant has its own use, with even the weeds having a purpose. As a healer, I must listen to the spirit of the plant to find out what disease it is meant to cure.

"So, you see, Maggie, what happens when the different parts of nature become out of balance. First, man wanted too much. Then, animals took their revenge too far. Finally, it was up to the plants to restore the balance. But if man had stayed within their bounds to begin with, there would be no need for someone like you or me."

Maggie realized in this belief system, balance was in everything. Women balanced men. Winter balanced summer. Fire balanced water. Plants balanced animals. Farming balanced hunting. And humans were responsible for keeping the balance within themselves and among the different elements of nature.

This idea was new to Maggie. Though she was certain animals did not talk or seek revenge, she did believe there was a balance to the earth and felt a connection with many of the Cherokee practices that worked to keep the equilibrium.

She worked among several women before her pregnancy as they gathered medicinal plants in the forest. She bent low, pulling up the roots in the patch of ginseng, when someone put their hand on her shoulder. Maggie looked up into the eyes of a young woman about her own age.

She spoke no English but knelt next to Maggie, pulling the root from one plant without disturbing those surrounding it. Then she did the same with another plant, again leaving those surrounding it. She pointed to Maggie, who did the same. When the woman was satisfied that Maggie understood the process, she went back to her own basket.

Later, when Maggie returned from the woods, she asked Oukonunaka about the practice. "We harvest only every fourth plant. We leave the others to grow for future use. It is part of nature's balance. Without balance, we bring on our own sickness or failed crops or poor hunting. Everything that happens that is not good is because we neglected our responsibility to keep the balance."

Oukonunaka sat down, his legs stretched out in front of him, and began tamping tobacco into his pipe. "You know, Maggie, balance doesn't just happen with harvesting roots and herbs. Our hunters also use balance. Four days before heading out to find food, our hunters purify themselves with washings, fastings, prayers, and rituals. They begin the hunt with a prayer asking for success. When they find this success, they pray for forgiveness for taking the animal's life, explaining that their need was great. To prove this need, we use every part of the animal, from the meat and skins to the bones and sinews. The only exception is when we leave part of the animal as a sacrifice or sign of respect to the animal's spirit."

As Maggie continued to learn about balance, she noted that people sought out the medicine man for more than illness and disease. They often consulted Oukonunaka about emotional issues or dilemmas in their lives – all things pertaining to some type of unbalance.

As a healer, and one who could talk with the spirits of plants, they believed Oukonunaka could help them restore the balance. Of course, those in the English settlement did not seek him out for this purpose, but the idea that balance was needed for the body and spirit made a lot of sense to Maggie.

The most unique aspect of the Cherokee healing practice, and one Maggie found fascinating, was the use of song. Often, Oukonunaka would begin to chant while working to heal someone of a disease or illness. If family and friends were present, they, too, would sing, offering the healing energy of their spirits to the process.

At first, Maggie found the ritual to be primitive. However, she soon noted the intonations provided a soothing effect on the patient. It was the same when Oukonunaka chanted his prayers over her during the new moons. Although she didn't understand what he said, the rhythmic sounds flowing from one note to the next calmed her, allowing her to commune with God more effectively.

In the beginning, she could find no discernable pattern to the tunes. However, she began to realize most of the lyrics were repeated four times before the song came to an end. And though she didn't recognize the words, Oukonunaka appeared to say the same thing every time, without alterations.

One of the most common chants Oukonunaka offered was known as the healing prayer. She asked him if he would teach it to her. He said, "I say this prayer over those who want to be healed and believe balance can be restored.

Grandfather,
Sacred one,
Teach us love, compassion,
and honor.
That we may heal the earth
And heal each other."

Maggie listened intently, leaning on the words. Love. Compassion. Honor. All characteristics she learned in church. This prayer seemed to be in perfect harmony with the God she knew. And the part about healing the earth and healing each other – isn't that what she did? What her mother did? Her grandmother? Didn't each, in their own way, try to use the earth's bounties as a way of healing one another?

"That is beautiful, Oukonunaka. A perfect prayer. And though it is lovely in English, would you teach it to me in your language?"

Oukonunaka looked surprised. "You wish to learn Tsalagi? It is not so easy for the English tongue."

"Nor is English easy for the Cherokee tongue, but you have mastered it. I will likely never speak fluent Tsalagi," she said, struggling over the foreign sounds in her mouth, then continued. "However, I want the words you use for healing to become part of what I do. Remember, I've come here to gain knowledge."

"Yes, Maggie, you have indeed. So, let me teach you." He spent time each day helping her to form her lips and tongue around the awkward sounds, correcting her when her voice went up instead of down. "Rising sounds are different from falling sounds. They mean different things. Be careful, or you may find yourself asking forgiveness of a bear!"

After many weeks, she was able to say the Healing Prayer and often murmured it in addition to her own prayers when she ritually washed in the river.

And with each utterance, she felt a peace that, this time, she would bring forth a child she'd have the opportunity to keep.

Chapter 12

Maggie
- Spring 1863 -

Maggie was nearing full-term. The baby squirmed inside her belly, the kicking alternating between her ribs and her bladder. "I believe this child is trying to dig its way out," Maggie exclaimed as the bulge rolled one way and then the next. Although she complained a bit about the punches and kicks, in reality, she thrilled to have such a strong, active baby growing within her.

"Have you given any more thoughts to names?"

She and Henry decided they would not reuse the name Henry. Though it was customary to keep trying for a son to carry on his father's name, both believed they already had that son, and he now lay buried with his grandparents near their homestead.

Henry scratched his chin and began throwing out names that made Maggie laugh. "Elder? Haskell? Zollie? Ruel? Ossie? Furman?"

"What horrible names, Henry! No son of mine is going to have the name Zollie McCoury. Do you want him to be teased his entire life? And I've noticed you are focusing entirely on boys' names. What if we have a girl? Do you plan to call her Furman?"

He grinned. "We could call her Furgirl!"

Maggie balled up the dish towel in her hand and threw it at his head. "I'm serious, Henry. This baby will be here soon enough, and right now, the child has no name. If we aren't careful, the baby will end up with a Cherokee name, and we'll have to live here next to the Qualla Boundary forever."

Maggie and Henry had begun talking about moving back home to Green Mountain Gap. Although Maggie loved what she was learning at the hands of Oukonunaka, both missed their home. With Maggie's parents gone, the land was all theirs. They could move into the big house, start farming, and raise their family. And Maggie could take on the role of granny woman.

With a thoughtful expression, Henry said, "Names are so important, Maggie. In many ways, I like the way the Cherokee do it, giving the baby a name at birth, and later, once the child shows who they really are, giving them another name to match."

Maggie nodded in agreement. "I think it is all part of their balance. They do the best they can in the moment and make the necessary changes to keep the balance once they have more information. But, in actuality, we do something similar.

"I'm Margaret Louise. I've been Margaret Louise, Maggie Lou, and just plain Maggie. Each name suits a different part of who I am. You are Henry Thomas. You could be Hank or Harry or even go by your middle name or initials. Plus, how many people do you know of who go by a nickname? Think about Red, in town. That surely ain't what his parents put on the church records, but he took it on because of his hair, in just the same way the Cherokee do."

Smiling, Henry reached out to take Maggie's hand.

"You are a wise woman, Maggie. You are going to make a fine mother and a fine healer."

"Thank you, Henry. But we still don't have a name for our baby." She looked at him pointedly.

Henry laughed out loud. "You are not just a fine mother but a determined one." He paused before saying, "I actually have been thinking of naming a daughter Caroline Ann. It was my grandmother's name. Caroline means a person who is beloved, and surely, if we have a daughter, she will be beloved. What do you think?"

Maggie threw her arms around Henry, the awkward bump keeping her from getting as close as she'd like. "I love the name, and I love the idea of a beloved child. If it is a girl, we will name her Caroline Ann. And if it is a boy?"

Henry swatted her playfully on the backside. "You are relentless! I've already named our baby girl. That's going to have to be enough for one day. Now, off to bed with you. I have a long day tomorrow helping Lucien prepare the garden plot for planting."

Maggie, despite being tired, turned from back to side to back again, unable to find a comfortable position. Just as she finally closed her eyes, a pain tore through her abdomen, making the breath catch in her throat. She stifled a moan, hoping not to wake Henry. Within moments, the pain eased, and Maggie closed her eyes again, wondering if the time had come.

She didn't have to wonder for any length of time, as the next pain came ten minutes later. Though it, too, was short-lived, she remembered the early pains when she birthed Henry, and these were similar.

Thinking of the baby boy she lost, Maggie's hands

turned cold, and she gripped the top of the blanket. She managed to carry the baby to term, but she had done the same thing with little Henry. She couldn't bear the thought of losing yet another child.

As the panic grew, threatening to overtake her, Maggie thought of her times with Oukonunaka at the river. All his words of assurance. His prayers. Even his use of beads to predict the future pointed to a healthy delivery. She quietly murmured the healing prayer, first in English, then in Cherokee, continuing to softly chant until her fingers loosened their grip, and her mind cleared.

Without making any noise, Maggie rose from the bed, slipped on her shoes, and made her way to the water. In between contractions, she washed her feet and her face while saying a prayer.

"God, it is time. The baby is ready to enter the world. I've done all I can do to bring the baby here safely. It is now up to You. I am grateful to You for my friendship with the Cherokee people and the things they have taught me about Your great creations – the life provided by the water, the healing provided by the plants, the food provided by the animals, the balance You created for all to enjoy. I ask thee now to help me in the coming hours and to allow this baby I'm carrying to be part of Your great plan. In Jesus' name. Amen."

Chapter 13

Maggie
- April 30, 1863 -

When Henry woke, he found Maggie sitting in the kitchen, gripping the edge of the small table in the corner of their room. "What's wrong? Are you sick?" He sprinted out of bed and to her side.

She smiled weakly, her face pale in the morning light. "Not sick, Henry. The pains started in the night. I've been managing them by breathing the way I was taught by the women of the village. I didn't want to wake you or Lucien in the night."

Henry's eyes were wild, darting from Maggie to the door and back again. "What do I need to do? Boil water? Gather towels? Find Oukonunaka?"

Maggie put her hand on Henry's forearm, forcing him to look down at her. "I'm fine, Henry. It has only just begun. Labor can take hours, even days. Though, I do think I would like you to let Oukonunaka know. Despite being the medicine man, he will not be permitted to participate in the birth, but he can come now and provide a blessing to make the delivery easy. He'll also bring Atsila, who will tend to me."

Henry turned toward the door, ready to find Oukonunaka, but Maggie caught his arm again. "Henry? You have enough time to put your pants on." Maggie laughed heartily until the next pain hit, spurring her husband into action.

In what seemed like mere moments, Oukonunaka came through the tiny home and into the bedroom where Maggie still sat in the chair, sometimes still and quiet, other times moaning softly and rocking her body to and fro.

He held her hand in his own as he crouched down to be eye to eye. "You are a strong woman, Maggie. It is time to use this strength to bring your baby into the world." Then he began a peaceful chant, one Maggie hadn't heard before. The intonations soothed her soul, reminding her she could do hard things, especially with God on her side.

Oukonunaka stood. "I will be nearby, Maggie. Trust Atsila to help you. Trust the Great Spirit to guide you. Trust yourself to bring forth a healthy child."

Maggie hated for her old friend to go. Though she was fond of Atsila, her presence wasn't as calming. When she entered the room and began the chant intended to frighten the baby from her womb, the lingering peace fled.

Oukonunaka had explained the ritual to her weeks before. "Atsila will come to your bed and shout at the baby to leave your womb. First, she will say the words assuming the baby is a boy.

> 'Listen! You little man, get up now at once. There comes an old woman. The horrible old thing is coming, only a little way off. Listen! Quick! Get your bed and let us run away. Yu!'

"Then, she will repeat it in case you are having a girl, saying the same thing, but will call the child 'little woman.'"

Maggie laughed at his description. "Do you think it works?" she asked.

He smiled at her. "The baby will do what the baby will do. However, we can certainly suggest what we would like to have happen."

While Atsila chanted in a loud, angry tone, she shook a rattle high and low, moving throughout the room. By the time she finished, Maggie's womb had begun to contract again.

Atsila, who spoke very little English, said, "See? Baby listen!" Then she prepared an infusion of wild cherry bark to help speed up the delivery. Maggie was certain the concoction would be far more beneficial than the chant.

As the labor progressed, Atsila became more insistent for Maggie to remain standing. "No sit, Maggie. Stand."

Maggie groaned against the pain, her knees growing weak and threatening to deposit her onto the floor. "I have to sit. I have to lie down. I can't." But Atsila held her under one arm with a tight grip, moving her across the floorboards, back and forth. Only when the contraction ended did Atsila agree to let her rest.

As the sun started to dip in the sky, Maggie's thoughts turned dark. She had been laboring all day. It was just as it had been with little Henry. She called frantically for her husband. "Henry! Henry!"

Despite Atsila's efforts to hold the door closed, Henry burst into the room. "I'm here, Maggie. I'm here."

"Oh, Henry. I'm so afraid. I'm trying so hard, but the baby isn't coming. What if I lose another baby, Henry? What if..."

Henry stroked her hair as he held her in his arms. "Shhh, now. Shhh. Remember everything Oukonunaka has taught you, Maggie. Remember the balance. It is up to you to keep the balance. And remember God, Maggie. Come on, say it with me,

'Fear thou not; for I am with thee: be not dismayed; for I am thy God: I will strengthen thee; yea, I will help thee; yea, I will uphold thee with the right hand of my righteousness.'"

Maggie began to recite the scripture with Henry. A calm assurance, like the one she experienced when Oukonunaka blessed her earlier in the day, overcame her. Henry repeated the words again. When he finished, she murmured, "Again, Henry. Please say them again."

Once Maggie calmed, Atsila removed Henry from the room with an insistent shove. "No men," she said as she pushed the door closed. "Bad luck."

But Henry's presence had been enough to remind Maggie of Oukonunaka's words about believing in the Great Spirit and in herself. Now, when the pains came, she repeated Isaiah 41:10, followed by the Cherokee healing prayer. By focusing on these things, she found she could bear the pain.

As the night darkened, Maggie spied the moon out the window, rising over the trees. She gasped when she realized it was a full moon. Tonight would be the Flower Moon celebration, the same celebration she experienced the first time she met Oukonunaka.

She imagined the food and the dancing. She imagined the celebration of new life to come. How fitting it was that her child would come during the celebration of new life.

Her child would be born as the first plants of the season grew – the very same plants that help man against sickness and disease. Her child would be born as the river began teeming with new life – the very same river she bathed in twice a day for the entirety of her pregnancy. Her baby would be born in the time of birth and renewal.

Sometime in the wee hours of the morning, before the

sun rose but long after the moon was high, Maggie started to push. Atsila had her crouch down, holding onto the table for support. With each contraction, Maggie felt the baby move closer and closer to its entrance into the world. Then, with an enormous effort from Maggie, the baby slid its way into the waiting hands of Atsila.

Maggie closed her eyes, panting from the exertion. The silence after all the grunting and moaning was eerie. Maggie began to chant softly, praying fervently that all the hard work had not been in vain. That her baby had survived.

After an eternity of worry, the infant let out a long wail. Maggie opened her eyes, taking in her pink daughter, who was loudly protesting her arrival. She held out her arms for the child and pulled her close, allowing Atsila to take care of the placenta and cord.

Finally, Maggie crawled into her bed, pulling the blanket over her tired, sweaty body. Despite the exhaustion, Maggie looked into her daughter's sweet face, unwilling to fall asleep for fear of missing these first moments with her precious baby. Henry was ushered into the room by a triumphant Atsila, and Maggie, with trembling arms, held out the child. "Henry, meet Caroline Ann."

Chapter 14

Josie Mae
- February 27, 1893 -

Josie Mae had long abandoned her knitting, listening with rapt attention to the tale of her mama's birth. When Granny finished speaking, Josie Mae could not contain her questions. "Why did Mama never tell me she was born near a Cherokee village – and with a Cherokee woman right in the room?"

Maggie startled at the sound of her granddaughter's voice. She had been so engrossed in her memories that she had forgotten Josie Mae sat a mere three feet away.

"I can't be sayin' why your mama didn't tell you the story. As for me? It's not an easy one to tell, being all wrapped up with the death of my mama and pa, my little boy, all my lost babies, and the innocence of my youth."

Josie Mae wrinkled her eyebrows. "The innocence of your youth? Whatever do you mean, Granny?"

Maggie ran a hand through her hair before clasping her hands in her lap. "Prior to meeting Degataga, I didn't understand that someone, like my mama, could hate another person simply because of the color of their skin or who their god was or even what kind of home they lived in. I believed what the Bible tells us about lovin' one another, and jus' figured everyone else did, too."

Josie Mae sat back in her chair, thinking about these words. "Granny? Do people still hate other people because of such things, or did that only happen back when you were young?"

Granny shook her head from side to side. "No, sadly, it still goes on. The Cherokee were driven from this land because they were different. There was a war back when your mama was a girl to end slavery, but many folks still don't want to associate with the freed blacks.

"And it isn't just about color. It's about religion, with those attending one church talking bad about those attending another, and most churches talking bad about folks who don't attend one at all. And those without money are often judged to be lazy or no good. Seems to be the way with some people, to hate others."

Josie Mae stilled, a thought forming that scared her a bit. "And Mama? Does Mama have that kind of hatred? Is that why she hasn't told me about the Cherokee?"

Maggie sighed deeply. "Your mama. Oh, I suspect she has some hate in her. Most of us do. I found some in my own body a time or two. But, no, I don't think it is hate that drives your mama. I think it is shame.

"See, your mama always wanted to be something more. A city girl. Educated. Refined. Anything touching her that isn't upper class – like me and this home and my working with the Cherokee – is like a smudge on her reputation. She don't hate the Cherokee because of their color or their religion. I don't even think she hates them at all. She simply doesn't see them as necessary because they don't fit into her world.

"But I don't want you to go thinkin' your mama isn't a good woman. She is. She loves you fiercely, and me, as well, despite the stain I bring. She is smart, independent, and wants to help others. Remember this, Josie Mae – everyone has good traits and bad ones. It's our task to make the good ones better and tame the bad ones into submission."

Josie Mae, who had listened to the story far too long to let it end without questions, asked, "What are your bad traits, Granny? The ones you have to tame?"

Maggie laughed out loud. "If'n you don't have any notion, then I must be doin' a mighty good job. And for that, I think we need to celebrate." She headed to the kitchen, cut them both a slice of cake, and put the kettle on to boil.

Not satisfied with the answer, Josie Mae persisted after shoveling in a forkful of the sweet. "I'm serious, Granny. What kind of things are you taming?"

Maggie set down her fork. "I'm not going to make you a list, Josie Mae, but here's one to help you understand what I mean. I lost a baby boy and several others before I had your mama. I lost several more after. I was never able to have another child, despite wanting one so badly. I've had to learn to be content with what the Good Lord has blessed me with and not spend my time wishing I got something else instead."

Josie Mae ducked her head, ashamed for pushing her Granny to say more about the lost babies. Maggie reached over and tussled her hair. "Don't you worry about it none, Josie Mae. It is always good to take a look at the things you are working on, even if it is difficult to do so."

Now Josie Mae looked into her Granny's eyes. "And... what do you think my bad traits are, Granny? What do I need to tame?"

Maggie, who had resumed eating, stopped again. "Child, you are still so young. You have many years before you have to fret too much about good traits and bad."

Josie Mae shook her head with emphasis. "I'm not so little anymore, Granny. I'm twelve, almost thirteen. Mama says I will be a woman soon. And you are letting me go with you to the Cherokee village because I'm old enough. And you told me the story about your babies."

She pushed her plate back on the table and went to the desk where Granny kept the writing paper. After rummaging for the pencil, she brought both back to where they sat. "I'm going to make two lists, Granny. The first list will be my good traits. The second list will be my bad ones."

She wrote "Good" on one side of the page and "Bad" on the other with a long line down the center. Then she sat with the pencil tip touching her lips. This was harder than she'd expected it to be. "Granny? Isn't thinking about the things you do well kind of like bragging? Doesn't the Bible say boasting is a sin?"

"It depends on what you're making the list for, Josie Mae. If you was makin' the list to show it off to your friends, why that would be boastin', and that would be a sin.

"But if you was makin' the list for your own eyes, so you could work on makin' your strong traits stronger, then it is actually a Godly activity. In Ephesians, it says to put off the old self, which is what a person does when they try to make themselves better than they were before."

Josie Mae continued looking at the column marked Good. When nothing came to mind, she shifted her gaze to Bad. Here, she seemed to have no issues. Lazy. Willful. Talk without thinking. Forgetful. Impatient. Jealous.

Maggie leaned over to study the list, and Josie Mae blushed hot for her Granny to read all those horrible traits written for anyone to see. Granny pointed, saying, "You ain't got nothin' on the good side. You needin' some help?"

When Josie Mae didn't answer, Maggie began ticking off things on her fingers. "Loving. Kind. Thoughtful. Helpful. Friendly. Honest. Cheerful."

Josie Mae started to laugh and held up her hand. "You are going too fast, Granny! I can't write them down as quick as you are saying them."

She put the pencil on the paper and went to her grandmother. Despite being almost a grown woman in size, she sat on her Granny's lap and looped her arms around her neck. "Thank you, Granny. Thank you for the list. And for the stories. And for just being you. I love you."

Chapter 15

Carrie Ann
- March 10, 1893 -

Carrie Ann pushed her way outside, careful to cover her face with a scarf. The bitter wind was vicious, biting anyone foolish enough to let a bit of skin show. In the two minutes it took to walk from her home to the doctor's office, icicles began to form on her eyelashes. She moved inside, stamping the snow off her boots as she crossed the threshold.

Dr. McKeithen looked up with a smile. "Is that you under all the wool, Carrie Ann? Or do I need to worry that some unknown intruder has come to make off with our meager supplies?"

Carrie Ann unwound the length of blue, knit by her daughter and given to Carrie Ann as a Christmas present. "It's me. No need to fret. Not that anyone would be out in weather such as this unless they were facing an emergency."

Daniel chuckled. "But, Carrie Ann, you are out in this weather! Is there some crisis I'm unaware of?"

Carrie Ann, growing tired of the banter, shrugged. "No emergency. Just work ethic. Imagine some poor soul needing medical attention and finding a bit of cold air kept the doctor and nurse at home."

She thought of her mama, likely huddled around the

stove in the main room of the house, of no use to anyone feeling poorly in town. This gave Carrie Ann a sense of smug satisfaction. She was here. Her mother was not. It would be foolish for someone to hike the miles out to consult with the granny woman when they could find modern medicine right here in town.

Of course, there wasn't a lot of medicine to be had at the moment. The sizeable snowfall this winter had cut Burnsville off from Asheville and any of the bigger cities to the East. That meant few deliveries for the apothecary.

As if reading her mind, Daniel said, "Even if they come, they aren't likely to find what they need. I didn't realize how cold things could become here. I should have ordered more supplies at the beginning of the cold weather. I pray, for the sake of those in town, some epidemic doesn't roll through before the roads open."

Carrie Ann shook her head as if dusting off his comments. "You couldn't have known because this kind of weather doesn't happen often. I was Josephine's age the last time we had a winter like this."

Poor Josephine. The child had been stuck out in the middle of the woods for weeks with only her grandmother for company. She must be going out of her mind with boredom. She said as much to Daniel.

"Boredom? Why would she be bored with your mother around? All that knowledge right in one room for the taking. I wouldn't complain about being trapped with her for a few days if she was willing to tell me everything she knew."

Carrie Ann sighed. They were back to this again.

"Let's just assume, for the sake of argument, that my mother had some things of value to pass along. I can assure you that after three weeks, you'd be more than ready to brave sure death at the hands of subzero weather than sit and listen to her ramble for one more minute. I just hope Josephine has the fortitude to stick it out. I'd hate to find her frozen on the path to town."

Before Daniel could reply, the door opened, letting in a blast of frigid air. It was Esther's husband, John.

"Sorry to be troublin' ya," he said, dipping his head first in Carrie Ann's direction and then toward Daniel. "But the baby's gotten croup. Esther's been walking him to and fro for two days. She's done worn out, but the baby? He's still coughin'. Was hoping you could come have a look? Didn't want to bring him out in the cold."

Daniel reached out his hand to John, grabbing him at the elbow as they shook. "No need to apologize, John. That's what we are here for. Let me grab my bag." Turning to Carrie Ann, he asked, "Do you mind handling things here until I return? Shouldn't be too long."

"Of course, Doctor." She rummaged in the cupboard, managing to find their last bottle of ipecacuanha. "Here, Doctor, you'll want to take this with you." In a quieter voice, one not meant for John's ears, she whispered, "We are out of liquid mercury." He nodded as he jammed his arms into the sleeves of his coat.

"Come, John. Let's see what I can do to help little Malcolm feel better and give that wife of yours a bit of rest."

Once the men departed, Carrie Ann decided it was time to understand the full extent of their problem. She pulled out a tablet and pencil to make an inventory of what they had left. As she lifted down each jar, one at a time, she wrote the name and the quantity of each. She also quizzed herself to be sure she still remembered what the drug was for.

"Tongaline is best used for rheumatism, gout, sciatica, and nervous headaches." She noted the jar contained about two ounces.

"Morphine relieves pain, headaches, menstrual cramps, asthma, and gastrointestinal diseases." This container was empty except for a slight powder residue. However, she wasn't too worried because they had several ounces each of opium and cocaine, both of which could help with similar issues.

"Bicarbonate of soda for indigestion and potassium iodide, also known as salt, for dysentery, epilepsy, and syphilis. Nux vomica for heart and respiratory complaints." She noted with satisfaction that they had enough of these to last until spring shipments could arrive.

Mercury was gone, as was arsenic. Finally, looking on the bottom row, she took down Folia Sennae, a drug used to treat fevers, finding they had enough for two or three doses, but no more. The caraway seeds were also used up, having helped Mrs. Robertson with her colicky baby. The benzoin, useful for coughs, was in low supply. And, she had just given Daniel the only remaining powder root of ipecacuanha.

Her shoulders drooped as she realized they would have next to nothing to offer patients with coughs and fevers, two of the most common ailments during the long winter months. She prayed the roads opened up soon so their supplies could return to normal.

As she finished straightening the jars, Daniel pushed into the room, the frigid air clinging to his coat. "You'd never know it was midday. It's as cold as it was before the sun came up." He rubbed his hands together with force and speed, hoping to create a bit of heat.

He removed his bulky jacket and leaned down to throw another log into the fire. Sparks rose up the chimney, and a burst of flames illuminated the floor around the fireplace.

"I think Malcolm's going to be fine. He's coughing, that's for sure, but I've seen much worse. I've got them creating steam for the child every two hours. I also told John to take his turn walking the boy. Esther's got to rest, or she'll be sick soon, too."

He handed her the bottle of ipecacuanha. "I asked John to come by tomorrow if Malcolm is any worse. If he is, we'll start him on some medications. If not?" He shrugged. "I hated to use the last of what we've got unless we have to." He shrugged again. "I wish I had some liquid mercury. That always makes the steam work better."

He turned, running his hands through his hair. "But, as my mother used to say, 'If wishes were horses, then beggars would ride.'"

Carrie Ann hated seeing Daniel look so defeated. Here he was, a Harvard-educated doctor who decided to take up residence in the little town of Burnsville. She knew she was the reason and felt both guilty and delighted. She still held him at a distance and wasn't sure she wanted a relationship, but she couldn't help worrying that he would eventually pack his bags and head to an area that appreciated what he had to offer.

Carrie Ann put her hand on his shoulder. "You did the right thing, Daniel. If he isn't too terribly sick, then we need the medicine on hand for a child who might be worse off."

He stepped away from Carrie Ann, not seeming to notice her casual use of his first name. "You may be right, Carrie Ann, but I don't like it. I don't like it one bit."

Chapter 16

Maggie
- March 10, 1893 -

Josie Mae scurried around the stove, helping Maggie cook the evening meal. The girl had already been out to the woodpile, bringing in as much wood as she could carry in two trips. "That's enough for now, child. You'll freeze to death out there," Maggie had scolded.

Now, Maggie rolled out the biscuit dough, cutting out large squares and placing them on the baking sheet. Josie Mae stirred the thick stew, making sure the soup didn't scald in the pan. Maggie caught her dipping in her finger and waggled her own finger at her. "But, Granny! How else am I gonna know if it needs more spice?" she asked.

"It's got plenty of spice, and you are well aware of it. You're just not willin' to be patient and wait for it to be sittin' in your bowl."

Josie Mae laughed as Granny said, "You can't fool me, no matter what."

"Fine! I'll keep my fingers out of the pot if'n you hurry and put those biscuits in the oven. I'm so hungry my mama can probably hear my stomach rumblin' all the way in town."

Maggie grunted. This cold snap better end soon. She wasn't worried about running out of food, but the larder was getting slim on flour and sugar. She hated the idea of rationing the breads and sweets, especially with the way Josie Mae was eating. Maggie was confident her granddaughter had grown two inches this winter, and all her dresses were hanging a bit short of the ankle.

As she finished up the biscuits, her mind turned to taming her bad traits – something she'd been thinking about ever since the conversation with Josie Mae two weeks earlier. She told Josie Mae about the babies but not the entire story.

It was true she had to learn to be content with one child. It was true this had not been easy. But what she failed to mention was she struggled against her own helplessness.

It made no sense to her that, as a healer, she had no ability to heal her own body. If healing had to do with balance, as she firmly believed, what was out of balance in her?

She didn't believe it was an herbal solution – she tried everything available to hold on to the babies which formed in her womb. No, it must be something else, and it was this something that nagged at her.

In Luke, it said, "Physician, heal thyself." And yet, no matter how she struggled, she failed. Even after all these years, she hadn't grown content with what God had allowed her to have.

And the exasperation didn't stop with her own body. She lost her precious husband. Her ma and pa. Nonetheless, folks in town looked to her to make them well with such certain faith. At times, she wanted to scream that she didn't have the answers. If she did, she would have saved those who meant so much to her.

She wondered if this was the opposite half of her gift. What was worse than knowing you had the ability to cure some but not the ability to cure others? She gave her arms and shoulders a quick shake, reminding herself her granddaughter was hungry and making a meal was more important at the moment than introspection.

"There. All done. Now, just ten minutes in the heat, and we'll be ready to eat."

No sooner had she popped in the biscuits than a loud banging began on the door. Standing up while brushing her hands on her apron, Maggie rushed to the door, swinging it wide, letting in a blast of cold and some unrecognizable soul. "Goodness! Come in!"

Maggie propelled the visitor through the doorway and toward the fire, closing the door with a firm shove. "Josie Mae! Put another couple of logs on and set the kettle to boil." She turned to the man – for he was undoubtedly a man by his size – with raised eyebrows. "What in tarnation are you doin' out in weather like this? And it fixin' to get dark soon?"

While she spoke, she worked to unwrap her guest, winding off the scarf and tugging at the mittens. As she reached for his cap, she realized who had come all the way to the holler. "John? John Stallard? Is that you?"

Maggie wasn't sure if he was nodding or simply shivering, so she pushed him a bit closer to the fire and wrapped him in a warm blanket.

"What is it, John? Is it Esther? The children?"

John stammered, syllables chattering from his lips without making full sentences. "Mal....colm.....sick......Esther...... fran.....tic.....must.....find.....Mag.....gie......."

Maggie turned to Josie Mae. "Help me pull off his boots,

child. We've got to warm him up." But, as she stooped to take hold of a heel, John jerked his foot back. "NO!" Then, with less force, "No….Maggie…..Got….to…..help…..Malcolm….."

Now it was Maggie's turn to be stern. "John Stallard! You know, good and well, I'm gonna do everything I can to help your child." She pulled him around to face her, staring into his eyes. "You realize that, right?"

He nodded weakly.

"But if'n things is so bad an extra five minutes is gonna make the difference, then it is too late for me to be much good. If I let you go back out before gettin' ya warm, you are likely to die from the cold. And what good would it be to Esther to lose her husband? Can ya tell me that?"

When John didn't speak, Maggie mumbled, more to herself than anyone else, "Comin' all the way out here on a day like this. Nearly freezin' to death and taking no notice of his own health. Actin' like I don't understand the situation." While she spoke, she rubbed his arms, moving her hands up and down and back again. "Josie Mae? Is the water done boilin' yet?"

"No, ma'am. It ain't bubblin', but some steam is risin'."

"That will be good enough. It's gonna be warmer than he is." Maggie stirred in some tea and a bit of sugar, pressing the mug into John's big hands. "Drink this. Go on, now. Drink it up." She nodded in satisfaction as he pulled the cup to his lips.

Once the cup was empty, Maggie said, "Now, tell me. What's wrong with Malcolm? What brought you all the way out here to me when a doctor lives and works right in town?"

John looked down at the floor, the blood rushing to his cheeks. "We done went to Dr. McKeithen earlier today,

Maggie. Esther, she didn't want to. She wanted me to come fetch you right off, but I said it made no sense to come out here. She wasn't happy but finally gave in."

Maggie prodded him on. "Go on, John. I'm not angry you went to the doctor. He's a good man. And you were right. It is senseless to be out here, yet here you are."

"Well, Dr. McKeithen came on out to our place. He looked at Malcolm. Listened to his chest. Said what we'd been sayin', that he had the croup. Told us to steam him every two hours. Gave Esther a talkin' to 'bout givin' the baby to me once in a while so she could rest. Then, he said he'd come back in a day or two, that Malcolm, though sick, wasn't too terrible bad."

John looked up at Maggie. "I asked him 'bout gettin' some medicine. Some of the fancy stuff from the apothecary meant for babies with croup. And he told me he was all out of the silver and only had a smidgen of the ip-something root. Said he hated givin' it away unless Malcolm got sicker. Then he was gone."

Maggie's eyes stretched open. "So, he didn't give Malcolm anything to help with the cough?"

John shook his head. "No, said he didn't have nothin' to give 'cept if Malcolm got worse. So, after walking the floor with the child another couple of hours, steaming him like the doctor said, Esther insisted I fetch you. She said you'd bring something to make him stop wheezin'. And here I am."

Maggie began barking instructions to Josie Mae. "Ladle some of the stew into a pot to go with me. Enough for the family. Leave a bit here for you to eat. Be sure to remove them biscuits out of the oven before they burn."

As Josie Mae hurried to do as she was told, Maggie

gathered what she would need to help the child. "John? Have you got any onions put up at home?"

Embarrassed again, he looked down. "It's been a hard winter, Maggie. We ain't got much of nothin' left in the root cellar. Got some turnips and a few potatoes. Still got us a barrel of flour, though."

"I'm not askin' so I can come by for dinner, John. I want to be sure you can make an onion poultice to place on Malcolm's chest." Then, to Josie Mae, "Once you finish preparing the stew, gather several bunches of onions." She pointed to the corner where they had an assortment of root vegetables hanging from the rafters.

"John, make yourself another mug of tea and drink it down while I finish getting together my things."

Maggie went into her storeroom and was soon joined by Josie Mae. "I got the onions. The biscuits are out of the oven. Did you want me to wrap them in a towel?"

"No, child." Maggie shook her head. "You have them with the stew. You'll be needin' them for breakfast in the morning." She stopped, holding onto Josie Mae's hands. "I'm gonna make it to Esther's tonight, but I'm not gonna be makin' it home. Once I leave here, you bar the door and don't open it. You got plenty of firewood. Plenty of food."

Josie Mae gave Maggie a quick squeeze. "I'll be fine, Granny. You worry about Malcolm. Make sure they're eatin' right, too."

Then Josie Mae turned to the different herbs. "I suspect you'll be needing some of this here mountain mint oil. It's good to add to steam when a person's got a cough."

She glanced at Maggie with expectant eyes. Maggie straightened her shoulders and smiled at her granddaughter. "Yes, Josie Mae, that is exactly what I'll need. I also want to make up a warm tea. They can put it in his bottle to help clear up the cough."

Josie Mae began sifting through the shelves. "I'd suggest some rosehips and red clover. Maybe some thyme?"

Maggie beamed. "You've been listening hard, Josie Mae. Gather some yarrow, lobelia, and golden seal as well. Oh, and can you grab some garlic, too? I should have had you find some when you were getting the onions."

Now it was Josie Mae's turn to smile. "I got some, Granny. I figured you'd want it in a tea or as part of the poultice."

Maggie grabbed Josie Mae in a bear hug. "Stay warm, hear? Don't open the door for anything. Not unless I'm callin' your name from the other side of the door. Understand? Make your breakfast in the morning. I'll be along once the sun is up."

Maggie brushed away a proud tear. "You have gone and grown up on me, Josie Mae."

Walking back into the main room, she told John, "Let's go hitch up the mules to the sleigh. It will be a might colder but a whole lot faster."

Once the animals were harnessed and ready, the two packed in the food and medicine, plus several warm blankets. Josie Mae waved them off, barring the door – alone for the first time in her life.

Chapter 17

Josie Mae
- March 10, 1893 -

Josie Mae listened as the jingling reins and clopping hooves receded into the distance. She realized she was still standing by the door as if expecting someone to come back at any moment. Her chest tightened, comprehending it would be hours before she saw Granny again. When the tears began to form and threatened to fall from her eyes, she gave herself a little shake.

"Josie Mae! Get ahold of yourself. What is all this blathering about? You ain't the one with a sick child. You ain't havin' to travel in the cold, in the dark of the night. You ain't got nothin' to be cryin' about." She swiped at the hot tears escaping down her cheeks and clapped her hands together.

She strode to the stove, looking over the night's meal. She would have two biscuits and the stew, leaving the others for morning. She'd cook up some sausage gravy and save a bit for Granny, who would be cold and hungry when she arrived.

Ladling the thick soup into a brown-flecked pottery bowl, she balanced the biscuits on the rim and settled into the chair. The fire was warm and bright, despite the fading light outside.

She soon realized eating alone wasn't the same as eating with Granny. Everything was silent except for the occasional scrape of a spoon or crackle from the fireplace. Then the wolf began to howl, the one that cried out nearly every night while they ate. Only this time, the noise felt threatening, as though he were planning to come to her door and swallow her up like Little Red Riding Hood.

She stamped her foot, angry with herself for such childish thoughts. "Josie Mae. Stop this instant. The wolf is the same wolf who cries each evening, and not once have you given it a second thought. The wolf is no more likely to come and eat you up than it is likely you'll meet the giant from Jack and the Beanstalk." She dug her spoon into the stew, forcing her mind away from the howling wolf.

"I need a plan," she thought. "Something to keep me busy. Something to keep my mind off the wolf and off Granny being gone." She shuddered, thinking of the long night ahead – alone.

She ticked off things she could do to stay occupied. "I'll clean up the dishes once I eat. Afterward, I can read from the Bible. Then I can practice my ciphering."

She was not as good at math as she should be, and her mama kept threatening to send her to the school in the next town. She didn't want to live in Burnsville with her mama and walk all that way every day to sit in a classroom.

"Then, if I'm still not tired, I'll pull out my knitting. It's a long way to Christmas, but I have five pairs of mittens, five scarves, and five stocking hats to finish up for the Stallards, plus everything I need to make for my own family. While I knit, I can begin to plan the trip we'll take to the Cherokee village once the weather breaks."

Thinking about her upcoming adventure brought a quick smile to her lips. She couldn't believe she was old enough to accompany Granny. Eventually, Granny had finished the tale of her mama's birth, though there was little left to tell.

* * *

When Caroline Ann, shortened to Carrie Ann, was five months old, Maggie and Henry made their way back to the holler. Maggie brought with her several Cherokee ways of healin', including the blessing song.

When they arrived back home and came into town, everyone was happy to learn they were alive.

"We know'd your ma and pa died, and you'd been sick. But when we came callin' to see to ya, you was gone. That Indian disappeared, too. Knowing that them Indians can't be trusted, what with bringing disease and trying to get revenge on us white folk, and with Jones saying that Injun was leading you through the woods, we just figured he'd taken you with him."

Maggie put her hand up to stop the flow of words.

"I refuse to let you talk about Degataga that way. He is not 'that Indian' but a Cherokee trader and son of the Cherokee medicine man. He did not bring the sickness with him. You know, as well as I do, the fever comes pretty regularly. Why, it came through town not six years back and killed off several of your own mas and pas."

Her eyes flashed as she looked from one person to the next.

"As for him taking us off? When is the last time you can recall someone being taken off to the Cherokee lands against their will?" She looked from person to person again, daring anyone to give her one instance in their memory of such a thing happening.

"Henry and I chose to go live near the Cherokee because Degataga saved our lives. I wanted to express my appreciation to his father. And I hoped to learn about some of their healing ways. With my mama gone, I wasn't gonna have that chance no longer."

She let the words settle in before going on. "But I got far more than a bit of healin' knowledge." She reached into the wagon and pulled out a cooing Carrie Ann. "Oukonunaka, the medicine man, helped me carry a child to term and bring her into the world."

Several of the women began to ooh and aah over the baby. "Henry and I," she looked to her husband and then continued, "we wanted to come home. To make this our home with our child. But we won't be staying if'n havin' Cherokee friends is a problem to ya."

She glanced around again, watching the women shake their heads no. Mary Jane, the one who exclaimed so freely that the Indian had kidnapped the two of them, spoke up.

"No problem, Maggie Lou. I mean, if you say he was good to ya, then good he was. We've been missin' your ma something fierce, what with no one nearby knowing anything about healin'. We surely need you here, Maggie Lou." Several others nodded.

At first, the townsfolk were cautious about Maggie's curious ways, which were so different from her mama's. But when she was able to help women bring forth their babies, or cure the colic, or tend to a fever, they became accustomed to her chanting. By the time Carrie Ann was a toddler, no one gave it a second thought.

Maggie began making a pilgrimage back to the Cherokee every spring to celebrate the Flower Moon with Oukonunaka and Degataga. During the visit, she would learn more about the customs of Cherokee healing and pray by the river. The learning was for those she served. The chanting was in hopes of conceiving another child.

Although she occasionally grew a baby for a season, it would never make it to term, despite the herbs and chants. It seemed Carrie Ann was to be her one and only miracle.

* * *

Josie Mae realized she had stopped knitting, and the fire had dimmed so much that she was having trouble seeing her hands in her lap. Had she been sleeping or merely day-dreaming?

She put down the needles, loaded up the fireplace, washed her face, and climbed into bed. Although many hours were left before Granny would come home, she was no longer afraid. Granny was right. She was all grown now. Grown enough to stay alone. And grown enough to visit the Cherokee village and begin learning their heal-ing ways.

Chapter 18

Carrie Ann
- March 11, 1893 -

As she left for home the day before, Daniel had asked Carrie Ann to stop by and check on Malcolm. "I just can't shake the feeling I should have done more. Offered more care." His shoulders sagged under the burden.

"Daniel! You did what you could. It isn't your fault our supplies are low. You didn't cause the weather, nor did you run out and halt the deliveries. No, instead, you went by their place, instructed them on the use of steam, suggested ways to keep Malcolm comfortable, and promised to follow up on the child's progress. What more could you do?"

With each declaration, her words grew louder and higher in pitch, like a teen girl throwing a fit, she realized. Lowering her voice in both volume and octave, she continued, "You are not a magician, Daniel. You are a doctor."

"Even so, Carrie Ann, the poor little thing was wheezing, and Esther looked like she was ready to drop. And what did I do? Suggest she nap and prescribe some steam without the added benefit of silver." He let his hands fall to his sides in defeat.

Carrie Ann had not slept well. She kept dreaming of a small child suffering from a cough. The child coughed and coughed until they began to turn blue. As she struggled to help the baby, it turned into Josephine. She woke to the sound of her own strangled cry and, unable to go back to sleep, spent the last half of the night struggling with the blankets.

By daybreak, Carrie Ann had already eaten breakfast, washed up the dishes, gotten ready for the day, and stood impatiently tapping her foot, waiting for an appropriate time of day to pay a visit to the Stallard home. When she decided everyone would be awake, she bundled up for the walk and strode with determined steps to the edge of town.

Before the house came into view, she caught sight of smoke rising from the chimney. She quickened her step, realizing she, like Daniel, was worried about the boy. But as she approached the porch, she stopped in her tracks.

Parked on the side of the house was her mother's sleigh. It was unmistakable, as few people owned one, and even fewer had one as old as Mama. "This used to be my great-granny's," she often said with pride while Carrie Ann tried to hide her embarrassment at riding in such an ancient piece of junk.

Mother's presence meant only one thing – John had summoned her to their home after he visited with Daniel. Like the doctor, John – or perhaps Esther – believed he hadn't done enough. But instead of taking it up with Dr. McKeithen, they simply sidestepped him and called on the granny woman. Carrie Ann wasn't sure if she should go in and check on the child or march right back to Daniel with the news.

However, curiosity got the best of her. She had to know how the baby was doing and what, if anything, her mother had given the child. She marched to the door and rapped with her mittened hand. John popped the door open and ushered her in. "Good morning, Carrie Ann! What brings you out our way?"

Carrie Ann took in the picture. At the table sat Maribelle and Lloyd, eating what looked like oatmeal. In the rocker by the stove sat Esther with a quiet Malcolm in her lap. The boy's night clothes were gaping open at the front, and a lumpy cloth laid atop his chest. He appeared to be sleeping. Her mother sat next to Esther, where she'd obviously been chatting with the woman before Carrie Ann's unexpected visit.

Trying to remain professional, she said, "Dr. McKeithen asked me to come and check on Malcolm this morning. He was concerned he had so little to offer the child. But," she said, waving her hand in the direction of the baby, "he appears to be doing quite well."

John stepped forward with a smile. "Oh, yes! He's mendin' quite well. Your ma came all the way here just as it got dark last night and stayed with us. She brought some mint oil to add to the steam prescribed by Dr. McKeithen. She also brung some herbs we've been making into a tea and putting in the baby's bottle. Seems to be soothing the poor little one's chest. And, of course, the onions she brought for a poultice. Smells like the dickens, but it's better than the wheezin'."

Carrie Ann's cheeks flushed with anger. She worked to keep her face blank and set her jaw, reminding herself an outburst would give her mother something to talk about and would likely not go over well with Daniel.

She was certain Malcolm had turned the corner on his own. Her mother's timing was nothing more than coincidence. With or without her onions and herbs, the child would be sleeping at peace this morning, but there was no way anyone in the room was going to believe it.

Instead of trying to persuade them, she said with as much brightness as she could muster, "I'm so glad he's doing better. I'll tell Dr. McKeithen that Malcolm won't be needing any of the ipecacuanha. Is there anything else I can do to help?" She added this last bit to appease Daniel, despite wanting nothing more than to remove herself from her mother's presence.

Esther answered, in a soft voice so as not to wake the sleeping child, "No, thank ya, Carrie Ann. We appreciate you coming out this way. Had we known you was thinkin' of comin', we could have saved ya the trip. But since you're here, can we offer you some breakfast? I got oatmeal on, and you're welcome to it."

Carrie Ann shook her head. "No, thank you. I've had something to eat. I'll just head on to the doctor's and prepare for today's patients."

Esther called to John. "John. Please pour Carrie Ann a cup of coffee 'afore she heads out again. No need sending her out into the cold without a warm belly."

Before Carrie Ann could protest, Maribelle said, "Come, sit next to me! I want to talk to you about bein' a nurse. I wanna be a nurse one day." Then, looking down, a slight blush coming to her cheeks, she added, "Like you."

This pleased Carrie Ann. In fact, she felt far more proud than she would have imagined possible. It was only a little girl's praise, and not even her own child's. As that thought sauntered through her mind, she stopped, the cup midway between the table and her lips. She turned in the direction of her mother. "Mama? Where is Josephine?"

Maggie stood, walking toward her daughter. "Josie

Mae is at home. I made sure she had plenty of wood and plenty of food. Since I've doctored up Malcolm, I'm heading back."

Carrie Ann's scowl was barely concealed beneath a smile of gritted teeth. Maggie had seen this look so many times and knew an explosion of words would be next.

Maneuvering to the door, Maggie said, "Esther, I'll be back in a day or two to check on him. Keep feeding him the tea. Do the steam every two hours, just like Dr. McKeithen said. In between, use the poultice. Make another if'n the one you have don't seem strong enough."

Turning to John while guiding Carrie Ann through the door, she said, "Thank you for letting me stay the night. I wasn't too keen on going back in the cold night air."

John moved as if to help her with the mules. "There's no need for you to go getting all chilled. I've got Carrie Ann with me. You stay in and make sure them children eat all their oatmeal. And be sure Esther gets a bit of something to eat, too." Then, in a conspiratorial whisper, she breathed, "She don't take good enough care of herself, John. It's up to you!"

In a matter of moments, they were alone. Maggie rushed her words, "Save your anger for the barn, Carrie Ann. There's no need in making a fuss within earshot."

Carrie Ann moved stiffly toward the wooden structure. As soon as the doors closed, she gritted out, "You left a child all night in the cold in the middle of the woods so you could put onions on a baby's chest? That's it, Mother. I'm finished playing these games with you. I'm collecting Josephine today. She's my daughter, and she's coming to stay with me, where she will have proper supervision."

Maggie pulled the reins over the mules' heads. "Josie

Mae ain't a child no more, Carrie Ann. She done changed from a child to an adult while you weren't lookin'. You're welcome to ask if she wants to come live in town with you, but I don't believe she'll be sayin' yes. And I won't be makin' her."

She turned to look at her daughter. "I do not doubt you love her, Carrie Ann, but you haven't been a real mama to her in years. That's been up to me. And last night? I believed she was capable of handlin' it on her own. If I didn't reckon she could do it, I wouldn't have come here with John. You ain't the only one lovin' the child – the young woman," she corrected.

With those words, she left the barn, Carrie Ann gaping at her back.

When the clopping of hooves faded, Carrie Ann eased out of the building and closed the door, making her way not to the doctor's office but home. Somehow, without meaning to be, she was all alone. Her mother and Josephine had one another. The doctor was closer to his patients than the woman who assisted him. Her husband had long since passed, and she had never entertained finding another one.

Even the one thing she had done well, becoming a nurse, wasn't turning out the way she had hoped. It seemed no one appreciated what she had to offer.

She crawled into bed and wept, hot tears rolling down her face.

Chapter 19

Maggie
- March 30, 1893 -

She breathed in deeply, allowing the cool air to expand her lungs. Maggie enjoyed being outside again after so many weeks cooped up in the house. The weather broke shortly after her emergency trip to help Malcolm.

Although still cold at night, the daytime hours warmed up enough to make a dent in the snow. Brown patches emerged under the bright light of the sun, and mud formed in the wheel ruts leading into and out of the homestead.

She noted the first crocus leaves pushing out at the edge of the field. Spring was on the way. Experience told her these first flowers might live through a snowfall or two. Nonetheless, within weeks, the frigid temperatures and snowy weather would end, not to be seen again until the following winter.

With the warmer days came the preparations for her trip. As she often did as of late, she wondered why she continued to do the things she had been doing.

Did it make sense to plant such a large garden when it was just Josie Mae and herself? Did it make sense to continue living so far away from town as the walk got more and more difficult for her each year? Did it make sense to drag her old body out of a warm bed to make house calls in the middle of the night? But more importantly, at least at this moment, did it make sense to keep going to the Cherokee village every spring?

The list of reasons to stop going loomed large. Degataga and Oukonunaka died several years ago. In fact, very few people recalled their first meeting thirty-one years earlier. Of course, everyone welcomed her when she came. Her arrival, her friendship with the medicine man, and the birth of her daughter were part of the story they told at each Flower Moon celebration. But those with firsthand memories were dwindling.

And if she thought getting to town was difficult, what should she call this annual spring pilgrimage? Treacherous, perhaps? That's the way it felt as an old woman with mules laden with wares to offer for trade.

Not only was the trip challenging, but it was lonely. She had been trudging through the mountains and sleeping in makeshift tents without Henry or Carrie Ann for almost two decades.

The thought of Henry caused a gripping in her heart. Still, after all these years, she missed him and their life together.

Carrie Ann was not quite eleven. Henry started coughing at Christmas. She ministered to him, making sure he drank enough water, forcing him to sleep with the stinky onion poultice, and plying him with the herbal tea concoction. Although, for a time, he seemed to grow stronger, the cough lingered and was still a problem when they made their way to the Cherokee village.

Oukonunaka blessed him, choosing to perform a rite usually reserved for Chieftains. Once settled back at the homestead, he grew worse, each day becoming weaker.

With nothing else to try, Maggie loaded him up in the wagon and drove him to the doctor in Asheville.

She knew the verdict before she knew the cause. The doctor's inability to look her in the eyes when he entered the room told her all she needed to know. Her husband was going to die. "It's the wasting disease," he informed her. Cancer. "There isn't much we can do. He's eat up with it. It's in his lungs. Likely in his kidneys and liver, too. That's the reason he looks so yellow."

Maggie had observed the yellowish color in her husband's eyes and the smell of ammonia on his breath. It's why she brought him here. She knew it was more than a cough, and she knew it was more than she could handle. And, it seemed, it was more than the city doctor could handle as well.

She took Henry back to the holler, despite the doctor's insistence he should remain in the hospital in town. What could they do for him in a sterile facility far away from everything he loved that she couldn't do for him at home? At least in his own home, in his own bed, he would have his family near.

Upon arriving home, Carrie Ann spent hours with her pa, reading to him, playing checkers, and talking about everything happening in her world.

"You'll never believe what happened today when I was feeding the chickens, Pa," she said with a grin. "You know ol' Henrietta, the one with the bush of red feathers on her tail?" She waited for her pa to nod before continuing. "Well, she must have decided she was the boss because she fluttered around the yard, scaring all the others into the trees. Not one other chicken could get near me and the bucket. I finally caught her under my arm so the others could eat. I think we need to call her Miss Bigwig instead of Henrietta. What do you think?"

Henry laughed. "Can't you just see that ol' chicken with a white powdered wig and hammering away on a table with a gavel?"

Carrie Ann continued the game. "And all the other chickens coming before Miss Henrietta Bigwig with their problems and concerns. 'Oh, Miss Bigwig, Georgette only lays an egg every other day but insists on getting the same treatment as the rest of the hens.' And then Henrietta bangs her gavel and says, 'Two weeks in the coop with no extra feed. Next!'"

Maggie loved hearing the two laugh and carry on, but as she cared for Henry, she recognized that he was growing weaker and weaker. After a particularly difficult week, Henry couldn't muster up the strength to get out of bed. Within days, he didn't have the strength to hold his head up to sip the broth. Before long, he seemed unable to swallow the broth she spooned into his mouth.

As Henry's illness progressed, Carrie Ann stopped going to her father's bedside. It was as if what she didn't see wasn't really happening. Maggie didn't blame her. She was a child and one who was losing her father, the man she adored. Maggie couldn't imagine losing a father at such a young age. Losing her own pa when she was newly married was difficult enough.

Henry had always doted on Carrie Ann. Despite being difficult and headstrong, Carrie Ann had always been attentive to her father. When she was moody, he could make her laugh. When she was inconsolable, he brought comfort. When anything Maggie said or did sent Carrie Ann into fits of anger, a simple word or touch on her arm by her father calmed her.

"I have no idea how you do what you do, Henry," Maggie told him one afternoon after a particularly grueling argument. "She either outright ignores me or twists every word I utter into fuel for her rage. But with you? You just have to breathe in the same room with the child, and she becomes docile. What is your secret?"

Henry shrugged. "You know how you have the gift of healing? Well, I have a gift, too. It's like I can see her soul, the way horse whisperers understand a wild mare. My Carrie Ann always pushes and pulls when others conform. She strains at the bit and tries to buck loose. But she's a good girl. Strong. Capable. Smart. She just needs a quiet voice in her corner to provide direction."

Maggie had no idea how Carrie Ann would manage once her father passed away. Who would be there to whisper the words she needed? Who would help her figure out her world? On the day Henry wouldn't take the offered broth, Maggie forced her daughter to sit and hold her father's hand. "You'll regret not saying goodbye while you have the chance," she explained. She wished she had been with her parents at the end to ease their transition to death. She still longed for one more moment with them and didn't want that longing to be part of her daughter's regrets.

Carrie Ann sat in the room next to her father with wooden arms and unseeing eyes until Maggie sent her to bed. That night, as she cared for her husband, holding his hand and whispering her love to him, he drew his last breath. And from that moment to this one, she missed him with her entire soul.

The following spring, when it came time for her yearly trip to the Cherokee village, Carrie Ann refused to go.

"I hate them, Mama. They dance and sing and pray, but for what? It didn't save Pa." Without warning, she blurted, "Neither did you! You killed him, you know! You and your Indian ways. All the stupid chanting and those herbs? You should have taken him to Asheville right away. Just as soon as he started to cough instead of waiting until he was yellow and sickly and ready to die. They would have been able to help him if you hadn't expected all the granny woman and Cherokee nonsense to cure him."

Maggie sat in stunned silence, tears stinging her eyes. Carrie Ann, growing energized by her accusations, continued. "You can sit there with tears and pretend you cared, but you didn't. If you really cared, you would have let a real doctor fix Pa.

Carrie Ann stood, back straight, arms folded across her chest, hands balled into fists. "I hate them Indians. I hate your fake healing. I hate you for killing my pa."

Pinpricks of tears formed, even now, all these years later. Carrie Ann had been true to her word. She had never visited the Cherokee again, and she did everything in her power to become what she believed was a real healer – someone who went to school and learned the right way to cure diseases like the one that took her father.

And yet, despite losing Henry, despite losing her own ma and pa, despite losing friends, Maggie still trusted in the healing ways. No, there wasn't a perfect solution. Some people, even with the best care, would die. Others, even without care, would survive.

But Maggie believed what she offered – her herbs, her knowledge, her beliefs, her hope – were needful and helpful. She also thought modern medicine, even with all its advances, did not hold all the answers, despite her daughter's insistence otherwise.

That, she decided, is why she continued to visit the Cherokee each spring. She used those weeks to renew her spirit and to remember why she chose to be a healer.

With a smile, she realized this year held an extra benefit. This year, her granddaughter would be introduced to the Cherokee traditions to add to her growing understanding of the healing ways she'd already begun to absorb. This year, Josie Mae would determine if she was called to be a healer woman like her granny and the many generations before her.

Chapter 20

Josie Mae
- April 28, 1893 -

The shooshing of feet along the paths outside their hut woke Josie Mae from a dreamless sleep. She and Granny had arrived at the Cherokee village two days earlier, but Josie Mae still hadn't recovered from the trek. When Granny said it would be long and difficult, Josie Mae had merely shrugged her shoulders. If Granny could go every spring, certainly she could do it, too.

But the phrase 'long and difficult' did not do it justice. At the end of the first day, Josie Mae wanted to turn back.

Her thighs were sore from riding. But worse than that, her feet and legs were sore from the times they could not ride and had to lead the mules over rocks and gullies. She was sure they spent the entire day climbing, except she remembered having to skip into a run to keep from falling down a hill. Of course, with every down came another up.

At the point Josie Mae was positive she could go no further, Granny pointed out a small clearing. "There it is. That's what I've been looking for. Every year, I spend my first night here. It's a good spot with a clean, running stream just a few yards away, and a nice flat space for sleeping."

Unfortunately, finding the campsite did not mean the

end of the work. They had to feed and water the mules, gather firewood for their campfire, and pull together some long branches to make a lean-to to cover them while they slept. By the time they got the fire lit and supper going, Josie Mae doubted she would still be awake when it was time to eat.

Josie Mae rested her arms on her knees and cradled her head. In a muffled voice, she asked, "How many days, Granny?"

Granny, who was stirring whatever she had cooking in the pot, said, "A week. Maybe ten days. It's taken me two weeks sometimes. It's difficult to say. Just depends on the weather and the water."

Josie Mae groaned. She could not imagine doing this six more times. Or maybe nine. Or maybe even thirteen. And when she realized they would have to do the same thing in reverse, she groaned again.

Granny came and stood next to her, the meal on the fire forgotten. "What's the matter, child? Are ya ailin'?"

Josie Mae shook her head. She longed to tell Granny it was too much. She wanted to go home. Nothing in the Cherokee village could be worth a trip like this.

But before she could form a coherent thought, Granny said, "Maybe your ma was right. Maybe this trip is too much for a young child. When we used to bring her, we had her Pa to do the walking and leading. She tried to tell me I was expecting too much. I'm sorry, Josie Mae. I'll take you back in the morning, and once you're settled with your ma, I'll head out again. Maybe you can try again in a few years."

At the thought of going back a failure and proving her ma right, Josie Mae sat upright, her tired eyes gleaming.

"No, Granny. I don't want to go back to stay with Mama. I said I was going to go to the Cherokee village, and that is what I'm aimin' to do."

She hadn't realized how much this trip meant to her until Granny suggested she not take it after all. Plus, she hated the idea of her mama being right, especially against her granny. At that moment, she determined she would make it and back home again, even if it required her to lash herself to the mule to make it happen.

She stood up, stretching her sore muscles. "That groanin' I was doin'? It ain't nothing but a bit of complainin'. You won't hear no more of it out of me on this trip, Granny. That's a promise."

Josie Mae had been true to her word. She didn't complain again, though the journey had not gotten any easier. They dealt with rivers swollen so high they had to change their route to find where it widened and wouldn't wash them downstream.

In the middle of one night, it began to rain. Not a gentle tap tap tap, but a downpour so strong they had to relocate so as not to slide down the hillside in the mud. The next day, trekking along was even more difficult as the sludge sucked at their boots, pulling them down rather than propelling them forward.

On the ninth day, when Granny said, "That's it! Over there! See the smoke, Josie Mae? That's the village," Josie Mae could have wept with joy and exhaustion. They made it. She made it.

Josie Mae did not expect such happiness at their arrival, but the women all came running to the clearing, chattering in words foreign to her ears. Each wore a broad smile and began helping them offload the mules. For the first time in over a week, Josie Mae didn't have to take care of the animals or make her own pallet for sleeping. She was simply allowed to sit and watch, as was Granny.

The two of them were led to a campfire and given a warm drink and fry bread. Josie Mae took a small sip, delighting in the sweet flavor. She raised her eyebrows at Granny, asking, without words, what she was drinking. "It's called spicebush tea. It's made by soaking honey locust pods in hot water. It's tasty, isn't it?"

As the night fell, they were provided with more food before being brought to a hut. Granny explained they would be living here during their visit. "We will meet with Illanipi, the medicine man, tomorrow. Tonight, he has begun the preparations for the Flower Moon ceremony. These rituals are sacred and cannot be changed, even for honored guests."

In the morning, Granny took Josie Mae to the settlement where her mama had been born. The town had nearly disappeared. A few dilapidated structures and a cleared area that was once a road were all that remained. "What happened, Granny? Why did the people move away?"

Granny smiled, but her eyes were sad. "The year you were born, Josie Mae, a fever spread far and wide through the mountains. Nearly everyone in the settlement died. Many in the Cherokee village did as well. The fever took Oukonunaka, who was a very old man. It took Degataga as well. It's the same fever that took your pa."

"The few who didn't die," Granny swept her arm in an expansive circle, "decided they needed to be closer to a real town. Most figured their loved ones would've lived if they'd been in Asheville or even a place like Burnsville. But you and I know different, don't we?"

Later in the day, Josie Mae had the opportunity to meet Illanipi, the medicine man. He was tall and bronzed with a thick black braid hanging to the middle of his shoulders. She was surprised he wore a white cotton shirt and pants like the men at home wore. Somehow, she figured the medicine man would look more like... an Indian?

As if he could read her thoughts, Illanipi began to laugh, the smile creasing his face at the mouth and eyes. "She thought I might be wearing feathers and carrying a spear!"

Now Granny laughed, too, and the heat rushed to Josie Mae's cheeks. How foolish and childish. This man would never take her seriously now. She swallowed hard and looked him in the eyes. "I'm sorry if I offended you. It's just that... I mean..." She took a deep breath. "There hasn't been a Cherokee trader in Burnsville for years. The only Indians I've ever seen have been in pictures. I..."

He held out his hand to her. "No offense taken, Miss Josie Mae." Then he smiled again.

"In two more nights, we will perform the Flower Moon ceremony. For our ceremonies, we dress more like our ancestors did. I'll have on a breechcloth and leggings, with two feathers hanging from my braid. The hunters will display their tattoos, and the women will have brightly colored skirts and beads. It will be a fine sight. Much better than the picture books."

She tried to smile in return, still warm from embarrassment.

"Once the celebration is complete, we will spend plenty of time together. Your grandmother informs me you may wish to be a medicine woman?"

She nodded, a rush of heat washing over her body again, only this time it was excitement. "Yes! I've been learning from Granny for years. I've been looking forward to this trip and meeting you. I want to understand what Granny has learned from you. It must be very important. Otherwise, why would she keep coming back all these years?"

She said this with an understanding of the toll the traveling took on her and realized the price must be even greater for Granny. With this knowledge, she determined to learn everything she could to make the sacrifice worthwhile.

Chapter 21

Maggie
- April 30, 1893 -

No matter how many times she participated, Maggie never tired of the Flower Moon ceremony. The sounds and fragrances and colors transported her back to her first visit with Degataga and Oukonunaka.

The first time was so unforgettable, as she and Henry were honored as friends. Others throughout the years held distinct memories, but tonight's celebration would be a highlight for her. She was introducing the third generation to the balanced ways of healing.

Maggie tried not to think about her daughter. Carrie Ann never understood what Maggie was trying to teach her about balance. The concept was one Carrie Ann had never mastered. To this day, she pushed and pulled, fighting her way forward. She was that way from birth, demanding and opinionated, never able to just be happy.

After Henry died, she became more obstinate and determined.

"Balance?" she would scream. "What kind of crazy notion is balance? I am not one with nature. I never have been, and I never will be. We aren't supposed to be, Mama. Don't you see that? We are here to rule over this earth and everything on it. Healing based on balance is foolish, and," she threw the next words like venomous darts, "potentially deadly."

Maggie shook her head to clear the thoughts of Carrie Ann. It was true her daughter didn't understand the healing arts in the same way as Maggie, but Carrie Ann was a fine nurse and worked hard to help her community. Maggie respected this but hoped Josie Mae would choose a path closer to her own. Josie Mae definitely had a different temperament from Carrie Ann. She appeared to have the extra sense to say and do just what was needed. She had the granny woman way about her.

As the evening drew near, she began talking with Josie Mae, reminding her of the events to come. "There will be food. More food than you've ever seen in your lifetime. More than anything we put out on Christmas. Many of these foods will be different from what we eat at home, but I want you to try them.

"After the food comes singing and dancing. The words will mean nothing to you, but don't focus on the words. Focus on the rhythm. Pay attention to the movements of the women. Listen as they capture the beat with their beads.

"Keep an open mind and experience the night as if you were a Cherokee. Become part of the ceremony. Remember, they are celebrating a time of rebirth. Spring has come after a long, hard winter. The plants are budding. The animals are coming out of hibernation. The river is preparing to lend its sustenance to the people."

Josie Mae nodded solemnly. Maggie picked up a brush and started stroking Josie's hair from top to bottom as she talked.

"We went through a cold winter, you and me. We spent

long hours cooped up in the house. We had no one else to talk to. We began to run low on some of our supplies. And then, the warmth came again. You remember how you felt on the first day you could stand outside and let the sun dance on your cheeks without worrying about frostbite? Tap into that feeling tonight, Josie Mae. Remember the cold and the gratitude for the warmth that followed."

Now, Maggie divided Josie Mae's hair into three long strands to create a braid. "This is part of the balance in nature. There is warm to the cold. There is summer to the winter. This is the same balance we use when healing people. We find their pain and discover ways to relieve it. Sometimes, it is with herbs. Sometimes, it is with words. Sometimes, it is with prayer. It is always with balance."

Maggie turned Josie Mae to look at her. "I don't expect you to understand everything right now. I just want you to begin to be open to the ideas you learn here. Be open to seeing how what the Cherokee believe is a continuation of what we believe about God. Can you do that?"

Josie Mae nodded again. Her eyes were wide and clear.

"Yes, Granny. I want to understand healing the way you do. I want to be able to help people with medicine like my mama, but also with nature, and with... concern. You have concern, Granny. You care about the people you help, like Esther. Because you care, you can help in ways Mama can't. I ain't sayin' she's not a good healer. I think she is very smart. I just think she's missing a piece."

Maggie pulled her close, murmuring into her hair. "I love you, Josie Mae. I think you have the makings of a fine granny woman." Then she walked arm in arm with her out to the fire circle.

Throughout the night, Maggie observed her granddaughter as she clapped in delight or swayed to a particular song. As the moon rose high in the night sky and the dancing became a steady beat, a young girl about Josie Mae's age came over and took her by the hand. Josie Mae looked at her grandmother to be sure it was alright but went without hesitation upon seeing Maggie's nod.

Josie Mae was led to the back of the line with the children and beginner dancers. The young girl, who spoke no English, began instructing Josie Mae, showing her the steps. Within minutes, Josie Mae was dancing with the others as if she had been learning the movements her entire life. Maggie sat back with a contented smile.

Illanipi, who was seated to her left, leaned over and said, "She is a fine girl, that granddaughter of yours. She is young. I sense she has a bit of impatience. But," he jutted his chin in Josie Mae's direction, "I see something in her I haven't seen in many. Her intuition is strong. She will be able to feel when the balance is wrong long before others. I believe, my friend, Maggie, she may be a stronger healer than even you or I."

Tears sprang to Maggie's eyes. She loved her granddaughter with a fierceness that sometimes surprised her and was proud of who she was and what she might become. Even if Josie Mae chose another path, Maggie believed she would find a way to be the best at whatever she set her mind to. She thanked Illanipi for his kind words.

"They are not simply kind, Maggie. They are true."

By the time the sun peeked over the horizon, both Maggie and Josie Mae were ready for sleep. They walked together to their lodge in an easy silence. Once inside, as they slipped beneath the fur blankets, Josie Mae cleared her throat.

"Granny, I know you are tired, but I just wanted to say thank you. Thank you for bringing me here. Thank you for believing I was ready to begin learning the things you understand about healing. Thank you for pressing against Mama and insisting I come. Thank you for giving me the strength to continue the journey when I wanted to give up."

Maggie rolled onto her side. "What do you mean, give you the strength?"

Josie Mae smiled as she stifled a yawn. "When you told me Mama said I couldn't make it. You knew it would make me determined to make it here. I just wanted you to know that I knew."

Maggie laughed out loud. "Illanipi was right. You are intuitive. Much more intuitive than I am sneaky, that's for sure. Now, go to sleep. With the festivities over, we have lots to do before we head back home."

As Maggie closed her eyes, her last thought as she drifted off was, "Illanipi was correct about more than Josie Mae's intuitive nature. Despite still being a child, she saw right through me. Without a doubt, she has the ability to be a better healer than me."

Chapter 22

Josie Mae
- May 10, 1893 -

The days since the Flower Moon had been filled from morning to night. Josie Mae and Granny spent nearly every waking minute with Illanipi, who began by showing the child where he kept his medicines. Each wall held layers of shelves holding endless containers of roots, powders, oils, and tinctures.

Upon entering the building, Josie Mae drew in a deep breath. She had never seen so many medicines in one location. Illanipi's collection made the small room in their cabin look tiny and pitiful. "Granny," she breathed. "Look at all these herbs! We'll never have space for as much as this!"

Granny laughed. "You are right, child. Be thankful we don't need all of this. Illanipi is the medicine man for all the Cherokee left in the area. Not only does he keep the ingredients needed to help them when they are sick, but he also keeps what is needed for all of their ceremonies. His job is significantly larger than our own."

Josie Mae beamed when Granny said 'our own.' This was proof she was beginning to view Josie Mae as a healer rather than a little girl. She walked along each wall, removing the lids from clay pots with care, smelling the various contents. Some were recognizable as soon as she inhaled. The sharp tanginess of lemon balm. The menthol scent of mint. The sweetness of thyme leaf.

But the jars contained others she didn't recognize. One smelled of dried grass. Another pungent, making her nose wrinkle. Another of cat pee.

She turned to the corner of the room where the roots hung in bunches. These were harder to tell apart without seeing their leaves. With so many, how was it possible to distinguish one from the next? Without thinking, she blurted, "How do you keep all these roots apart? Mixing up goldenseal root with yellowroot could mean giving someone a flu cure when they have a sore throat!"

Immediately, she balked. She had been rude without meaning to again. When would she learn to think before she spoke? "I'm sorry. What I said was disrespectful. I'm sure you would never confuse the two. I just... I would. Get them confused, I mean." She stammered until she ran out of words, then she looked helplessly at Granny, hoping she might rescue her. But Illanipi broke the awkward silence first.

"Josie Mae, do not be embarrassed by your questions. If one does not question what they see, if one is not willing to question what they think, then one will walk away with no knowledge. You are here to learn, yes?"

Josie Mae nodded, still ashamed of her outburst.

"Then you must ask. Your question is a good one because, as you stated, goldenseal root and yellow root, especially at certain points in the drying process, look very similar – and neither has a distinctive scent. Yet, both are used for different ailments in the body."

He reached out his hand and led her to the corner

until they were standing under the hanging bunches. Once below the roots, he instructed her to look up. A big smile broke out across Josie Mae's face. There, on the crossbars, were words written in Cherokee. "It's just like in our store-room, Granny. And at the apothecary at Mama's!"

However, many Cherokee medicine practices were not like the things she learned from Granny or her mother. She discovered for the Cherokee, healing was a community effort. When a family member was ill, several people would gather and pray, believing their collective spirit would guide the healing process. In fact, the more people who participated, the more likely it was the sick person would find health again.

She asked Granny about the idea when they were alone. "Isn't it odd they would invite so many people into the patient's room? It can't be good for the person who is ill, and it may make entire families sick."

Granny nodded. "Yes, but in a way, we do the same thing."

Josie Mae cocked her head to the side, trying to remember such a time.

Granny continued. "When we go to church, do we not pray for the sick and afflicted? Do we not offer up our collective prayers to God on behalf of those who are hurting in hopes our prayers as one body will be more effective than the prayers of just one?"

Josie Mae straightened. "Yes! We do. It is similar, isn't it?"

"There are many similarities you will discover between the Cherokee people and our own. Some of the ways of the Cherokee can be used without any changes. Like how they turn certain barks into tea or how they combine herbs to create just the right treatment for a wet cough."

Josie Mae listened, leaning toward Granny to catch each word.

"On the other hand, the Cherokee have beliefs that are similar to ours but not the same. For instance, they believe every single thing on earth has a spirit, and the medicine man has the ability to ask these spirits how they can best help in any given situation.

"We don't believe the same thing about spirits. So, let me ask you a question. How might you use this Cherokee understanding, given you don't believe you can talk to and receive answers from plants?"

Josie Mae grew still. Her mind was twisting and turning, trying to figure out how to make use of something that seemed so much like a fairytale. A few thoughts turned into the beginning of an idea.

"I don't believe plants can talk to me, but I do believe plants, when used in certain ways, are beneficial to man – for food, for medicine, for shelter, for tools. As a healer, it is my job to learn these uses. But..." She hesitated. She wasn't sure if she should go on, but Granny's nod encouraged her to continue.

"But I also understand God is in charge of everything, including the plants. I've watched you use a remedy one way for some people and another for someone else. You said you had a feeling that adding a particular herb would be helpful.

"Maybe the feeling you had is what Illanipi would call hearing the plant speak. I think it is God whispering in your ear, telling you the plant has something to offer on His behalf." She stopped, quiet, pondering her words.

After a long silence, Granny whispered, "You are very wise, Josie Mae. Intuition does come from God. It is a gift

He bestows on some, while He gives others gifts such as strength. As you continue to learn about healing, always remember this is His gift to you. Use it for the benefit of those around you."

For the rest of the week, Josie Mae listened to Illanipi, careful to find a way to balance the Cherokee ways with her own, just as Granny instructed.

Of course, the one thing she had most wanted to do was to learn a Cherokee blessing. Granny had always been adamant that a medicine man be the one to teach her. "I am nothing more than a student. I cannot speak the language. I cannot communicate with others. What I say is simple memorization, like a fancy bird that mimics what it hears. Parrots do not make good teachers."

However, when Josie Mae asked Illanipi to help her, he said the time had grown too short on this trip. But he did give her the Cherokee alphabet and help her learn the sounds of the letters. "Take this with you and practice. When you return next year, I will begin teaching you to speak our language and understand our ways."

Although Josie Mae was disappointed, she determined to study each day so, that the following spring, she would be ready.

She packed up the alphabet and the rest of her things. She and Granny would start their journey home in the morning. Granny had spent the day packing up herbs and roots for her own use, as well as jewelry and other small trinkets to trade at the store in Burnsville.

As she climbed into bed, she fingered the bracelet given to her by Halona, the girl who taught her to dance at Flower Moon. She had Illanipi translate for her as she presented the gift.

"This is a friendship bracelet. I have one just like it." Halona held out her slim wrist, showing off the colorful beads found encircling it. "We will both wear them until we meet again." Halona hugged Josie Mae and disappeared among the women of the village.

Josie Mae no longer saw the trip to the Cherokee as something to dread. Instead, she looked forward with great anticipation to the coming year when she would come again to reestablish friendships, participate in the Flower Moon, and learn more about healing.

Chapter 23

Carrie Ann
- May 30, 1893 -

Carrie Ann couldn't remember a time she had been this angry. She was fully aware she was partly to blame for the entire situation, which only added to her emotional state. When she said no, she should have stood firm. Instead, she gave in to her mother and Josie Mae, and now? Now, her mother, in one short trip, had indoctrinated her daughter.

Her mind had been on a low boil since the evening before. Carrie Ann had not had the opportunity to talk to Josephine after the trek. The doctor's office was slow, so she asked Daniel for the afternoon off. It wasn't as if he didn't take plenty of afternoons to fish and hunt.

Prior to heading out to her mother's house, she gathered up a package for Josephine – several new balls of wool for her Christmas project, some fabric scraps for the patchwork quilt they were making together, and her favorite molasses cookies.

Despite the physical distance between them, Carrie Ann loved her daughter immensely. She often wished life had been different. If Tavish had been a good man and not perished from fever, she would have continued living in Asheville and raising more children. Now that Josephine was nearly grown, they would be friends. She imagined them sharing recipes and swapping gossip.

She shook her head to clear her thoughts. Of course, if she had remained in Asheville, she would have never gone to school to be a nurse. There just wasn't any use in looking back. Instead, she would focus on what she did have.

Carrie Ann set off, resolute, and enjoyed her walk down the path. The day was warm and sunny. The bees hummed from one miniature blossom to the next while birds called overhead. It was the perfect late spring day, and she was happy to be visiting with her daughter.

As she stepped into the clearing of the cabin, she spotted her mother out in the garden. "Planting herbs for her doctoring, no doubt." Although the thought prickled, she swiped it away. She wasn't going to let her mother ruin her afternoon.

She pushed open the front door without knocking and found Josephine sitting at the table with her chalk and tablet. Her first thought was, "Good, the child has finally buckled down to learn her sums." Then she wondered, "Can I convince her to attend the local school next year? Several of her friends at church walk each day. It wouldn't be too burdensome, at least during the warmer months."

Carrie Ann smiled warmly, but as she started to compliment Josephine on her studies, she realized she wasn't working on arithmetic problems. Carrie Ann's jaw dropped, and she reached out to snatch the tablet. "What is this?" she demanded when looking at the squiggles and lines.

Josephine, twisting her mouth to one side as if she didn't understand what was causing her mother's angst, said, "The Cherokee alphabet. Illanipi gave it to me. He said if I studied hard..." but Carrie Ann cut her off before she could go any further.

"Illanipi? Who is Illanipi? And why would you think studying the Cherokee alphabet was something you should be doing?"

Tears sprang to Josephine's eyes. "Illanipi, Mama. That's the medicine man Granny... I mean, grandmother and I visited. He said..."

Carrie Ann shouted, slamming the tablet onto the table. "I don't care what this Ippillapi said."

At that moment, Maggie came into the room. "His name is Illanipi. He gave the alphabet to Josie Mae because she was curious about their language. He has promised to help her learn some words if she studies hard before next spring."

Carrie Ann squared off with her mother, ignoring the fact that Josephine was still in the room, listening to every word.

"I can't believe you, Mother. I simply cannot believe you. You know I do not approve of your old-fashioned healing ways. And you know I do not approve of those Indians you call your friends. I only allowed Josephine to go with you because I was certain, by doing so, she would finally rid herself of the foolhardy idea of following in your footsteps. I should have known you would make the whole thing seem so alluring."

She turned to her daughter. "So, you think learning the Cherokee beliefs is so charming, do you? I suppose you are trying to seek after your grandmother's precious balance. But let me ask you one question, Miss Josephine. Did she tell you it was the Cherokee blessings and Cherokee medicine that sent your grandfather to an early grave? Did she happen to mention that if she had taken him directly to the doctor's office in Asheville, he might still be alive today instead of eaten up with cancer?"

Josie Mae began to sob. "Mama, it ain't true."

Carrie Ann, waving her hand toward her mother, said, "It isn't true? Do you have knowledge of the truth because she told you so? And do you think she would tell you the whole story? Don't be naïve. Her mountain doctoring was useless, and now she's trying to train you to learn the same foolishness."

Maggie slammed her hand on the table, causing Carrie Ann to suck in her breath. "I've had enough. Do you hear me? Enough! This is my home, and you have no right to come here and throw around your accusations. Your father had cancer, Carrie Ann. And not just any cancer, but lung cancer. There ain't nothing a doctor can do for lung cancer."

She walked to the other side of the room and pulled Josie Mae close against her chest, smoothing her hair, and shushing the child's sobs. Then she turned back to Carrie Ann, continuing in a quieter voice.

"Don't you think I wondered if I should have taken him to Asheville sooner? Of course, I did. Don't you think I blamed myself for not understanding he didn't just have an ordinary cough? But Carrie Ann, you need to understand something. I talked with the doctor. I asked him if your pa would have lived if we had made it to him earlier. And do you know what he said?"

Carrie Ann looked at her mother blankly.

"He said no. He said I could have brought him the day he first coughed, and the outcome would have been the same. Cancer is cancer, and nobody's got a way of fixing it. Not you. Not Daniel. Not the doctor in Asheville. Not anyone."

When Carrie Ann said nothing, her mother pointed at the door. "I think it's time for you to leave now. I'm sorry you came all this way for nothing, but Josie Mae and I have things to do today, so we don't have time for visiting. We'll come calling on you in town soon."

Carrie Ann had been so stunned she simply turned around and walked out of the cabin that had, at one time, been her home. She didn't see any need to try to force Josephine to come with her. It was too late. Her mother had already poisoned the child against her. And, once again, it was her own fault.

The argument had been yesterday. She sent word to Daniel that she would be taking another day. She claimed not to feel well and let on it might have something to do with womanly issues, just to be sure there'd be no questions upon her return.

She sat in her kitchen, going over yesterday's events in her mind. She wasn't wrong about this. Her mother was, without a doubt, using Josephine's trusting nature against her. She was too naïve to see her grandmother's beliefs were outdated and potentially harmful.

Carrie Ann remembered sitting at the ceremonies as a young child. She had to admit they were enchanting. It is no wonder Josephine wanted to learn more.

And this line of reasoning brought her back to this entire problem being her own fault. She should have never left her daughter in the care of her mother. Of course, if her mother hadn't helped her, Carrie Ann would have never gone to Boston to be a nurse. She would have been stuck on the farm to this day. She shuddered at the thought.

No, those early years were not to be helped. But once she finished her studies and came back to Burnsville to work with Dr. McKeithen? That is when she made her mistake. She should have insisted Josephine live with her. She should have insisted the child go to school. She should have insisted Josephine, if she wanted to be a healer, learn from her and Daniel rather than her mother.

And now it was too late. She could drag her daughter here, but she wouldn't stay. She was old enough to begin making her own decisions. In a few short years, she'd be thinking about marriage and children. The choice would be hers. Carrie Ann had been too busy to raise her own child, and now, she realized, she was living the consequences.

Chapter 24

Maggie
- July 27, 1893 -

In the latter part of June, Maggie and Carrie Ann established a truce of sorts, but only for the sake of Josie Mae. Maggie thought of the long nights listening to the child sob. Josie Mae believed she was the cause of the entire problem between the two adults in her life. Nothing Maggie said could convince her otherwise.

Maggie, unable to bear her granddaughter's distress for another moment, had determined to go into town. She found Carrie Ann sitting with the doctor on his front porch. "Good morning, Daniel. Carrie Ann." She nodded to both. She noted Carrie Ann's mouth had straightened into a thin line. As Maggie continued to speak, Carrie Ann's eyes narrowed and the muscles tensed in her arms, like a cat ready to pounce on its prey.

"I hope you don't mind, but I've come to whisk away my daughter. It's been too long since we had lunch together, so I packed a bit of food on this fine day." Maggie lifted the basket, tipping it in Daniel's direction. "The weather is perfect for a picnic, and just to be sure Carrie Ann would agree, Josie Mae baked her favorite – oat cakes."

Daniel slapped his knee. "Why, Carrie Ann, it appears

I'm losing my nurse for the afternoon. Go and have a wonderful visit with your mama."

Carrie Ann began to protest. "I couldn't, Dr. McKeithen. We've been so busy lately. Hardly a chance to breathe between patients." Then, turning to Maggie, she said, "You understand, don't you, Mama?" Although the words were pleasant enough, Maggie detected an icy sting.

Her response would have been the end, except Daniel was on Maggie's side. "Nonsense! The day is too beautiful to waste sitting around here just in case someone comes by. I was even thinking of putting a note on the door saying they could find me down by the river. In fact," he stood up, "that's exactly what I'm going to do. You go have a picnic with your mama, and I'll see if there's anything biting."

He turned to Carrie Ann. "Go on, now. Gather up your things. I'm locking up."

With his proclamation, Carrie Ann had no choice. As they walked down the street toward the outskirts of town, Carrie Ann breathed out a harsh whisper between tight lips. "I'm not going to eat lunch with you, Mother. However, I was not going to create a scene in front of Dr. McKeithen or anyone else who might be eavesdropping. Our family issues are no one's business but our own."

Maggie realized her assumption was correct. The doctor's easy manner suggested her daughter had not confided in him about the argument, and now, her words confirmed it.

She was not surprised by this admission. Carrie Ann was not one to discuss her private affairs with others and would be very careful not to be seen in a poor light, especially by someone she held in such high regard. Maggie was also aware Daniel did not hold similar opinions about healing as her daughter and had some of the same intuition she'd discovered in herself and witnessed in Josie Mae.

Maggie slipped her arm through her daughter's, adding a bit of grit to her own voice. "You are going to eat lunch with me, or at least hear me out. I would let this whole matter go on as it stands if it weren't for Josie Mae."

Carrie Ann tried to come to a stop, but their interlocking arms propelled her forward. "That's right," Maggie continued. "Your daughter, Josephine. She has spent the last weeks crying, sure this is all her fault. Nothing I say convinces her she has done nothing wrong. How is a child of twelve supposed to figure out her mother and grandmother don't get along, and her existence has nothing to do with it?"

As they reached the edge of town, Maggie stopped, releasing her grip on Carrie Ann. "The problems between us? I don't have any idea what to do about them. You've had your own way of viewing the world since you were a baby. Even though I didn't understand what drove you, I've always been proud of you."

Carrie Ann glanced up at her, disbelief filling her eyes.

"It's true, Carrie Ann. I wanted a child more than anything I ever dreamed of. I was only able to bring you, and you alone, into this world. Despite our differences, I've been proud of how you took charge of your life and made decisions that suited you.

"You were nothing more than a toddler, and everyone who met you knew you were destined to be your own person, with your own views. It was exasperating as I tried to teach you about life, but in my heart, I couldn't have been more pleased to be rearin' someone who already knew her way.

"Sure, I wished your path was the same as mine. What mother doesn't?" Maggie stopped and let the sentence sink in, hoping Carrie Ann would recognize how their relationship mirrored the one Carrie Ann had with Josie Mae.

"But truth be told, I was so thrilled when you went off to nursing school. My own daughter, smart enough to become a nurse. And then to find a way to bring all that learnin' back to her hometown to help the people she loved. I'm still proud."

Maggie reached into the basket, pulling out a small blanket. She smoothed it over the ground and began setting out the rest of the contents. She lowered herself down, her old knees creaking, and patted the space beside her. "Sit down, Carrie Ann, please?"

Carrie Ann, surprised by her mother's earlier declaration, sat down.

"We don't see eye to eye on most everything, but we have the same purpose. We both want to help folks." Carrie Ann started to protest, stating her mother's way of helping was not helpful, but Maggie held up a hand.

"Let me finish. We both want to help folks. Yes, differently, but the intent is the same. Do you agree?"

A resigned sigh escaped from Carrie Ann's mouth. She hated the way her mama doctored but had to admit she did it to be helpful. "Yes, fine. We both want to help folks." But she couldn't stop herself from adding, "Even if you don't do it right."

Maggie raised her eyebrows with a slight smile. "Point taken. And then there's the matter of Josie Mae, Josephine." Maggie stared deep into her daughter's eyes. "We both love that child more than life itself and want what is best for her. Correct?"

Carrie Ann closed her eyes, not wanting her mother to witness the emotions sure to show in them. "Yes, yes, of course."

Carrie Ann, despite being angry with her mother, knew Maggie only wanted the best for her granddaughter. She had been a rock, taking them in when Josephine's father died. She had been willing to care for Josephine while Carrie Ann went to school. She loved the child and, Carrie Ann knew, Josephine loved her back.

"And it's because of this mutual love for Josephine we must make a truce. The poor child is torn. Should she love her granny or her mama? Which one should she follow? Or perhaps, should she be allowed to follow her heart?"

Maggie stopped talking and picked up a slice of ham. She had nothing left to say. The rest was up to her daughter.

Carrie Ann pulled her cookie into pieces, mulling over her mother's words. First, she was surprised her mother used the word proud. She would have never thought her mother found any value in what she did. Had she always been pleased with her, and Carrie Ann just missed the signs?

And there was the knowledge her argument had wounded not only her mother, as she intended, but also her child. This thought brought tears to her eyes. Poor Josephine. It wasn't fair that she got sucked into the fight merely because she loved both women.

Carrie Ann cleared her voice. "Thank you for coming out here, Mama. I agree Josephine should not be made to suffer simply because we refuse to get along, but I'm still angry." She wanted her mother to be aware the truce did not mean defeat. "I believe you are pushing Josephine toward something that is harmful, and I'm confident she will see it in time."

Carrie Ann stood, having not touched her lunch. "In the future, we will keep our disagreements private. I will do my best to respect you and your home. I'm certain you will do the same. Whatever Josephine decides about her life's path is, of course, up to her. If it's alright with you, I'm going to drop by now. I'd like to tell her we've made up, so she needn't worry about it any longer."

Maggie nodded her consent.

"I'd prefer to be alone with her. I don't think I'm ready yet to pretend we are a happy, loving family."

The picnic lunch had been a month earlier. Carrie Ann now came by after church each Sunday for dinner. Maggie and Josie Mae made frequent stops to visit Carrie Ann when they were in town. By all accounts, everything was as it should be – except both Maggie and Carrie Ann knew they were far from happy and loving.

Chapter 25

Carrie Ann
- August 4, 1893 -

"Hello, Mama! It's good to see you again." Josie Mae raised up on her tiptoes to plant a quick kiss on her mother's cheek.

Carrie Ann smiled at her daughter. "It is good, Josephine. But I'm surprised you are here. Mama just came at the beginning of the week for supplies. And I'll be by on Sunday like normal." She stopped short, her tone becoming more clipped. "Is everything alright, Josephine? Mama isn't sick, is she?"

Josie Mae shook her head. "No, Mama. Everything is just fine. It's just that... Well... I have a favor to ask of you." She looked at her mother from under her long lashes.

"Well? Don't stand there staring at me with doe eyes. What brought you all this way? Come now. Don't leave me in suspense." Although she tried to sound as if she were teasing, there was an urgency in her voice as she considered all the possibilities.

"Well, you know I'm thinkin' about being a healer, like Granny." Carrie Ann sucked in her breath, letting the air escape between her clenched teeth.

Josie Mae hurried on, noting her mother's irritation at the topic. "I don't think I should choose to be something when I don't have anything to compare it to. All I really understand about healin' is what I've seen Granny do. And that doesn't make any sense when I have a mama who is a nurse. So..."

She swallowed hard before continuing. "So, I was thinking maybe I could work with you a couple of days per week during the good weather to learn about what you do."

Mistaking the look on Carrie Ann's face to mean she wasn't happy with the proposition, Josie Mae rushed on, assuring her she'd be no trouble. "I won't get in the way. I'm not expecting money. I..." She held up her hands and let them fall to her sides, head hung down. "Never mind. I guess it was a foolish idea."

But before Josie Mae could move, Carrie Ann had her by the arm. "It's not a foolish idea, Josephine. Not foolish at all. I just didn't expect you to say what you said. In fact, I'm truly surprised."

Josie Mae lifted her eyes. "Really? I thought... Well, your mouth? I mean. You looked upset. I figured you thought I would be a bother. I don't want to be in the way. I just want to see what you are doing. Learn what you have in the apothecary. Maybe..." Her face broke out in a hopeful smile. "Maybe be with you when you work with patients?"

Carrie Ann began to laugh. She hadn't seen her daughter this curious in a long time. It reminded her of when Josephine was a little girl with pigtails, running headlong into whatever adventure lay ahead. She missed those days with her daughter, the days when hugs and kisses were plentiful, and laughter came easy. "I can't promise you anything without talking to Daniel. I mean, Dr. McKeithen." The blood rushed to her cheeks. She wished she hadn't made that blunder. She didn't want Josie Mae thinking she was too familiar with her boss, nor did she want her to assume it was appropriate to refer to him as Daniel herself.

Josie Mae's face didn't even register the slip, obviously too excited to care what her mother called the doctor. "Will you ask him, Mother? Soon? Today?" The words rushed out of her with no pauses between the questions.

"Dr. McKeithen is making a house call. He will be back here shortly. Do you want to wait here? I'll talk to him about it, and we can work out the details."

Suddenly, Josie Mae pulled her arms around her waist and looked toward the door. "Oh, no. I mean. You should ask him without me here. He might feel like he has to say yes when he wants to say no if I'm sitting here watching him. No. I'll go back home and help Granny with the cookin'. You can tell me what he says when you come out to the house on Sunday."

She began to back out of the building, obviously not wanting to be around when the doctor came in. Carrie Ann could feel the child's embarrassment, but before she let her go, asked, "Josephine. Does your grandmother know about this? It would be cruel to bring it up when I'm visiting if she is unaware of your plan."

"Oh, yes! Granny knows. In fact, it was Granny's idea. She says a good healer should be willing to learn from anyone who has something to teach.

"She says she learns from Illanipi and from you and Dr. McKeithen. She sometimes learns something new when tending to someone on their farm – you know, about an old family remedy or something they brought over from the Old Country. She says a person is never too old to learn and should spend their whole life trying to be better than the day before." With those words, she turned and nearly skipped down the street.

Carrie Ann wondered aloud. "What in the world is Mother up to? Why would she suggest such a thing to Josephine?"

Carrie Ann jumped when Daniel answered. "Who is 'she,' and what did this mysterious 'she' suggest to your daughter?"

"Oh, my. I didn't see you there. I thought you were out." She sputtered and gestured with her hands, a flustered movement at having been caught ruminating out loud.

"I'm stealthy," Daniel replied with a grin. "So, what has you so ruffled?"

"Mama..."

Before she could say another word, Daniel groaned. "Please, no. Don't tell me you and your mother are at it again. What terrible crime has she committed this time? Healed another poor soul by talking off their wart?"

This was something Daniel was immensely curious about because, before moving to Burnsville, he'd never heard of such a thing. Around these parts, however, it was a skill many granny women, including Maggie, claimed to possess.

If someone had a wart, rather than treat it with a poultice of thyme and rosemary as he would prescribe or rub it with a potato and bury the potato as many of the superstitious would advise, Maggie simply whispered to it. Within the week, the wart was gone.

He asked Maggie about this ability, and she shrugged. "I don't know why it works. Seems to have something to do with the balance I try to practice. I tell the wart what needs doing, and the wart listens and does it."

With a low growl, Carrie Ann muttered. "No, she isn't talking off warts or whispering away the fire in a burn or blowing the thrush from a baby's mouth. At least not that I'm aware of." She wondered why he thought it was so humorous to bring up her mother's idiosyncrasies, knowing how they upset her.

She took a deep breath. "No, what she is suggesting this time makes logical sense. Which means I wonder what she's up to. It isn't like her to think clearly or push her granddaughter to learn something useful."

Daniel guffawed, bending at the waist and laughing. "Really, Carrie Ann, you need to give your mother a bit of a break." He wiped his eyes. "So, what is it she's suggested?"

Carrie Ann, irritated by his laughter, considered not telling him, but she thought of her daughter's earnest face. "First, let me say I agree with what she is proposing. I think it makes sense, and I hope you will, too. It's her motives I question." She proceeded to tell him Josie Mae's request.

Daniel loved the idea. "She can tidy up, keep me up-to-date on the paperwork, learn about ordering the meds. Yes, she will be a great help. Plus, with another person here, I may be able to do a bit more fishing!" He laughed at her expression.

"Oh, for heaven's sake, Carrie Ann. It was a joke. I do wish you could be more relaxed."

She hmphed in his direction. "So, I should tell Josephine you are willing to have her here in the office?" At his nod, Carrie Ann finally smiled. She couldn't wait for Sunday to deliver the good news.

Chapter 26

Josie Mae
- September 4, 1893 -

Josie Mae reached into the corner with the broom, making sure the apothecary was spotless. Of course, she had already swept the floor twice, dusted the shelves, adjusted the various assortment of jars, and washed the windows. She sighed to herself, not wanting to catch the attention of her mother.

Josie Mae started coming to the office with her mama almost a month earlier. When she began, she expected a lot of hands-on learning, like when working with Granny or Illanipi. But her mama's way of teaching was different.

"You can't start in the middle and work your way to the edges," she said when Josie had asked a question about morphine. "You have to start from the bottom and work your way up. Questions about the drugs and how they help with illness are far too advanced." Then she handed her a dust rag and suggested she make herself useful.

An entire month later, and Josie Mae was no closer to learning anything of value. She still didn't understand why morphine was so much better at dampening pain than willow bark. She also wanted to figure out if it made sense to begin a treatment with something weak, or was it better to give a patient the strongest drugs possible?

This last question wasn't only about pain but about any illness. She knew many different cures existed for the very same condition. She had trouble distinguishing when to use which one, and why these cures worked for some people but not others. Did healers have a way to determine what would work before trying? But each time she tried to broach the subjects on her mind, her mother brushed her thoughts aside.

She also noted, with exasperation, she rarely had the opportunity to spend time with Dr. McKeithen and had, not even once, been with him alone. Josie Mae felt certain he would be willing to discuss her questions, but she never got the chance to ask.

When Mama told her about the agreement, she explained that Josephine would learn to do paperwork and how to order medicines. She might even be given the opportunity to see patients. But so far, all she'd been allowed to do was sweep and dust and run errands.

She was not unwilling to help. She would do anything needed to make sure Dr. McKeithen didn't regret allowing her to be there two days a week. It's just she didn't feel like she was helpful at all. And quite frankly, she was beginning to think the trek into town wasn't worth it.

Josie Mae balanced the broom in the corner behind the door and turned to face her mother. "Mama?" She waited for Carrie Ann to look up from the book she was reading. Once she was certain she had her attention, she cleared her throat and gripped the counter for support.

"Mama, I want to do more than sweep and dust. I'm not learning anything about being a healer. The closest I've come is memorizing the names of all the jars on the shelf, but it does me no good because I have no idea what they do or how they are used."

"You've done what? Memorized the names of all the containers? Josie Mae, there is no need for storytelling. The only way to know all the names is to read them."

Josie Mae turned her back to the wall of shelves and began to recite, starting from the top shelf. "Potassium acetate, potassium nitrate, spirit of juniper, peppermint, lactopeptine, strychnine, emetine, morphine, quinine, caffeine, salicylic acid, salicin..."

While she recited, Dr. McKeithen came into the room. "... chloral hydrate, diastase, mannitol, and laudanum."

She flipped around in time to see her mother's mouth hanging open and a huge smile spreading across Dr. McKeithen's face. Josie Mae returned the smile as he clapped his hands. "Why, Miss Josephine! I had no idea we had such a scholar in our midst. I don't believe I could name all the drugs we have on hand, and definitely not in the order I have them stored on the shelf. Bravo!"

While Josie Mae blushed crimson, he nodded toward Carrie Ann. "Did you hear her? She got every single one of them right. I began following along as soon as I knew what she was doing. She didn't leave out one. Not a single one!"

He glanced back at Josie Mae to find her standing with her arms wrapped tight around her middle. "I'm amazed by you, young lady. Without a doubt, we are wasting your talent having you dust and sweep floors. Come here, with me. I have a job for you."

Dr. McKeithen took Josie Mae into the little office used for accounting. In it was a tiny wooden desk, sheaves of paper, pencils, erasers, order forms, and envelopes of various sizes. Carrie Ann stood in the doorway, both immensely proud of her daughter and concerned that Dr. McKeithen was going to give her too much responsibility.

"Every two weeks, I have to take inventory of the drugs on the shelf. I keep this master list." He handed the paper to Josie Mae. "You should feel right at home with these, Josephine. I have listed every drug we have in the apothecary. But here," he pointed to a second column, "are the quantities I always want to have in stock. So, your job will be twofold."

He held up one finger. "First, you must determine how much of the medicine we have and compare it to the amount we should have."

He then held up a second finger. "Second, you need to order the quantity needed from the different supply houses. This second part is a bit trickier. So, for now, focus on the first task, and mark what we need to purchase here."

He pointed to a third column. "Once you have that information, come to me. I'll explain my system, and you'll see why I have the jars on the shelves the way I do."

She looked at him, eyebrows drawn into a question. "I'll give you a hint. It has something to do with where the supply comes from."

Josie Mae's eyes lit up. She had been wondering about the order. It wasn't alphabetical. She didn't think it had to do with what the drugs were used for because, when Dr. McKeithen made up a prescription, he always pulled from several sections of the apothecary. She had never considered he kept them grouped together by supplier.

Josie Mae buzzed down to her toes. She couldn't wait to begin. "Should I start now? Do you want me to use the scale on the counter, or do you have a different one for this job? Is it best to bring down one jar at a time, or do you do it in batches? Do I have to worry about cleaning the instruments between uses?"

Dr. McKeithen held up his hand, rocking himself around in a circle. "Woah, Josephine! All those questions are making me dizzy!"

Carrie Ann broke in. "Yes, Josephine, that is quite enough. You are obviously not ready for such a task."

Josie Mae's face fell, but before she could think of something to say, Dr. McKeithen cut in.

"No, Carrie Ann. She's fine. I love her excitement. And she is right. I gave her two tasks but didn't give her any information on how to perform them. Instead of going ahead and doing what she was told and making mistakes along the way, she began asking specific questions to help her understand. Obviously, I'm not used to having an apprentice. Thank you, Josephine, for helping me be better at this new role of mine."

Apprentice! Dr. McKeithen called her an apprentice. This was far more interesting than cleaning the same floor over and over again. Her joy threatened to leap out of her body.

Dr. McKeithen continued. "It's almost time for you to go home. You're coming again tomorrow, correct?"

Josie Mae nodded with enthusiasm, wanting to dance in little circles but knowing it would not be an appropriate thing for an apprentice.

"Can you come in an hour early?" he asked.

Josie Mae looked to her mama. "Mama? Will it be alright with you? I'll likely not have time to help you wash up after breakfast."

Carrie Ann waved the words away. "Of course, child. I spent many years washing my own dishes before you started staying the night with me once a week. I can certainly do so again in the morning."

Josie Mae turned back to Dr. McKeithen, nodding vigorously.

"Good. We'll begin first thing tomorrow. You can follow along, asking questions as I work on the first containers. Afterward, I'll let you do a few with my guidance. If all goes well, you can complete them tomorrow. We'll worry about step two the next time we are ready to order. What do you think?"

Without considering her actions, she ran to Dr. McKeithen, throwing her arms around his middle, saying a muffled thank you into his shirt. Then, she ran to her mother, giving her a big kiss on her cheek.

Finally! She was going to be a real apprentice.

Chapter 27

Maggie
- September 5, 1893 -

Maggie listened as Josie Mae gushed. She'd been talking nonstop for an hour, but Maggie had no intentions of asking her to stop. Maggie was thrilled Josie Mae was learning something from Dr. McKeithen.

"And you know how I just dusted and dusted. Why, there wasn't a speck anywhere, but still, I dusted. I tried to tell Mama I was bored, so bored I had memorized all the names of the jars. I wanted to tell her I'd rather understand what use the things in the jars had, but before I could say anything, anything at all, she said I was a liar!"

Maggie let her eyes grow into big circles. "It's true, Granny! Well, of course, Mama didn't say liar. She said storyteller, but you and I know it means the same thing. So, anyway, I started repeating all those names, and Dr. McKeithen heard, too. And now I get to help order the medicines!"

Maggie smiled. This was the fourth retelling, as if Josie Mae were still trying to believe it had happened.

"So, I went early, early this morning. Mama had barely gotten out of bed when I left the house. I got to the office before Dr. McKeithen had even opened the front door, but when he did, I was waitin'. He said I was as eager as a hound pursuing its prey. Isn't that funny, Granny? I ain't never heard such a thing as that."

Maggie stifled a laugh. She was doubtful Josie Mae knew about fox hunting with hounds, so she probably had no idea what Daniel meant. However, it didn't seem to stifle her excitement.

"After we went inside, he brought down the first jar. It had potassium acetate in it. I knew the name, of course, but what I didn't understand was what potassium acetate did for folks. So, while he was measurin', I watched him careful like, but I also asked him about the white powder. I noted it didn't smell like anything at all. In fact, it could have been nothing more than bread flour by the looks of it.

"So, I said, 'Dr. McKeithen? Just what is potassium acetate used for? I mean, why do you need it here at the apothecary?' And do you know what he said, Granny?"

Josie Mae was so into the retelling of her story she didn't wait for a response.

"He said it was a diuretic. And since I didn't have any idea what that meant, I asked. And he said it was a fancy way of saying it would make someone pee. Well, I got kind of red in the face talking to a man about peeing, but he didn't seem to think there was nothing wrong with it. So, I said, 'Granny uses dandelion or hawthorn to help folks pee.' And you know what, Granny?"

Once again, she did not wait for a response. "He said he had never been taught about dandelion or hawthorn. Can you believe it? No one ever explained to him about how dandelion can make folks pee."

With so much of the story left to be told, Maggie adjusted herself in the chair. She was growing too old to sit in one position for too long without her bones starting to complain.

"So, when he took down the next jar, potassium nitrate, he didn't wait for me to ask him what it was for. He just right out explained it to me. And guess what? It helps folks pee, too. In the same way we've got several remedies for the same problem, so does Dr. McKeithen. But he also said potassium nitrate can help people with a toothache. If they put the powder on their sore tooth every day, the ache will go away."

Josie Mae took a breath to ask a question in which she expected an answer. "I wasn't able to tell him what we used for a toothache. I couldn't rightly remember. I promised to bring him the names of our remedies next week. What do you use for a toothache, Granny?"

Granny sat forward. "Well, there's a couple of things to try. Chewing on yarrow root can be helpful. Sometimes, drinking a tea made from marigold leaves works. If a person has access to it, cloves, like the kind you buy at the store for making Christmas pudding, can also help. Of course, the best thing for a toothache that won't go away is letting the doctor pull it out."

Josie Mae involuntarily touched her cheek with her hand, grimacing. "I don't think I'll tell him about that. I don't want any part of someone losing one of their teeth. I've seen the tools Dr. McKeithen uses, and they don't look friendly."

Granny laughed out loud. "No, you're right, Josie Mae. Getting a tooth pulled isn't much fun. But neither is having a toothache. I guess a person's got to decide which pain is gonna be worse, 'cause they're gonna have pain. It's a matter of which one do they want."

The rest of the afternoon, Josie Mae talked about the different medicines she learned about. Dr. McKeithen didn't give her explanations on everything. Once Carrie Ann came to work, Josie Mae was left to measure the remainder of the ingredients on her own. However, he taught her about quite a few, and she planned to ask him about the others the next time they worked together.

"I have an idea, Josie Mae." Maggie reached into a burlap sack sitting by the side of her chair. "I got this for you. I was saving it for your birthday in November, but I think maybe you should have it now."

She pulled out a notebook and handed it to Josie Mae. The cover was red with green vines and yellow flowers. Inside were dozens of lined, blank pages. On the inside cover, Maggie had written, "Always listen to the whispered voices, Love Granny."

Josie Mae ran her fingers first over the front and then over the pages. She looked up, eyes glassy. "Thank you, Granny. This is the most beautiful book I've ever seen. It's nearly too pretty to mess up with a pencil."

Maggie waggled her finger. "It's no such thing. It's meant exactly for writing in, and I hope writing is what you'll do. With you learnin' so much, it might be useful to start putting it down. Kind of like your own remedy list."

Josie Mae nodded and began thinking out loud. "I could write all the different plants and medicines I know and what they do. Or I could write down all the different diseases and mark down which plants and medicines could help. Which way is the best way, Granny?"

Maggie shrugged. "It's your book, child, and as such, it needs to be useful for you. There isn't a right way and a wrong way. Not this time."

Josie Mae was thoughtful. "I think maybe putting it by disease would help. Of course, I don't have names for all the diseases, but I could always leave space on every page for others."

She riffled through the pages, tapping her chin. "I mean, since I already have four different cures for needing to pee, I could list all of them together. If I find out other cures, I could add them to the list. Then, when I'm the granny woman, if I have someone who needs to pee and can't, I can just look at my book."

She closed the notebook, looking again at Maggie. "But Granny? How do I decide whether I should use potassium nitrate or dandelion? Or if dandelion is better than hawthorn? How do you do it?"

Maggie considered her granddaughter's question thoughtfully. She was certain, more than ever, that Josie Mae would make a fine healer someday. She was also certain, more than ever, that suggesting she apprentice in town was the right thing to do.

Had she had the opportunity as a young woman, she would have taken it, but there wasn't a local doctor any closer than Asheville. With the training Josie Mae got from her, from the Cherokee, and from Dr. McKeithen, she was sure to learn the best ways to relieve those who were hurting.

Josie Mae interrupted her ruminating with, "Granny? How do you know?"

Maggie shook her head. "You don't, child. You have to use the gift I told you about. Do you remember the gift?"

Josie Mae nodded. "Intuition?"

"Yes, intuition. Balance. Listening to the plants. Hearing your patients. Listening to what they say after starting the treatment. Being willing to admit you were wrong and trying something new. All of this will help you decide."

She leaned forward and held her granddaughter's hands in her own. "Keep in mind, Josie Mae. Not everyone can be healed. Sometimes, God says it is time for someone to go, so go they will. It won't matter what you give 'em or what you don't give 'em."

Josie Mae rubbed her thumb across the top of Granny's hand, noting the lines and creases. "You mean, like grand-daddy?"

Maggie nodded, thinking, "Yes, exactly like that."

Chapter 28

Carrie Ann
- September 27, 1893 -

Carrie Ann tidied up the back office. She spent the after-noon making sure patient charts were up to date. Although Dr. McKeithen seemed to have a way with people, he didn't have the same propensity toward paperwork. He'd scribble a sentence or two with every intention of going back to fill in the details later. However, Carrie Ann learned very quickly when working with Daniel that these intentions rarely became realized.

So, she took it upon herself to take his sparse notes and create actual documentation of the visits. Oftentimes, she had to ask him to clarify something he wrote or, more likely, explain what he hadn't written.

Like earlier today, when she read, "Sore throat. Usual." What did Daniel mean? Was it typical for Sue Ellen to have a sore throat? Did he mean to write unusual, think-ing her sore throat was out of the ordinary and some-thing to watch? Did he mean he gave her the standard care when presented with a sore throat? And, if the latter, which standard care? The reason behind the sore throat could easily change what they used to treat it.

In this case, he meant he followed the standard pro-tocol for a sore throat. Carrie Ann took advantage of this example as a way to begin her lecture on being thorough.

"You do realize these notes are pretty much worthless to anyone who wasn't in the room with you, right? Sore Throat. Usual. That could mean so many different things. If I had to treat Sue Ellen without you, I wouldn't have any idea what you'd done before or why."

Daniel, screwing up his mouth and working hard to not look irritated, answered, "But you don't have to treat Sue Ellen without me. I'm right here. If you have a question, you can ask."

She rolled her eyes. "Trying to reason with you is like trying to reason with my daughter, though I expect it from her. You, on the other hand? You should – and I daresay do – know better."

Daniel's sigh only spurred her on. "Let's say some epidemic, heaven forbid, came rolling through and sent you to bed, weak with a fever. And let's say Sue Ellen came to this clinic with a sore throat which, despite treatment, was still painful. I'm here. You are not here. I look at this chart, and I have no idea – none whatsoever – what you have done or what I should do next."

Daniel raised his eyebrows, a smile threatening to form on his face. "You could always ask Sue Ellen what I gave her. She's likely to be able to tell you." As she pursed her lips, Daniel laughed out loud.

"Fine. Fine. I'll try to do better. But I hate writing it all down. Maybe I ought to have been a healer like your mama. She just keeps everything in her head, and no one bothers her to do more than that."

Carrie Ann put the back of her hand over her eyes, rubbing in frustration. She was so tired of Daniel's obsession with her mama.

"Speaking of Mama," she said, her words coming out a bit shriller than she meant. She cleared her voice and tried again. "Speaking of Mama, I do wish you wouldn't include Josephine in your fascination with that woman. It isn't as if she isn't exposed to enough of my mother's backwoods medicine without you pumping her for details while she is here."

Daniel looked puzzled. "Pumping her for details? What are you talking about, Carrie Ann?"

Pointing a finger in his direction, she said, "You know exactly what I'm talking about.

"Just yesterday morning, as Josephine was working on the inventory, I heard the two of you chatting about remedies. I was thrilled when you explained how chloral hydrate can help someone fall asleep, especially if they are anxious or troubled by something. There is such value in her understanding the use of these medicines. But then?"

She began drumming her fingers on the wooden counter. "Then, you asked her what her granny would give for sleeplessness."

She looked at him pointedly. "But it didn't stop there. Josephine mentioned St. John's Wort as well as rosemary, and the two of you began talking about herbs brought over from Europe that grow well locally and how these newer plants have changed how my mother practices healing versus someone who didn't have access to these herbs. What were you thinking?"

He shook his head and sucked in a deep breath.

"Carrie Ann, you have got to get this problem with your mother under control. You look for problems where none exist. All I was doing was helping Josie Mae see how remedies change as we learn new information.

"For years, in North Carolina, no one had the ability to use something like rosemary. Now? Your mother grows it in her garden and dries it for medicine. It is no different than before I came here and set up this apothecary," he said as he swept his hand in a circle around the room. "People once relied only on something like St. John's Wort, and now they have access to chloral hydrate."

He walked over to where she stood and put his hands on her shoulders. "However, Carrie Ann, when it comes to insomnia? It is possible that for some people, using your mother's herbs would be a better fit. That's why I don't see any problem explaining what I do and learning what your mama does."

Carrie Ann shrugged off his hands, letting them fall to his sides.

"It is perfectly fine for you to believe what you want to believe. You are a grown man with a strong education in science and medicine. My daughter, on the other hand, is very impressionable. She doesn't have your background and can be easily swayed to think her granny's little herb garden in the sideyard is as effective as the medicines here. She might even decide there is no need to have a real doctor in town."

Daniel shrugged. "Maybe there's not."

He walked out of the office with an "I'm going to eat lunch with the boys," leaving her standing with her mouth agape. No need for a real doctor? If he didn't understand his worth, it was no wonder some people, like Esther and her family, didn't either.

She straightened the papers, thinking about Esther. Carrie Ann had been to their home several times, checking on the children, Malcolm's growth, Lloyd's development, and now, with Esther once again with child, her health.

Although Esther never uttered a harsh word and always thanked Carrie Ann for dropping by, she said they were doing fine, thanks to Maggie.

Carrie Ann began to mutter to herself. "Maggie, indeed. She's probably having Esther dip in the river twice a day and, while dancing naked in the woods, sing songs to the pregnancy goddess. Then, heading home and drinking some tea using only her left hand and stirring the concoction counterclockwise."

Carrie Ann paused long enough to snort. "Some good that will do when Esther starts experiencing problems." But as she thought about Esther's last delivery, Carrie Ann stopped muttering, remembering that her mother was the one who helped Dr. McKeithen deliver a healthy baby.

She stomped her foot. "No! That is not the way it happened. She made a lucky guess one time, and now she has Daniel, Esther's family, and Josephine all believing she knows what she is doing. But not me. I know the truth. She was responsible for my pa's death using the same healing she claims saved Esther. Her methods aren't anything more than wishful thinking, and I don't want any part in it."

Chapter 29

Maggie
- September 29, 1893 -

Maggie couldn't believe it was already the end of September. Little Malcolm was not so little anymore. She realized, with a start, the boy would soon be a year old. He was nearly walking, pulling up on chairs and taking tentative steps if the right bribes were held out. She noted he especially liked anything dipped in honey, so she was sure to bring a little with her whenever she visited.

That's where she was headed today. Maggie was concerned because Esther was with child again, although she had made it through the early stages of pregnancy without losing the baby. This was something to be thankful for. However, Esther looked tired and pale most of the time, so Maggie stopped by often with the excuse of checking in but with the intention of helping a bit with chores.

Of course, Maggie was getting on in years, and some of the work that needed doing left her back and hips aching. But she was willing to do what was necessary to help a friend.

As she approached the porch, the door opened, and Esther came out with two empty buckets. She set one down and raised her hand in a wave. "Hello, Maggie! It's so good to see you. I was just heading to the well to bring in some water."

Maggie walked briskly up the steps and took the bucket before Esther could pick it up again.

"You're my guest," protested Esther, but Maggie just laughed. "I ain't never been guest enough not to be helpful when helpful is what was needed."

The two women linked arms until they reached the well, then chatted while filling the buckets.

"You're beginnin' to show. The baby must be growin' just right."

Esther smiled, gently rubbing the swell under her apron. "He moves all the time now." She looked earnestly at Maggie. "I'm sure it's a 'he.' I can just feel it all the way to my soul."

Maggie nodded. Boy or girl, Esther would love the child if they were able to get it here into this world. "It'd be good to have another boy. Maribelle might wish she had a little sister, but strappin' boys will help John around the farm."

As they walked back to the house, a bit slower because of the weight, Maggie asked, "And how is everyone else faring?"

Esther smiled. "The kids are growing like weeds. Did I tell you? Lloyd said bread. I know it ain't much, but he's never said a word. Never done more than point and grunt. You tested his hearing and said everything was fine, but I was beginnin' to wonder. But he said 'bread' loud and clear and pointed right at a new loaf I'd baked. I was so happy I would've given him the whole thing except we needed it for dinner. Maybe folks is right. Maybe he is just a child with a slow start."

Maggie had her doubts, with Lloyd already nearing four years old, but she wasn't willing to snatch the hope from Esther's grasp. "Likely so. Some young'uns just don't need to talk much. Once they got somethin' to say, they say it."

Maribelle was sitting in the main room, keeping an eye on her brothers. "Hello, Miss Maggie! Mama had me watchin' the boys while she got us some water. It's a big job now, but Mama says I'm the girl to get it done." Maribelle beamed with pride.

"Remember, Miss Maggie, how I said I was gonna be a nurse like Miss Carrie Ann?"

Maggie nodded.

"Well, I done changed my mind. I'm gonna be a granny woman like you. My mama says you saved her life more'n once and, if'n it weren't for you, baby Malcolm wouldn't be here with us. So, I figure Nurse Nightingale would have been a granny woman, too, had she known of 'em. I 'spect she didn't since she didn't grow up in the mountains."

Maggie smiled down at the child. "Well, you know, Maribelle, my daughter is a nurse like Florence Nightingale, and I'm a granny woman like you said. We both do a lot for our little town. Whichever you decide will be just fine, that's for sure."

Maribelle stood up, brushing her hands on her skirt. "Well, I done made up my mind already. I'm gonna be a granny woman. Mama says if'n the baby comes alright, I might be able to help."

Maggie tried to hold her smile on her face, thinking Esther's labors never went well. There was no place in the room for a child.

"But she already done warned me if'n it don't go so well, like with Malcolm, and Pa has to fetch you, then

I'll have to watch my brothers and keep 'em out of trou-ble. She says I can be in charge of the boiling water and towels. So, either way, I'm gettin' to be a little bit like a granny woman." She grinned at the thought of helping birth her little brother or sister.

Maggie wanted to believe Esther would bring this lit-tle one into the world with no issues, but she wasn't coun-tin' on it. By the look on Esther's face, neither was she.

"Maribelle kept on pesterin' me about helping you when you came to deliver the baby. I told her if'n you was here, it meant the baby was being particular. And, when babies are being particular, the granny woman has to keep her whole mind on her job, so she'd not be able to be in and askin' questions."

Maggie smiled, relieved to understand Esther had no intentions of allowing Maribelle in the room during the delivery. But the promise was enough to satisfy a child humming with anticipation.

"Well, since I'm here, is there anything I can do for ya? I've got the whole afternoon with nary a thing to do."

That wasn't entirely true. Maggie knew she could be canning the last of the vegetables from the garden, mak-ing applesauce, drying herbs, splitting logs, and a number of other chores to ready the homestead for winter. Still, she was here to help Esther for the rest of the day, so help she would.

Maribelle went to the bean patch and picked the last of the snaps. Maggie, after making sure the child under-stood how to break them in half, got the canning pot ready. "Let's get these beans set up today, and we can start on them apples if you'd like. I think we can put up a dozen quarts or so before I have to leave for home."

The two women worked for hours. Maggie noticed

Esther moved more slowly than usual, often sitting to wipe her brow and take a deep breath. The next time she came, she'd bring her the ingredients for the tea she learned about this past spring. Illanipi told her he had begun having pregnant women and those overcoming a long sickness drink a concoction with oatstraw, red clover, nettle, raspberry and dandelion leaves, horsetail, and rose hips.

When she tried it and made a face, Illanipi laughed. "Many of the women have made such a face," he replied, "But none of the men." Maggie assured him the men didn't like the flavor either but were too worried about looking strong. He nodded in agreement.

"Here," he said, adding a bit of mint. "This makes it easier on the tongue."

Maggie made a mental to bring the herbs. It might put a little color back into her friend's cheeks.

As the sun began to dip toward the horizon, Maggie reluctantly made her way back to her homestead. There was so much more work to be done to ready Esther's home for winter. John started working at the Bremen place during the harvest, bringing in essential supplies. But his absence meant many of the chores landed on his wife.

"Take it easy now, hear?" Maggie called as she left. "I'll be 'round again next week. We'll finish up them apples. I'll bring Josie Mae with me. Between the three of us, we can accomplish a lot."

Maggie waved as she faced the path leading toward town. But she looked toward the house one last time as she rounded the bend in the road. She couldn't shake the feeling something wasn't right. She just didn't know what.

Chapter 30

Josie Mae
- October 4, 1893 -

Josie Mae scrambled out of bed. She spent the night at Mama's house after working in the apothecary the day before. Although she typically went back to Granny's house on Tuesday night, she was needed at Esther's house this morning.

Rather than walk the miles to Granny's and then back again today, she stayed in town. Her intention was to beat Granny to the Stallards and get a head start on any work around the place.

Her mama didn't understand her excitement. "It seems mighty strange to me you are so eager to help with chores at Esther's home when you don't show the same enthusiasm for chores around here."

Her mama was right, of course. She wasn't fond of doing chores for the sake of doing chores. But she wasn't 'doing chores' at Esther's house. She was helping the family prepare for winter because they weren't going to be able to do it all themselves. She loved the idea of helping others.

"Oh, Mama. It's not the same, and you know it. Working around the house is just boring. But being helpful to friends, especially when it involves Granny, means there will be plenty of stories and chatter and fun mixed in. If'n chores could be like spending the day at Esther's, well, then, I'd be much more willin' to be part of 'em."

Her mama grinned, though she tried to hide it. Mama never liked to show it when she thought something Josie Mae said was particularly insightful. Josie Mae, wanting to prove her mama wrong, at least a tiny bit, helped wash the supper dishes without being asked and grabbed the broom to sweep the front porch.

Once she was finished, she raised her eyebrows in the direction of her mama and said, "Well, I'm off to bed. I've got a big day tomorrow, and it will start very early. I'll be gone before breakfast."

The dawn light was just beginning to peek out over the horizon, casting long shadows across the floor. Although the morning was frigid for early October, she dressed in layers, knowing the work and the afternoon sun would change the temperatures from cool to quite warm.

She went to the kitchen pantry and, being sure to remain quiet, pulled out two leftover biscuits and a small hunk of ham. Wrapping them in a napkin, she put the food into her pocket and headed out the door.

Josie Mae appeared to be the only soul awake at this hour, though she was certain it wasn't true. Most folks rose at dawn, but they just hadn't come to town yet. Instead, they were busy tending their animals and making breakfast for the family.

She nibbled on one of the biscuits as she walked. Her goal was to start stacking the firewood into neat rows near the cabin, so Esther wouldn't have so far to go.

The little one was going to come toward the end of the winter, which meant she would be hauling wood for the fire with a swollen belly. Granny explained trying to do such things was more challenging when you had a baby taking up space inside.

John was busy working on another farm, trying to bring in some money before the freezing temperatures set in. He'd been chopping wood all summer but just hadn't had the time to stack it proper. Although it was a big assignment, Josie understood how important it was to have the firewood handy. So, as soon as she arrived, she began the task.

She already had three long rows before Granny got to the farmhouse. "My goodness, child! Would you look at that! You are doing a fine job. Fine indeed. Have you seen Esther yet this morning?"

Josie Mae shook her head. "No, ma'am. I've heard 'em moving about inside, but I just kept on workin'. I figured they'd come out here soon enough."

Maggie stepped onto the front porch, giving a quick knock. Esther pulled the door open, looking paler than she had just a week ago.

"Come on in, Maggie. Sorry, I ain't quite ready for you. I'm not sleepin' so well. Just feel kind of achy and out of sorts."

Maggie's brows knit with concern. "No pains, Esther? You don't think you are in labor?"

"Oh, no, Maggie. Nothin' like that. Just... well, just uncomfortable. The baby is moving and kicking. I'm grow-ing, so I figure the baby is, too. No, I don't think it's nothin' to worry about." She smiled, though her eyes held some worry, as she added, "Do you?"

Maggie shook her head. "Nah, I don't think so, Esther. But you are lookin' a might pale and run down. Not sleepin' will do that to ya. I got a tea that might help some. In the morning when you're makin' oatmeal for the children, you can add a bit of oats to these herbs. She pulled a small sack out of her coat pocket. "If'n you can, drink it twice a day. I'm gonna warn you. It ain't the tastiest, but I've added some mint to make it tolerable. Let me make you a cup, and while I'm at it, I'll put breakfast on the table."

She looked around. "Where's John? Josie Mae's been here since first light, but she said she hasn't seen anyone. Is he leavin' so early every day?"

Esther waved her hand toward the door. "He didn't make it back last night. Happens some. If'n he gets too busy and works 'til dark, he beds down in the barn. Saves him the walk."

Maggie nodded. "His being gone is likely a big part of why you ain't sleepin' well. It's a good thing I brought the tea."

Once breakfast was ready, Maggie called out to Josie Mae. "Child, come on in and have something to eat."

Josie Mae, wiping a bit of sweat from her brow, shook her head. "No need, Granny. I brung some biscuits and ham from Mama's." She pointed at the pile of clothes against the house. "I still got some left. I'll grab a bite when I'm hungry. I want to finish stacking these here logs."

Maggie smiled. "I'll send out Maribelle when she's done eatin'. Don't know how much help she'll be, but it will keep her out from under our feet in the kitchen. Do you think you can handle havin' the boys out here, too?"

"Sure, Granny. Maribelle can keep an eye on the boys, and I'll make a game out of them helpin' me stack wood. It will be nice to have some company."

When the children spilled out the front door, Josie

Mae called them to her. "Maribelle, put Malcolm down right here." Josie Mae had created a small circle out of sticks, which wouldn't keep Malcolm from escaping but would slow him down a bit. "Now, run back inside and fetch a couple of blocks to keep him occupied."

Once Maribelle returned, Josie Mae said, "We are going to play a game. It's a race to see who can be the fastest. See the pile of wood over there? I'm gonna count to 100. I want to see who can bring me the most logs. Do you understand, Lloyd?" Lloyd didn't look at Josie Mae or answer her question, but when she said "GO!", he ran for the woodpile along with Maribelle.

Josie Mae counted slowly, giving the children as much time as possible to collect the wood. This made her job a lot easier since she wasn't having to haul it as well as stack it. Lloyd liked the game and rushed back and forth, making it difficult for his older sister to keep up. By the time she got to 100, both Lloyd and Maribelle collapsed in a heap, causing Malcolm to clap with glee.

"I declare. I think it was a tie. You are both winners!" She pulled the ham out of her pocket, giving each child a small bite as a reward.

One after another, Josie Mae made up games to occupy the children. By the time Granny called them for lunch, she had stacked all the wood into five tightly packed rows as high as her hands could reach.

She was tired and sweaty. She rubbed a rough hand across her face, noting she had skinned up her knuckles. Maribelle, Lloyd, and Malcolm looked just as tired and grimy. But she had completed the job.

As Josie Mae washed up to eat, Granny moved about the kitchen smelling of sweet, cooked apples. Granny was a healer, but she did more than heal. She was someone others could count on, whether for a dose of the right herbs or a helping hand with the canning.

"That's how I want to be," thought Josie Mae. "I want to make folks feel better, but not like Mama and Dr. McKeithen. They only pay attention to wounds or illnesses. I want to heal people of their fear and anxiety and burdens, too." It was at that moment she knew for sure she would become a healer just like Granny, and the thought made her smile.

Chapter 31

Maggie
- October 8, 1893 -

Maggie called to Josie Mae, "Hurry up! We're going to be late. Pastor Elliston hates it when folks are late to the service!"

Josie Mae skittered back into her room, calling over her shoulder, "Just one more minute, Granny. I almost forgot Malcolm's present."

Today, instead of meeting back at the house for Sunday dinner, the two, along with Daniel and Carrie Ann, were heading to Esther's house for a birthday celebration. Malcolm turned a year old the day before, but being a Saturday, and with John still finishing up work in the next town over, Esther invited several over after church.

Maggie was bringing a ham. Carrie Ann was bringing something sumptuous she called potato casserole, a recipe she took from one of those fancy magazines she had delivered from Asheville.

Even Dr. McKeithen became involved, purchasing a cake from the bakery. "I don't cook, but I do know good food when I see it. I've been hankering for one of those cakes for weeks now, and this seems like the perfect time," he explained when asked to join them on Sunday.

Josie Mae flew past her grandmother and out the door.

"Granny, if you are waitin' on me, you're backin' up!" she laughed.

Maggie joined her outdoors, and the two climbed into the wagon where the ham was already nestled in the corner under a blanket. "Do you think he'll like this top? It ain't new, but I don't play with it anymore. Maybe Maribelle or Lloyd can help him spin it until he's big enough to do it himself."

Maggie leaned to her right and gave Josie Mae a squeeze. "He'll love it. I don't believe I've ever met a boy who didn't like a top."

On her last visit to Esther's, Maggie noted Malcolm had no shoes. She arranged for a pair to arrive on Esther's porch earlier in the week without a note. She didn't want her friend to feel like a burden, but Maggie knew they didn't have the money for new shoes for the child. She'd let Josie Mae's toy and the ham be their gift. The shoes would simply remain a mystery.

The two of them scurried into the church and took their seats just as the pastor began. He greeted folks and said a prayer before they all sang "Onward, Christian Soldiers." Once everyone settled, he started preaching. The topic, who is your brother, seemed timely, given the harshest part of the year was upon them, and during the harshest part was the birth of the Savior.

Maggie drifted from the pastor's words, thinking about brothers and sisters, and what the Good Book meant. In her mind, her brother was someone in her midst. It didn't matter how well she knew 'em. If'n they were within her little circle of light, then they were a brother. And if'n that person needed a helpin' hand? Well, she would do what she could.

Just then, Malcolm tried to run for the back door —now

that he finally figured out the walking process. Maggie reached out and scooped him into her arms, delighted to see the tiny brown shoes tied to his feet. "Not so fast, little man," she whispered. She sat him down, turned him toward his parents, and gave his fanny a pat.

He smiled broadly as he ran again, this time toward his family. Esther caught Maggie's eyes above the heads and mouthed, "Thank you." Maggie just nodded until Esther mouthed, "Shoes. Thank you for the shoes."

Maggie tried to look confused, acting like she didn't have a clue what Esther meant. It wasn't too difficult because she was confused. How in the world had she figured it out? Maggie had been so careful, wrapping the gift in a burlap seed sack and paying a penny for a young boy in town on errands with his pa to deliver it for her.

"Now, you just leave it on the porch. Don't say nothin' to no one. If someone asks what you're doin', just say deliverin' this package. Then, turn and run. Ya hear? It's a surprise, and I don't want ya spoilin' it." When he returned, he assured her he hadn't met up with anyone the entire time. Maggie gave him another penny for a job well done.

But now, somehow, Esther knew. Or maybe she just guessed. Perhaps she knew when it came to being brothers and sisters, Maggie was one of her best. They caught eyes one more time. Esther winked and turned back to the preaching.

Once the congregation uttered the final Amen, everyone streamed outside into the churchyard. The adults stood in groups chatting while the children played tag.

The day was bright and sunny for October, so folks wanted to enjoy the warmth while it was still possible. It wouldn't be long before the Sunday morning churchgoing population would thin out considerably. Maggie and

Josie Mae often didn't make it to town during the coldest weather, as was true of many other families living deeper into the holler.

Finally, Maggie helped Esther gather the children. She piled the family into the wagon, and Josie Mae sat in the back, allowing Esther to have her seat. Malcolm climbed into Josie Mae's lap and promptly fell asleep, his head lulling against her chest.

When they pulled up to the house, Josie Mae called out, "Granny? Can you come take Malcolm from me? He's so tired, he ain't stirring at all, and it's like trying to haul around a sack of onions."

Maggie scooped the little boy into her arms. She touched her hand to his cheek and then his forehead. Was he warm, or was he just hot and sweaty from playing? As she felt his head again, he opened his eyes and scrambled to be set down. "You all good?" she asked him before letting him go run with his siblings.

The rest of the afternoon was spent talking and eating. Malcolm was fascinated with his top and pushed it into his mother's hands over and over, wanting to see it spin. Josie Mae took over the spinning before letting Maribelle take her turn with the child.

She even worked with Lloyd, showing him how to use the top. "What happened to the one you got at Christmas, Lloyd?" Then, again, twisted her fingers and let the top fly. Although he, too, enjoyed the spinning, he didn't try to make it happen on his own.

As the air grew cooler, everyone began to say their goodbyes, one by one. Maggie and Josie Mae were the last to leave, despite having the longest drive. "Thank you, Esther, for the fine Sunday dinner. I'm so glad we got to celebrate little Malcolm's birthday with you."

Esther shook her head. "No, thank you, Maggie. Without you, Malcolm wouldn't be here and havin' a birthday. And now, I've got the chance to bring another little one into the world." She patted her belly with a contented sigh. "So, thank you, Maggie. For everything." She threw her arms around Maggie but had to lean forward to avoid her growing middle. "I love you, my friend."

"And I love you."

"Now, scat on home before it gets too dark to see."

Maggie laughed. "I've been back and forth to your house so many times that the mules don't even need me to do the steering. But it is time for us to go. I'll see you later in the week." Maggie kissed her cheek one more time and climbed onto the wagon.

As they rode back to their little farm, Josie Mae said, "Did you listen to what the preacher said today? About brothers?"

Maggie nodded.

"I was thinkin' about it. About brothers and sisters. Mama ain't got any real ones. Neither do I. Neither do you. That's three generations with just one child. I always thought I was kind of alone. I mean, I know I got you and Mama, but I mean alone, like with no siblings. But the preacher says we are all brothers and sisters, so I guess that means I'm not alone at all. I got more siblings than I can count."

"Hmm... I don't think I ever thought of it that way before, Josie Mae. I always looked at it as folks kind of like kin, but not actual kin."

"Me, too, Granny. Until today. Somethin' he said made me realize we are all related to one another. We all came from Adam and Eve, so that means we are all kin. We are all brothers and sisters. I'm kin to Esther and her family, Illanipi and his family, Dr. McKeithen, Pastor Elliston, and on and on and on."

"Well, now, Josie Mae, what are you going to do about it?"

Josie Mae wrinkled her brow. "Do?"

"Sure. When we learn something new, it's as useless as not knowing if we don't do something with it. You learned everyone you've ever met, and even those you haven't, are your kin. What are you going to do with that extra understandin'?"

Josie Mae rested her chin in her hands. "Well, Granny, I think it means I should treat everyone like I do my own family. Care for 'em. Help 'em. Like it says in Romans to rejoice with them that do rejoice, and weep with them that weep."

Josie Mae leaned over and put her head on Maggie's shoulder. "Did you buy Malcolm those shoes?"

Maggie straightened up. "Why ever would you say that?"

"Because it is somethin' you would do. You are always helpin' others. Rejoicin'. Weepin'. Healin'. Granny? When I grow up, I wanna be like you. I wanna be a granny woman and help people. That's how I'll show 'em they are my kin."

Maggie slipped her arm around Josie Mae's shoulder. "That would be a fine way to do something with what you've learned. A fine way."

Chapter 32

Josie Mae
- October 10, 1893 -

Josie Mae ran all the way from town and now hung onto the front steps. She had to find Granny right away but didn't have the breath to call out to her. She stumbled up the stairs and pushed open the door to discover the room was empty.

Wild with worry, she flew back through the door and jumped off the porch, making her way to the back of the house. She spotted Granny out by the barn. Josie Mae began to run again, waving her arms over her head.

Maggie saw her and, first walking, then running, made her way to Josie Mae. "What is it, child? Why are you all frantic and out of breath? Is it your mama?"

Maggie's face turned grim as she held Josie Mae by both shoulders. Josie Mae sucked in as much air as she could and blew out the one word. "Esther."

Maggie started pulling Josie Mae toward the house while rapidly firing questions in her direction. "Did she send for me? Is it the baby? Is she having pains?"

Josie Mae could hardly keep up as Granny pulled her along by the wrist. "No. Not... baby..." She panted.

With those words, Maggie slowed her pace, though still made her way swiftly into the house to gather things into her medical bag. "Take a sip of water, Josie Mae. Then sit down and tell me what is happening with Esther."

Josie Mae gulped some water, choking a bit and spilling it down her front. She collapsed into a chair and began to explain despite her breathlessness. "Esther came lookin' for me... she knew I was with Mama... she said it's Malcolm mostly... but seems Maribelle may be getting it, too."

Maggie spun around. "Getting what, Josie Mae? Getting what?"

"Fever." Josie Mae gasped.

Maggie ran her hand through her hair. A fever. Malcolm had been warm and not just playing after all. He seemed so lively at the party. She hadn't thought of it again. "How long has he been sick, Josie Mae? And Maribelle? How long has she been ailin'?"

"Esther says Malcolm woke up yesterday feeling poorly. She figured he had too much to eat or played too hard at his party. He's also cuttin' the back teeth, so she thought maybe he was just irritable and rubbed some Valerian root on 'em. But last night, he got to actin' real sick. And this morning, Maribelle started actin' poorly."

"Is John still working out on that other fella's farm?"

"I ain't sure, Granny. She didn't say. When she saw me walking toward the general store, she just asked if I was comin' home today, and if'n I was, would I ask you to come out to see them when you could. She was acting calm, but I could see she was scared. I told her I'd come straight here, so I ran the whole way."

Maggie squeezed Josie Mae's arm. "Thank you. You did a good job. I'm going to go on over and see what I can do to get those fevers under control. If John is home, I'll likely be back tonight. If he's still out, I'll stay. There's ham and biscuits. Some apples."

Josie Mae nodded. "Don't you worry none about me, Granny. I can take care of myself. But..." She hesitated. "I was wonderin' if maybe you might need me to help? What with two kids ailin' and Esther pregnant, I might be able to do a bit to make things easier on everyone."

Maggie considered it. She hadn't heard of any fever going around. It was probably just the kind of thing kids pick up as winter sets in. And Josie Mae was right. She would be a big help, especially with two sick young'uns.

"Why, thank you for offering, Josie Mae. I think it is a fine idea, and I'll be happy to have your company. Bring along your sleep sack just in case we have to bed down there tonight. We'll most likely have to take turns sleeping, so one will do. Go ahead and pack up something for supper, too. No need making Esther cook for us while she's trying to tend her sick children."

Josie Mae did as she was told, packing up all the biscuits, some ham, and a handful of apples. "Want me to gather up the evening eggs for tomorrow?"

"Yes, do that quickly, and I'll finish collectin' my things. Then we'll head on to Esther's. I don't want her becoming too anxious. It won't be good for the baby."

When the pair arrived, Esther pushed the door open and ushered them inside. "I've got 'em over here by the fire. Maribelle keeps complainin' she's cold. I figure Malcolm probably feels the same way but can't tell me so."

Maggie laid her hand on first one child and the next. "No doubt they're running a fever." She tilted Maribelle's chin up. "Do ya hurt?"

Maribelle nodded. "My throat." She touched her neck, then put a hand on her forehead. "And my head." She began to cry.

"Hush, now. Cryin' ain't gonna make you feel any better. In fact, it might make you feel worse. I've got something to help with your throat and head. I'm gonna make you something to drink. You'll start feeling better right away. Hush now."

Turning to Josie Mae, she said, "I want you to put together the fever tea. Put the water on first, and then you'll find what you need in my bag. Once you've done that, come and rock Malcolm and help him drink it down. He's not gonna be able to do it so well by himself."

She turned to Esther. "How are you feeling? And Lloyd? Any symptoms?"

Esther shook her head. "I'm tired, but ain't nothin' new. Lloyd hasn't complained, and I keep feelin' his head. He don't seem to be hot to the touch."

Maggie nodded. "And John?"

Esther shrugged. "Ain't seen John. He didn't come home last night and, with it gettin' dark, likely ain't comin' home again tonight."

"If'n John don't come home this evening, Josie Mae and I will stay with you so you can rest. Then, I'll send her out to the farm at first light. John needs to be here to help you. If you get too worn out, you could catch the fever, too. We don't need you doin' anything that will make the baby come too soon."

Esther pushed her hair out of her eyes. "Whatever you think is best, Maggie. That's why I asked you to come."

Josie Mae finally got Malcolm to finish his tea, and he fell asleep in her arms. She rocked him till she was sure he wouldn't wake and gently moved him to a pallet on the floor next to the stove. It would be easier to keep him warm and check on him this way.

Granny was tending to Maribelle. She kept crying until Granny began singing. Sometimes she sang hymns like those from church. Other times, she sang the Cherokee chants Josie Mae wanted so badly to learn. Each time she started the Cherokee blessing songs, Maribelle would grow still. There seemed to be some magic to the words.

Although the children remained feverish, they were no worse in the morning. Josie Mae had slept relatively well. Malcolm only woke once, and Granny said she'd stay up with Maribelle. As soon as it was light, Josie Mae stuffed a biscuit in her pocket and hitched the wagon.

"Take the road past Micaville. You'll see it going up to the North Toe River fishing hole. 'Bout halfway to the river, the Bremen place will be on yer right."

Josie Mae repeated the directions. Upon Granny's approval, she said, "I'll be fine. I'll pick up Mr. Stallard and bring him home. They can't have much use for him now with the weather turning cooler."

Although Josie had traveled before, she had never been so far on her own while driving her own wagon. She knew not to push the mules too fast. As Granny said, they were plodders, not trotters. But they were faster than walking.

Once she passed through Micaville, a town about a quarter of the size of Burnsville, she began to look for the road leading to the fishing hole. She began to fear she had missed it but then spied the track on the left leading between the tall pines. After just a few more minutes, she saw a house off in the distance. "This must be the place."

She snapped the reins, guiding the mules to the right, and pulled up to the house. A woman wearing an apron stepped outside. "Can I help you?"

"Yes, ma'am. I'm Josie Mae. I'm a friend of John Stallard.

Two of his children have come down sick, and his wife, already being big with child, needs him to come home, if'n it's possible."

The woman nodded. "I recall John. He's a good worker. He'll be back by the field. They're pulling up the last of the corn today. I think we was sending him back tonight or tomorrow anyway. Tell him to stop by the kitchen on the way out. I'll have something for the two of you to eat, and I'll have someone gather his pay together."

"Thank ya, kindly. Before I find Mr. Stallard, would it be too much trouble to ask to water the mules? If'n you got a well nearby, I got me a bucket in the back."

"You go on and fetch John. My son will tend to the mules. They'll be fresh and ready to go by the time we finish loading the wagon."

Josie Mae stopped, confused. "The wagon loaded?"

Mrs. Bremen laughed. "Oh, of course, you wouldn't know. John's been working for trade. He'll be happy you got the wagon here. That'll keep him from having to borrow one from a friend. Unless, of course," she mused, "you happen to be the friend."

By the time Josie Mae came back with John, the mules had been watered, sandwiches were sitting on the seat, and several burlap sacks with what appeared to be food were stacked in the wagon. Mrs. Bremen waved.

"Thank you, John. We welcomed having you. You are a hard worker. If'n you want to, we'll gladly hire you on next year. Take care of that wife of yours and those children." She threw her hand into the air in a wave and went back inside.

John leaned back. "How sick are they, Josie Mae?"

She shook her head. "Not too bad, I don't think.

Malcolm is feverish and whiny. Maribelle has a fever and sore throat, but she settles easy. Mostly, I think Granny was worried about Esther doing too much and bringing the baby on early."

"Thank you for coming, Josie Mae."

Josie Mae smiled. "That's what brothers and sisters do," she thought.

Chapter 33

Maggie
- October 14, 1893 -

Maggie pulled up in the yard at Esther's. Once John returned home, the two women headed back home.

"Keep giving the young'uns the tea," Maggie instructed John. "Keep 'em by the fire." John nodded his understanding.

"I don't think it is much of anything. Likely just a touch of something that should pass. We are going to head home now. I'll be back in a few days. Send word if'n you need me before then."

Now, as she began pulling stuff from the wagon, she realized everything seemed too quiet for midday. In fact, there wasn't even smoke curling out of the chimney, and despite being warm for October, a fire was needed for cooking.

Moving with haste, she grabbed the rest of the things – herbs, food, her healing bag – and knocked on the door. When no one answered, she pushed the door open. Sprawled on the floor were John and Esther and the three children. Esther pulled her head up and whispered, "No. Please. Don't want you to get sick."

Maggie stepped back outside, realizing the air was likely bad with sickness. She fashioned a kerchief over her nose and mouth, creating a small pouch she filled with a mixture used by her great-grandmother and brought over by her Scottish ancestors – valerian and rhubarb root, mint, horehound, germander, rose, fennel, and juniper.

Then, once again, Maggie entered the house, moving in a direct line to the windows and throwing them open. Both Esther and John watched from their makeshift beds on the floor as Maggie touched each child's head.

"They're feverish, like you," she stated before going in search of blankets. After wrapping up the children, being careful not to jostle them, she restarted the fire. They would need the heat, especially while she let in the fresh air.

Next, she gathered in some firewood, making a large stack next to the stove. "You've got to keep this fire going, do you hear me? I'm going to have to go home and tend to Josie Mae, then I'll be back. But you've got to take care of things until I come back."

Maggie set the pot on to boil. "Have you been drinking the medicine?" Esther shook her head. "Not since yesterday. Just too weak."

Maggie gathered the tin cups and filled each with her fever tea. She helped Esther and John to a sitting position before saying, "Sip this. Slowly. But you need to drink it all. Every drop."

She turned to Maribelle, who stared with feverish, unseeing eyes. Maggie propped the girl in her lap and began spoon-feeding the mixture into her mouth. She did the same with Lloyd. Turning to Esther, she said, "Do you still have bottles around? If we can get him to suckle, it will be the easiest way to get this into him."

Esther lifted her hand toward a cupboard and let it fall again. Maggie found a bottle and filled it with the warm liquid, placing the child between his parents and propping his head on Esther's lap. "Can you hold this while he drinks?" Esther put her hand on the bottle as Malcolm began to swallow.

Now she turned to John. "When did you come down with it, John?"

John coughed, clearing his throat. "Started feeling poorly two nights ago. Woke up yesterday so tired I couldn't hardly pull myself out of bed. Found Esther layin' in here with the kids. I tried nursin' everyone, but I got so weak." A tear rolled down his cheek, and he brushed it away with a swipe from the back of his hand.

"Sore throat?" Maggie asked.

He nodded, "Though I ain't complainin' of it the same way Maribelle is. She's been saying it feels like she's swallowin' glass." Maggie looked back at the silent child, wondering how long it had been since she had said anything at all.

"Any other complaints? Coughing? Runny nose? Stomach problems?"

He shook his head at each. "I cough now and again, but it ain't nothin' to call a doctor over. I'm just so weak, and I keep shakin' then sweatin' then shakin' again."

Maggie touched his forehead. He was as hot as the children. "That's the fever, John. We gotta get that under control."

Maggie wondered if they had the same fever that killed her mama and pa. Of course, there were several to choose from, so it didn't really matter. What mattered was getting them well. "I'm gonna make up a syrup to take in addition to the tea."

John nodded as he tried to stop his teeth from clanking. "Wrap up, John. You got the chills again. Every time you're chilled, you gotta wrap up. Every time you're hot, you need to use a wet rag."

She mixed together some corn liquor, salt, and linseed oil, adding a bit of honey so the children would swallow. "I'm gonna close these windows now and head back. I've got to take Josie Mae to her mama's house, and then I'll be back. Remember, keep the fire going. If the children start to shiver, pull a blanket on them. When they start to sweat, use a wet cloth. Keep drinking the tea."

She removed the kerchief once she was out of the yard and pushed the mules toward home. As soon as the cabin came into sight, she began hollering. "Josie Mae! Josie Mae!"

Josie Mae popped her head out of the door, concerned. "What is it, Granny?"

"Josie Mae, the Stallards are even sicker. John and Esther's done got it, as well as all three children. They can't tend themselves. Found 'em on the floor with no fire goin' or nothin'. They's all burnin' up with the fever."

Josie Mae ran to the wagon. "Oh, Granny! What are we going to do?"

Granny waggled her finger. "We ain't gonna do any-thing. Your mama would rightly have my hide if I exposed you any further to a fever. It was one thing when I thought it was just little sickness between the kids, but now that I realize it's spreadin'? Well, I'm just glad you didn't come down with it."

Maggie was silently berating herself. What had she missed? Why did she assume it was just a little sickness? Why didn't she head to town sooner to check on the fam-ily? Then, realizing she had exposed her granddaughter to something much worse, Maggie turned to face Josie Mae. "You ain't feelin' poorly, are you? No chills? No sore throat?"

"No, Granny. I feel just fine. Honest."

"Good. Now pack you some things. I'm takin' ya to your ma's house. I don't have any notion how long I'm gonna be gone."

Josie Mae put her hands on her hips in much the same way her mama did when she was being stubborn. "I'm not going to Mama's house. I'm either going with you to help, or I'm staying right here. I know how to tend myself. I'm not a child."

Maggie mirrored Josie Mae's stance. "Josephine Mae! I do not have time for you to be sassin' me. I said to pack your things, and that's what I meant for you to do."

Josie Mae sucked in a breath, hearing Granny use her full name instead of Josie, but she held her ground. "No, Granny. I ain't tryin' to be sassy. I just don't think it makes any sense to go into town. Who's gonna feed the chickens? Who's gonna finish drying up them herbs we picked yesterday? Who's gonna finish up the applesauce?"

Maggie didn't shift her stance or soften her mouth, but Josie Mae went on. "Plus, think about it. If'n there's a fever goin' round, it means the air all over town is likely to be bad. Mama and Dr. McKeithen will be busy tendin' to folks, too. I can be alone there with the bad air, or I can be alone here. And if'n I'm here, I can keep everything running."

Maggie dropped her arms to her sides and sighed deeply. "I ain't rightly sure when it happened, but just yesterday, I was arguing with a child. And now? I'm arguing with a full-grown woman."

She made her way up the steps. "Fine. I'm leavin' ya here, along with the mules and wagon. I want you to be able to come to town quickly if'n you have to."

Josie Mae started to protest, but Maggie held up her hand. "There ain't no other way I'm lettin' ya stay out here. I ain't takin' much, and what I do need, I can carry in my satchel."

"Why don't I drive you back to Esther's and then come on home again? You shouldn't be walkin' all that way, Granny."

"What about the bad air? You know, the air in town you don't need to be breathin' so you're stayin' out here?" Maggie raised her eyebrows while pointing a finger at Josie Mae's chest.

"Fine," Josie Mae said. "I'll drive you until we reach the creek on the far edge of town. You can walk the last mile on your own. At least let me do that for ya."

Maggie nodded, not really wanting to travel the entire way on foot, knowing she would need her energy in the coming days. "I'll be needing more fever tea, and get me what's needed for the flu syrup."

Josie Mae stopped. "You thinkin' it's flu, Granny?"

Maggie shrugged. "Could be. I'm just tryin' to find what will work best to bring down that fever."

Maggie had no idea what it was. Childhood fevers didn't usually affect adults, so she doubted it was scarlet fever with both John and Esther down sick. It was still early to be flu, but she couldn't rule it out. It might also be throat distemper. Or even the fever that took her parents or Josie Mae's father.

Josie Mae scurried around the house, gathering Granny's list and stowing it into her satchel. Granny gathered another dress and an apron. "If'n you decide to go to your mama's, send word by the Stallards' so I know where you're at. I don't want to come back here thinking you've gone missin'."

"I won't be going anywhere, Granny. I'll be right here. If I don't hear from you in two days, I'll deliver more supplies." She held up her hand as Maggie tried to interrupt. "I'll wear a kerchief. I'll bring you a change of clothes, some biscuits, soup, and a fresh supply of herbs. I'll just leave 'em in the yard and holler that I've been there."

Maggie gave her a hug. "I don't know what I would do without you, Josie Mae."

Josie Mae jumped up into the wagon and patted the seat beside her. "I guess it's your lucky day, Granny, because you don't have to do it without me." With that, Josie Mae turned the team and headed toward town.

Chapter 34

Josie Mae
- October 16, 1893 -

Josie Mae dropped Granny near the edge of town and turned back toward the cabin. That had been two days ago. She spent her time doing the chores Granny would have done had she been here. She put up the last of the apples, arranged the herbs so they would dry evenly, gathered eggs, and made her meals.

This morning, she cooked up an extra batch of biscuits and, using the chicken she caught the day before, finished making some hearty soup. She knew from experience there was nothing better tasting than soup when you'd been sick. She pulled out another dress and apron for Granny and collected together everything needed to make more tea and syrup. Once she packed it into the wagon, she started for the Stallards' place.

She wasn't aware of anyone else in town having the fever, but she went the long way around, circumventing most of the shops and homes, just in case. As she came to the edge of Esther's property, she gave a shout.

"Hello, Granny! It's me, Josie Mae. I done brung some biscuits and soup, plus other things you'll be needin'." Josie Mae made sure her kerchief was in place before jumping down from the wagon.

Granny pulled the door open but didn't step outside. "Go home, Josie Mae. It's bad here. Real bad." And then Granny slid down the edge of the door onto the floor. "Granny!"

Josie Mae ran for the door, not caring about fevers or bad air. She just had to help Granny.

Even with the kerchief, the odor coming from inside caused her to gag. She held her arm over her nose and mouth, kneeling in front of Granny. Before placing a hand on her skin, Josie Mae knew she had a fever. "Granny? Granny! Can you hear me?"

The old woman groaned. "Go home, Josie Mae. It's bad catchy. Go home."

Josie Mae pulled Granny onto the porch and covered her with her coat. Then she peered inside. Esther and John were lying next to one another with baby Malcolm in between. Maribelle and Lloyd were at their feet. No one appeared to be moving. Josie Mae wondered if they were all dead.

But as she drew nearer, she discerned the shallow rise and fall of Esther's chest and then Malcolm's. She held her hand on John's chest. Nothing. She pressed her ear against his heart and detected a faint thud. He was alive, but just barely.

Maribelle was cold to the touch and, Josie Mae realized, stiff. The child was gone. For how long, she could not be sure.

Lloyd opened his eyes, intent on her actions. "It's okay," she murmured. "It's okay." Josie Mae pulled him away from his sister, moving him to share the space with Malcolm between his parents. "Close your eyes now, hear? Just close your eyes and go to sleep. I'm going to cover you right up to keep you warm."

She made a little mound with the blanket to keep him from seeing what she had to do next. With her back to Lloyd, she fitted the blanket around Maribelle until it covered her small body and hefted the child over her shoulder, taking her out the back door.

Someone was going to have to bury her, and Josie Mae realized it would have to be her. But first, she needed to tend to those who were living.

Like Granny had done when she arrived two days earlier, she opened up the windows to let out the bad air. Then she stoked up the fireplace and set about making medicine for those who could still swallow.

She grabbed a blanket as she went onto the porch and wrapped it around Granny. Josie Mae propped the older woman against the wall.

"Here, Granny, take this syrup." Once she swallowed, she handed her some tea. "I know you're weak, Granny, but I need you to drink this tea. Every drop. I'm gonna check on the others. When I come back, I want to see every drop gone, ya hear?" She turned back to the house before waiting for the answer.

Josie Mae couldn't rouse John or Malcolm, but she was able to encourage Esther and Lloyd to sip the syrup. As soon as they swallowed, she brought them tea.

Realizing Lloyd was too weak to hold a cup, she filled the baby bottle and propped it up for him. He suckled until he fell asleep. Josie Mae spoon-fed some to Esther before dribbling little bits into John and Malcolm's mouths. Once finished with the tea, she hustled back out to Granny.

"Good job, Granny. You done drank all your tea. I've got some soup. I'm gonna go fetch it. I want you to eat somethin'. Who knows how long it's been since you last ate. I need you to get your strength, Granny."

Josie Mae ran to the wagon and lugged the crock into the house. She filled a small bowl with the still-warm soup and brought it out to the porch. "Can you manage it by yourself, Granny?" The older woman took the spoon. "Yes, child, but I may just drink it. See if you can encourage Esther to take some."

Josie Mae did as she was told, though she noted Granny hadn't asked her to give any to John or the children. Did she realize Maribelle was gone? Did she assume no one else was going to make it?

She held Esther's head in her lap and ladled broth into her mouth. Once, she added another spoonful too soon, causing Esther to sputter and choke. "I'm sorry, Esther. I'm sorry. Let's slow down a might. There you go."

Esther closed her eyes, and Josie Mae reached over to John. He hadn't moved since she'd arrived, and although she gave him some tea, she wasn't sure if he swallowed any or if it had just run down the side of his face and onto the bedding beneath him.

She pulled her hand back. Like Maribelle, John was cold to the touch. Had he died as well? And if he did, how was she going to lug him out of the cabin by herself without alerting Esther?

Josie Mae eased Esther's head to the pillow and made her way back outside. "Granny, Maribelle is dead. I took her out back until I can bury her. I think John is gone, too. I don't see his chest rising, and he's cold. So cold. How am I gonna get him out of the house? If Esther sees me take him, I'm afraid of what she will do. Granny?"

Maggie looked at her granddaughter. In a quiet, slow

voice, she said, "See if you can encourage Esther to come sit with me. Tell her she needs some fresh air. It will do her good and that you got your granny sittin' on the porch, too. You'll have to help her. Then you're gonna have to drag John out the back. I'm sorry, Josie Mae. I'm so sorry." She put her hands over her face.

Josie Mae straightened. "Granny, I need you to be strong. I can't do this all by myself. I'm gonna get Esther out here, but you've got to stop crying. I need you to be a comfort to her. She's gonna figure it out, and I don't know what to do for someone grieving their husband. I need you, Granny. Please."

Maggie dropped her hands, sniffing back her tears. "Bring Esther. I'll do the rest."

Josie Mae urged Esther out the door into Granny's care. The older woman seemed to have perked up a bit, as if the tea and soup gave her some energy. As Josie Mae headed back inside, Granny started to sing a quiet song as Esther began to cry.

Josie Mae's heart ached, but she couldn't deal with her own pain. She scooped up Malcolm and took him to Granny. Then, she scooped up Lloyd and put him in his mother's lap. Finally, she set about the task of pulling John outside.

* * *

She lay on the ground, looking at the sky, sucking enormous gasps of air into her lungs. Where she'd found the strength was a mystery, but John was wrapped in a blanket next to his daughter. She could still hear Granny singing.

Josie Mae climbed to her knees, pushing herself upright. She headed to the shed. "I'll have to dig a shallow grave for now," she thought. But, as she grabbed the shovel, she discovered a huge tree had fallen toward the back of the property.

It appeared John had been trimming the branches off, little by little. What caught her attention, however, was the enormous hole left by the roots where they had pulled free from the ground.

Josie Mae inspected the opening. It was deeper than anything she'd be able to dig and was plenty wide enough for John and Maribelle. She'd bury them together, and if Esther wanted a different kind of burial, they would worry about it later, after the sickness passed.

She hauled John, then Maribelle, to the lip of the tree throw and rolled them in. She would have to cover them, but she needed to check on Esther, Granny, and the boys. Granny was still singing. Esther was asleep with her head on Granny's shoulder. Lloyd was leaning on his mother's chest, watching Granny's lips move with her words.

"Let me make you some more tea. I'll put the water on." But before Josie Mae could turn away, Maggie nodded toward the child in her arms, shaking her head back and forth.

Josie Mae struggled to breathe. Not another child. Esther can't have lost her husband and two children. She reached down to take Malcolm in her arms, hoping Granny was mistaken. But the child's lips were blue, and his arms were cold. She turned away before Esther noticed and hurried him in the direction of the oak keeping watch over his father and sister.

Josie Mae crawled in, arranging those she placed inside. She tugged John's arm over his children and covered them completely with the blanket. She pulled herself out just as a terrible screeching sound knocked her to the ground. The tree, which had been on its side, reared up until it stood tall once again, its root ball and trunk filling in the hole holding the three souls.

Josie Mae lay in the dirt, panting, realizing how close she had come to dying. She knew better than to crawl into a tree throw. She'd been told since she was a child it wasn't safe. Fallen trees often stood up again when the weight changed because of the loss of branches or leaves or even water.

Josie Mae began to sob, first from fear and then from sorrow. For the mittens and scarves that she knitted, which would not be worn. For the girl who would never be a nurse. For the boy who would never learn to spin the top on his own. For the man who would never see his family again. For Esther and all those she lost. For Lloyd, who would likely never remember his siblings.

She sobbed until she had no tears left. Then she did what she needed to do. She tended to those who were still living.

Chapter 35

Maggie
- October 31, 1893 -

Maggie opened her eyes a slit at a time, squinting against the light. She gingerly raised herself up onto her elbows, trying to guess the time. It had been two weeks since she came down with the fever, and although the chills and sweats had stopped, the profound exhaustion lingered.

Three days after losing John and the children, Esther's fever broke. Josie Mae cleaned and cooked and cared for Esther and Lloyd until Esther had the strength to do so on her own. Then Josie Mae drove Maggie home.

Maggie had wanted to stay. Despite being so ill, she knew her friend needed her support, but Josie Mae was insistent. Maggie couldn't blame her. Josie Mae was hardly more than a child who had been pressed upon to do some tough things. Burying Esther's loved ones had been easy compared to dealing with the woman's grief.

As Esther's fever fog cleared, she began asking after John. "I haven't seen John. He didn't go back to work at the farm, did he? He's barely gotten over the fever. Maggie! You shouldn't have let him go."

She turned to Josie Mae. "Josie Mae, honey. Take your wagon and go fetch John. It makes no sense for him to work right now. If'n he's well enough to work, then I need him here with me to take care of the children."

Josie Mae froze in place. "Ma'am?" she whispered.

"Go and fetch John, child. Go on, now."

Josie Mae swung her head toward Maggie, desperate for Granny to be the one who told Esther the truth. However, Maggie hung her head as her tears flowed in a silent stream onto the blanket around her shoulders. Josie Mae realized Granny was too sick and too tired. The task was hers alone.

She sucked in a deep breath and faced Esther, but as she tried to explain, her words faltered. "Esther. John... he's... he's not workin', ma'am. He's..."

Esther pushed herself upright, going to the porch. "John! John!"

Josie Mae went to her, laying her hand on the older woman's shoulder. Esther shrugged it off as she moved onto the front stairs. "Come to think of it, I haven't seen Maribelle or Malcolm either. Those two are good at disappearing when there are chores needin' to be done."

Esther began calling again. "John! Maribelle! Malcolm! Get yourself to the house right now. Do you hear me? Right now!"

Josie Mae, unable to bear the woman's pain, started to cry and tried again to put her hand on Esther's shoulder. This time, Esther jerked away. "No! No, it's not true! John is out back working on that tree. And the children are just playing a game. John! Maribelle! Malcolm!"

The names echoed across the yard until the sound faded away. Then Esther dropped to her knees and sobbed. The sobs turned to screams as she tore at her face with her fingernails. Josie Mae grabbed at Esther's hands, doing her best to hold Esther's grief in her young arms 'til the woman was spent. The next day, Josie Mae gathered up Granny and drove them home.

Maggie wanted Josie Mae to check on Esther, but she was adamant. "No! I'm not going back there. I can't go back there." She began to sob. "Please, Granny, don't make me go back there." Between her sobs, Josie Mae whispered over and over like a refrain, "So much death – so much grief."

Maggie held her granddaughter against her chest, brushing her hair back from her face. "No, no, you are right. Can you go to your ma? Don't go too close in case you bring the fever with you. Just ask her to check in on Esther and Lloyd. Tell her they had the fever. That I have the fever. That John and the two children didn't make it. She'll know what to do for Esther."

That had been ten days earlier.

Maggie, now fully awake, called to her granddaughter. "Josie Mae? Where are you, child?"

Josie Mae appeared at the door. "I'm here, Granny. How are you feeling this morning? Are you about ready for some oatmeal?"

Maggie nodded. "Oatmeal sounds good. Thank you."

Josie Mae held out a hand to help Maggie to her feet. "You have a much better color today, Granny. I'm pretty sure you are on the mend now."

Maggie reached out to touch Josie Mae's face. "And you? Still no fever?"

Josie Mae shook her head. "No. I used the cloth over my face the whole time I was at..." She hesitated before saying the woman's name. "Esther's." Josie Mae closed her eyes, breathing in a slow, steady way, looking into Granny's eyes. "And I've been taking the herbs just like you said. I don't have no symptoms. It's been long enough now. And with you gettin' better? I think it passed me by."

"Good. That's good." Maggie said a silent prayer of gratitude she hadn't lost her granddaughter to the sickness.

"Mama says she can't figure out where the fever came from. No one else in town got sick, and she ain't heard of anyone round about with it."

She looked her Granny straight in the eye. "She's livid, you know. Says you should have never put me in danger. I tried tellin' her you didn't. I came on my own. If I hadn't, you'd have died like John and the children." Josie Mae stopped, unable to speak, tears springing to her eyes.

Angrily, she slapped at the rivulets making their way down her cheeks. "I done told her it was my doin', but she's angry. Says as soon as you're well, the two of you are going to have a talk. I think she wants me to come live with her in town."

Despite the tears, her eyes flashed, "I'm not goin'. She can't make me. I'm too grown now to be told where I'm going to live and what I'm going to do."

Maggie reached out and held her granddaughter by the shoulders. "Hush now. Don't worry yourself none about it. Your ma and me have had plenty of problems in the past. Many over you. And we've always found a way to work them out. We'll do it again this time. I promise."

She pulled the girl into another hug. "I promise," she whispered into her hair. "Now, let's eat that oatmeal you made. And then, I want you to take me to town."

Josie Mae's shoulders stiffened beneath the hug. "I ain't going to Esther's," she stated, each word clearly enunciated and evenly spaced.

Maggie shook her head, holding her granddaughter at

arm's length. "No, no, you're not. You'll drive us to your ma's. I can manage the short distance to Esther's on my own. You and your ma can have a nice visit, and then I'll come by and get my lecture over with. We'll stick around for the Halloween festivities in town. Maybe stay the night with your ma if she's willin'."

Josie Mae relaxed a bit, but her voice remained firm. "Fine. I'll visit, but I'm not staying."

"Of course, Josie Mae. You don't need to convince me. I'm on your side."

Chapter 36

Carrie Ann
- October 31, 1893 -

Carrie Ann grabbed her daughter around her middle with one arm and touched her from head to hips and back again with the other. "You feeling alright? No aches? Fever? Chills?"

Josie Mae squirmed, trying to free herself from her mother's grasp. "No, ma'am. I ain't feelin' poorly at all." Josie Mae glanced up at her granny, who was still sitting in the wagon. "And Granny is feeling better every day."

Carrie Ann let her gaze shift to her mother. She nodded, though no approval reached her eyes. She shifted back to her daughter. "I'm glad you are here. We have a lot to talk about." With that, she glanced once again to her mother.

"I'm headin' over to check on Esther and invite her and Lloyd to come into town for the Halloween celebrations. She needs to get away from the house, and it won't do her any harm to visit with a friend for a while."

Maggie held Carrie Ann's eyes. "I'm assumin' you've been over her way to check on her? How is she doing?"

Carrie Ann's eyes blazed. "Yes, I've been checking on her and Lloyd. They are doing as well as can be expected, given what they've been through. Of course, she lost the baby."

Maggie sucked in her breath. So much loss.

Carrie Ann continued as if she didn't catch her mother's distress. "I still do not understand why you..."

Maggie held up her hand, cutting off what was sure to be a reprimand.

"I realize you are angry. But I want you to remember you are angry with me, not with Josie Mae, and certainly not with Esther. I'm going now for a visit. I promise to return in plenty of time to have a discussion about what I should and should not have done. Then, my hope is we can enjoy the festival. Can I trust you to appreciate your time with Josie Mae and leave your indignation for me?"

Carrie Ann's hands had gone to her hips while her mother spoke, and she had a great desire to climb up on the wagon and slap the woman who gave birth to her. Her mama's righteous attitude always left Carrie Ann feeling like a little girl who, once again, was in trouble. This, despite it being her mother who was obviously in the wrong.

She let her hands drop to her sides, fingers balling into fists, willing the rage inside to calm itself. It would do no good to start an argument now, in front of Josephine.

With a measured tone, Carrie Ann said, "Of course, Mother. Anything I need to say is for you and you alone. Josephine and I will catch up on the local gossip. I'll fill her in on all the goings on she's missed these last couple of weeks. Should I expect you for lunch?"

Maggie shook her head. "No, I'll eat with Esther, but I'll be back midafternoon. The town shenanigans won't start until evening, so we'll have plenty of time to discuss whatever is on your mind."

Carrie Ann pushed her lips into a smile, though she doubted her attempt fooled anyone. She also doubted there would ever be enough time to discuss everything on her mind. "Fine, Mother. We'll see you this afternoon. Give Esther our love."

Now, that is something she truly meant. Carrie Ann liked Esther, and the poor woman had been through so many things in her life. She could not imagine how Esther would go on living, having lost her husband, two children, and another in her womb. She wondered what she would do if she were in that miserable woman's shoes and shuddered at the thought. It had been difficult enough losing her own husband despite the poor state of their marriage. No, she wouldn't wish this kind of loss on anyone.

Josie Mae hopped up onto the wagon to give Granny a hug. "Be careful, Granny. Don't go trying to do much more than drive this wagon to Esther's and back. You don't have enough strength to be anything more than a listening ear, hear me? Don't go tryin' to do any chores or fixin' meals. If'n she needs help, just take note and tell me about it. I'll work somethin' out with folks round about to fix what she's lackin'."

She planted a kiss on the older woman's cheek to erase the sadness lingering there and hopped back to the ground to stand beside her mother. Carrie Ann, shamed by her daughter's show of concern, echoed Josie Mae's sentiment. "Yes, Mother. Don't overtire yourself. The ladies in town have all said they can help Esther get back on her feet."

Maggie pulled away. Carrie Ann realized, with a start, that despite her anger, she did love her mother and was concerned for her health. How she could feel both the need to hurt her mother and hold her tight was a puzzle that she wasn't sure she would ever solve.

This conundrum had often been true in their relationship. Carrie Ann wanted her mother's approval and pushed the approval aside when offered. She wanted her mother's love but rebuffed her mother's efforts to show it. But Carrie Ann saw her mother doing the same things, pushing her daughter away, always trying to prove her ways were best, never allowing Carrie Ann to shine. She wished they were different, but no amount of wishing was going to change the facts.

So, she reached down and took Josephine's hand in her own, hoping to focus on a relationship that might still bear fruit. "Come on in, Josephine. I'm assuming you had breakfast, but I've got coffee, and Mrs. Briddleton brought by some apple tarts from her bakery yesterday."

The two bustled around the kitchen as they put together the midmorning snack before settling into rocking chairs by the fireplace. An uneasy silence was eased only by the scraping of their forks against the small china plates.

Carrie Ann cleared her throat. "We've missed you at the office."

Josie Mae stiffened, and Carrie Ann realized it sounded more like a reproof than a compliment. She continued, praying her next words would smooth over her first ones. "It will be so good to have you back. You do so much for us. I can't fathom how we ran the place without you." With satisfaction, she noted Josephine relaxing into her chair again.

"Poor Dr. McKeithen has had to do his own ordering. He was muttering to himself as he tried to figure out what he needed. He'll be pleased to have you back. I'm hoping you can start again soon?"

Carrie Ann let the question hang in the air. After some thought, Josie Mae nodded. "Yes, I should be able to leave Granny alone for a day or two. She's no longer sick and feverish. She's not as strong as I'd like her to be, but if I do the chores and make sure she has some easy-to-prepare meals, I think she'll do alright."

After speaking, she looked at her mother. "I've missed coming to the office. I learn a lot with Granny. But I learn a lot from you and Daniel..." She backtracked his name when Carrie Ann gave her a sour expression. "Dr. McKeithen, too. I'm glad I have the opportunity to do both."

The pair nodded while turning their attention back to their apple tarts. Though silent again as they ate, their words had evaporated the uneasiness.

* * *

Carrie Ann and Josie Mae looked up to the rumbling of wagon wheels. Carrie Ann took notice of her mother's tiny stature and experienced a twang of impatience. She needed to steel herself against such feelings if she was going to make her demands known to her mother.

She hated to ruin what had been a wonderful couple of hours with her daughter, but she felt certain by the time she and her mother talked it out, the enjoyable morning would be a distant memory.

"Josephine, I have a few things I need at the store. Would you mind going to pick them up for me?"

Josie Mae sighed deeply. "You aren't terribly subtle, Mama. If you want to talk to Granny alone, then just say so. Since I don't want to listen to the two of you argue –

again – I'll gladly run your errands." With that, she tossed a quick wave to her approaching grandmother and headed into town.

Carrie Ann winced. She thought she was being clever, but she should have known Josephine was too old to be fooled. The child knew she was angry and planned to have a talk because Carrie Ann told her as much. She wished she had been more straightforward. She made a mental note to remember her daughter was no longer a child, and she needed to treat Josephine as the young woman she was becoming.

Maggie pulled up to the porch and climbed down from the wagon, dropping with heavy feet to the ground. "Carrie Ann, I realize you want to have our chat, but can you fix me a cold iced tea first? And maybe something to eat? I'm plumb wore out from my visit. I don't even believe I have the energy to climb these stairs, though the rocking chair does look inviting."

Carrie Ann reached her hand out to her mother, pulling her toward the rocker. "Of course, Mother. Sit here while I pour us both a little drink. I have some apple tarts from this morning. Will that do?"

Maggie nodded as she closed her eyes, appearing to doze. When Carrie Ann appeared with a tray, Maggie opened her eyes.

"Esther is barely functioning. She's managing to feed Lloyd, but I don't know if she is doing much eating herself. I don't think she's doing much work around the house, either. The floors need sweeping. Dishes need washing. And, quite frankly, both Esther and Lloyd's clothes need a good scrubbing."

Carrie Ann began to scold her mother, but Maggie

quickly stated, "I didn't tend to none of it. I just listened to Esther while Lloyd played on the floor with a wooden spoon. He was fascinated by the way the spoon cut the light and made shadows, completely unaware of his mother's anguish."

Maggie looked up. "Esther could use some help. I don't think she's done a lick of housework. There's a few things that need tending before the snow sets in for good, as well."

Carrie Ann nodded. "I'll tell the Ladies Auxiliary from church tomorrow at the Wednesday night prayer meeting. They'll make sure she's okay until she gets back on her feet again."

"Thank you, Carrie Ann. You'll see for yourself this evening. She finally agreed to spend a little time in town for the festivities for the sake of Lloyd. I think he's the only thing that forces her out of bed. I just can't imagine..." Her words trailed off.

Carrie Ann, realizing there would never be a good time to start the conversation, rushed in before she changed her mind. "Mother, we need to talk. About Josephine. About you and Josephine."

Maggie set down her tea, wiping her mouth with the back of her hand. "Let me help you. What I have to say will save lots of time."

She sat up straight and cleared her throat. "I am not Josie Mae's mama. You are. You do not believe it is in Josie Mae's best interest to be learning my ways of healing. Just look at the consequences with Esther's family. That should be enough to convince me what I do is not real medicine. Not only are the outcomes bad, but I also exposed your daughter to a horrible illness that took three lives. Four if you count the unborn child. That alone is inexcusable."

She paused a moment, asking, "Have I got it right so far?"

Carrie Ann's mouth opened, but she said nothing. What could she say?

So, Maggie pressed on. "You do not believe your daughter should remain in my care given my recent poor decisions. You believe it would be best for Josie Mae to reside with you in town and maybe get some schooling once the winter weather clears. And finally, you believe, having killed my dearest friend's family, not to mention your father, I should stop practicing healing and let you and Dr. McKeithen take over."

Carrie Ann's mouth continued to gape open. Her mother had touched on every single point, even a few she wasn't sure she would have mentioned. With her anger deflated, she had nothing left to say.

Maggie closed her eyes again and began rocking. In a gentle whisper, she said, "I know you disapprove of me, Carrie Ann. Of my healing. Of the way I choose to live. And that's well within your right to do so. I don't suppose your opinion will ever change. But it ain't within your power to do much to change me now. Or Josie Mae, for that matter."

She allowed her eyes to open, staring at the wooden slats covering the porch. "For years, you made choices to leave Josie Mae in my care. You had your reasons. And I supported you and cared for your child and loved her just as a grandma would. I never let her forget who her mama was or that her mama loved her unconditionally." Maggie stopped, letting her words sink in.

"But she is no longer a child, Carrie Ann. She has her

own dreams and is creating her own path. It's too late for you to insist on her going to school or living here in town with you. Or much of anything. In just a few years, she'll be starting her own family and making her own mistakes."

Now Maggie focused on her daughter's face.

"As to me, don't you think it haunts me, losing those I love? Being unable to save your pa? My babies? Esther's family? All the others?

"Every single one I've lost is notched on my walking stick – the one I carry when I'm out gathering roots and herbs. I carry the dead with me to remind me I'm not God, and I can only do so much. I carry the dead with me to encourage me to continue to learn more. It's why I go every year to the Cherokee village. It's why I encourage Josie Mae to learn everything she can from you at the clinic. Those I lost are the reason I carry on."

Maggie reached out for Carrie Ann's hand. "Please know I didn't intend to expose Josie Mae to the fever. She came of her own accord. Thank God she did, or we'd all be dead. But I would have never sent for her. You aren't the only one who loves that child."

Maggie dropped her daughter's hand and leaned forward, putting her face in her hands. "I understand what you want, Carrie Ann. But Josie Mae doesn't want to live here, and I'm not going to force her to do so. And I'm not going to stop healing. Or teaching. Or learning. That's my piece. Now, if you have anything more to add..."

Carrie Ann leaned forward, mimicking her mother's pose, while slowly shaking her head back and forth. Her mother had said it all.

Chapter 37

Maggie
- November 8, 1893 -

Maggie tried to enjoy the Halloween festivities in town, but she didn't feel right about being happy when Esther was so despondent. Maggie, of course, wasn't surprised when Esther made no effort to clean herself up or find a costume for Lloyd. Thankfully, Carrie Ann found something for the boy to wear so he could participate with the others.

While the children bobbed for apples and listened to ghost stories, Maggie and Esther sat together on the tailgate of the wagon. Several women stopped to offer their condolences to Esther, but she did little more than mumble in their direction.

Finally, Esther began to speak, her voice rasping and cracking, as though she hadn't used it in a very long time. However, once she started, her words tumbled forth like a raging river. She mourned her husband. She mourned her babies – those long gone and those she lost to the fever. She lamented her fate.

"I keep askin' myself why the Good Lord left me here when He done took everything from me I love," she cried.

Maggie glanced toward Lloyd, thankful he was too far away for his mother's woes to reach his ears.

"I must have done something pretty awful. And now I'm paying for it. But why He had to make Maribelle and Malcolm and John pay with their lives over whatever I did just doesn't seem right. 'Cept now I have to live knowing it was me who killed 'em."

Maggie shook her head. "You know that ain't the way it works, Esther. God ain't punishing you any more than He was punishing Job when He took his money and his family and his health. It's just the way God works."

But Esther wasn't hearing any of it. "I'm the one thing that's the same each time something bad happens. I carried each of those babies to the grave. Me. I gave the fever to John. Me. I couldn't keep Maribelle and Malcolm safe from the fever. Me. It would be better if'n I just died and got it over with."

She looked over to where Lloyd sat in a circle with a group of children carving pumpkins. "But I can't leave him here alone, now, can I? You know as well as I do that something's wrong with him. He doesn't say anything. In his entire four years, he's uttered one single word. He doesn't smile or laugh. He doesn't hug and kiss. He just sits there, like he's doing now, lettin' the world go on around him. It's okay for now, but it ain't gonna stay that way. The folks in town is already talkin' 'bout him not being right in the head. He ain't likely to never leave my care, and that's if'n he's lucky. One little mistake that scares some woman or a child, and they'll send him away to live in an asylum."

Esther rubbed her eyes before looking over to Lloyd once again. "So, despite me wanting to leave this sad earth, God gets the last laugh, forcing me to stay when all I want to do is disappear."

Maggie's lips pressed together, and her eyes narrowed. "That's no way to talk, Esther. No way at all. Things are rough, that's true. You are hurtin'. But you've got lots of reasons to live, not the least of which is that little boy. I'm not gonna sit here and listen to you pine for death. Nor am I going to let you believe that Lloyd has nothing ahead of him in life." Despite her words, Maggie understood that Lloyd's future was grim, but she wasn't going to heap that on her friend right now. That was something they would deal with when the time came.

They sat in strained silence until, shuddering, Esther exclaimed, "Did you hear that?"

Maggie held her breath, leaning in and listening for the noise that caught her friend's attention. "Hear what, Esther?"

"The wind. It sighed. It done blow over the feet of my poor dead husband and children. And it's a comin' for me next."

Maggie trembled. Everyone knew hearing the wind sigh on Halloween night meant certain death. She wanted to tell Esther she was being ridiculous because the wind always made a sighing sound. However, she wasn't immune to superstitions, and she couldn't force the words from her lips.

Instead, she grabbed her friend's hand and denied the wind's very existence. "No, I didn't hear a thing. And neither did you."

When Esther took Lloyd home, Josie Mae and Maggie settled down in the extra room at Carrie Ann's house. Maggie did not fall right to sleep, worrying instead about the fevers and whether she missed something. Could she have prevented the deaths? Should she have called on Dr.

McKeithen and Carrie Ann? Did she try to save them on her own because she believed in her abilities or because she was too stubborn and proud to ask for help? Could the doctor and his nurse have saved Esther's family?

She also worried about Esther and how long it would take her friend to find the spark to live again. She worried about Lloyd and whatever it was that kept him silent. And finally, she worried about the sighing wind. The sky began to lighten before she finally closed her eyes.

Now, a week later, it was time to visit her friend again. Maggie was significantly stronger and would help Esther with some simple chores. They would talk. Maggie would help her see life was still worth living. She would work with Lloyd to help him speak. She would be the sister the pastor spoke about in his sermon back on the last day that Esther's family was whole and happy.

It was a perfect day to go. Josie Mae had begun working at the clinic again and wouldn't be back until the next morning. So, Maggie gathered up some things to make an easy lunch and hitched up the mules.

It had turned much colder, and the skies took on a gray cast that barely let the sunshine through. Maggie bundled into the traveling blanket and made a mental note to return before dark. It would be too cold to ride at night and come home to a hearth with no fire.

Despite the chill, Maggie enjoyed being out. The leafless trees stood tall along the road, creating wondrous patterns with their branches. Flocks of tiny, plump chickadees with their black caps and bibs called out a rapid chickadeedeedeedeedee overhead. Squirrels played hide-and-seek among the bushes.

"There is always life in these mountains," she thought

as she caught sight of a white-tailed deer frozen in place as the wagon passed. "In the cold, in the heat, in the rain, there is always life."

That's what she needed Esther to understand. Even in the depths of her sorrow, there was life to live. She would have to find a way to help her friend see that, despite the hard times, there was a reason to go on.

She came into town and decided to stop at the store to pick up a few things before heading on to Esther's homestead. The snow, though a dusting right now, was bound to begin falling in earnest. It was past time to make sure her supplies were in order.

"Good morning, Myles," she said to the man behind the counter. "I've got a list. Would you mind helping me gather it up and load it onto the wagon?"

"Well, howdy, Ms. Maggie. Glad to see you are no longer ailin'. I've been wondering if you needed anything. Been thinking I should drop by and see."

"That's mighty kind of you. But looks like I saved you a trip."

They both chuckled. Myles looked over the list and began hauling the heavier items – bags of sugar and flour, a barrel of molasses, and several bags of grain for the chickens – while Maggie gathered some spices, coffee, cheese, and candles.

Once everything was packed up and ready to go, Myles asked, "Will Josie Mae be able to help you carry this into the house? It's too much for one person to handle."

Maggie nodded. "Yes. She'll be back tomorrow. I'll just leave it in the wagon in the barn until morning."

"Good. That's good. Well, then, I'll see you the next time the weather breaks. Hopefully, we'll have an easy winter – however, watching the squirrels gathering those nuts? Seems they have a bit of knowledge we ought to take note of."

As Maggie drove away, she mused that Myles was probably right. The acorns came in heavy this year, and the bees had secluded themselves in their hives earlier than usual. Both were sure signs of a hard winter. That would be two in a row. She wondered how many weeks she and Josie Mae would be stranded together, though she didn't worry. They enjoyed one another's company and would find plenty to talk about.

She approached the edge of town and turned into the lane leading to Esther's house. The house stood quiet. No smoke rose from the chimney despite the cold.

Maggie shivered with a sense of foreboding. "Esther? ESTHER?" She called in a loud voice to her friend but got nothing back in reply. She scurried out of the wagon and thrust herself up the front steps, calling again. "Esther?"

As she reached the door, she realized it was ajar. She pushed her way into the room. Everything was neat and tidy. All the dishes were done. The beds were made. And oddly, the ashes had been removed from the fireplace.

Maggie shivered again. Where was her friend? She didn't have any family near, not any Maggie knew of. Not any who ever came during all of Esther's hardships. It seemed unlikely she would leave her home for some far-flung relative, especially as the weather turned colder.

Calling her name again, Maggie rummaged in the drawers. Esther's clothes were folded neatly in one, while John's were neatly folded in another. Lloyd's stuffed bunny sat on his pillow.

She hadn't seen them in town, but she wasn't really

looking. Maybe they had to drop by the doctor or stop at the bakery or say thank you to the ladies who had been out to help. All of these ideas were far more likely than visiting a long-lost relative.

But then her mind went to the missing ashes. She placed her palm on the hearth. It was as cold as the room. No fire had been lit here this morning. But the clothes. The bunny. Nothing seemed right.

Rushing back outside, Maggie made her way around to the barn. "Esther? Are you out here?" Maybe they were feeding the chickens. Or perhaps she'd find the wagon missing, a clue they were not at home.

As she rounded the house, she stopped short as she caught sight of them. Esther and her son, swinging from the branch of the tree serving as the burial place for her husband and two children.

Maggie wasn't aware she had begun to scream.

Chapter 38

Josie Mae
- December 10, 1893 -

Josie Mae tidied Granny's room again, though it didn't need it any more now than it did earlier in the day. She fluffed the spare pillow. She refolded the extra blanket. She ran the feather duster across the table and window ledge. She reheated the hot tea, which had grown cold waiting for Granny to take a sip or two.

While she moved about the room, she spoke to Granny about the weather outside, the fuss the chickens made as she threw their meal to them this morning, which herbs were ready and which ones were still in various stages of drying, what she had on the stovetop for supper, and the things she was learning from the *King's American Dispensatory* Dr. McKeithen had given her as a gift.

She could have talked about anything. Or nothing. Because Granny hadn't said a word since she finally stopped screaming hours after she found Esther and Lloyd.

Although weeks had passed, Granny had not spoken. Or responded. Or done anything of her own accord. She ate when someone pushed the spoon into her mouth. She drank when the cup was pressed to her lips. She used the toilet when led to the chamber pot. She bathed when placed in the tub in the living area.

She only did two things unbidden. Sleep and cry.

Her mama said it was shock and, eventually, Granny would move beyond the pain of seeing her best friend like that. But Josie Mae saw no signs of Granny coming back to her, though she spoke to her and tended her every day.

The last time her mama had come to the house, she insisted Josie Mae was too young to be Granny's only caregiver. "Sweetheart, this is too difficult for you. Granny needs too much care. I think we should bring her into town. She can stay at my house. Between you and me and the ladies from the church, we can..." but Josie Mae hadn't let her say anything more about it.

"No. Granny belongs here on the farm. In her own bed. Surrounded by her own things. Being tended to by me and not a bunch of women who will go home to their families and spread gossip to the neighbors."

Josie Mae heard what the ladies were saying about Granny as they came to the house under the pretense of being helpful. They'd stand around in clumps and whisper in that way that wasn't really a whisper.

"It's nervous exhaustion," one exclaimed. "Poor dear. Let's hope she doesn't have to go to an asylum." Another, who wasn't as kind, whispered, "She stares right through you, like she can see your soul. Crazy as a loon, I say." Of course, the one who caused Josie Mae to end the visits from the Ladies Auxiliary was the preacher's wife, who stated matter-of-factly this was God's punishment for carrying on with "them Cherokees."

So, Josie Mae tended to her grandmother, making sure she ate, drank, bathed, and used the toilet. She talked and sang. She read aloud from the Bible and from her medical book. She asked questions despite never getting answers.

But Josie Mae knew Granny was aware. She caught Granny following her around the room with her eyes. And whenever Josie Mae mentioned anything about medicine, Granny turned her head to the wall.

Josie Mae settled in the chair next to the bed where she kept her knitting and her books so she could be with Granny as much as possible. She touched the Bible and said, "Granny? With today being the Sabbath and all, I 'spect it would be a good idea to read from the Holy Book. Is there anything, in particular, you'd like me to read?"

Josie Mae began flipping through the pages and stopped abruptly when a hoarse whisper came from beneath the covers. She dropped to her knees and leaned toward Granny. "Did you have something you wanted me to read, Granny?"

Granny sighed and shook her head. "Go." Then she closed her eyes.

Although this was not the word Josie Mae hoped Granny would say first, it was a start. She pushed back on her heels and said in a fake, bright voice, "I guess you'd like to rest now. I understand. We'll read the Bible before prayers tonight. I'll be in the next room if you need me."

One word. It showed Granny had not lost her mind. She knew what she wanted, which was to be left alone. And for now, Josie Mae would give her what she wanted.

* * *

Over the next two weeks, Josie Mae began bargaining with Granny, who still only said one word – go. "Well, Granny, this is how it is going to work. You want to be left alone. I want you to eat this bowl of oatmeal. You eat that," she gestured toward the bowl sitting on the bedside table, "and I'll sit in the other room to do my morning reading."

Granny, without looking in Josie Mae's direction, snatched the bowl from the table and began to eat. Josie Mae retreated to the chair by the fireplace.

But Josie Mae was getting tired of the game. Granny was no longer in shock the way she had been when she first came home. Granny wasn't well, but she also wasn't crazy.

It was three days before Christmas. Although she had made a present for Granny, a beautiful red scarf with the softest wool she'd ever touched, she felt certain no gifts would appear for her on Christmas morning. She wasn't even sure if her mother would make the trek to the farm.

They didn't even have a tree. But that, Josie Mae realized, was something she could change.

"I'm going out, Granny, which should please you because you'll have your precious alone time. But when I come back, I'll be popping corn for decoration. I expect you to help me string it."

Granny looked away, but Josie Mae reached out her hand and turned Granny's chin toward her. "There is only one thing I want for Christmas. You. My Granny. The woman who loves me and loves life and loves Christmas." With that, she stepped outside into the cold winter air.

Finding a tree wasn't complicated. However, maneuvering the saw in the snow wasn't as easy as Granny made it look each year. She fought with the branches and was breathing in heavy puffs before she finally had the tree lying on its side. She secured it to the sled, the way she'd seen Granny do, and began hauling it home; once again, realizing how challenging the task really was.

She sank down into the snow and began to cry, not because of the tree but because she missed Granny. She missed their long conversations and Granny's unique insights. She even missed their disagreements because, at least then, Granny engaged with her.

She looked at the sad little tree tied to the sled. She didn't want to celebrate Christmas alone, pretending everything was normal. Maybe she should just leave the tree on the side of the path. But she was enough like Granny to finish a job once she started, so she brushed the snow off her mittens to begin tugging again.

By the time the tree was in the house and standing in the corner, Josie Mae collapsed into the chair facing the fireplace. She began to weep once again until she felt a hand on her shoulder. With a sniff, she looked up to see Granny in her dress and shoes.

"I'm tired, Granny. I need you to be the granny and let me be the child, at least for a day or two."

Granny gave Josie Mae's arm a squeeze. Though she didn't say a word, Josie Mae understood her grandmother was giving her the gift she most wanted. She would get to be a child for Christmas.

Chapter 39

Maggie
- December 23, 1893 -

Josie Mae was the only reason Maggie was out of bed and pretending to be interested in the holidays. Finding the girl crying while struggling with the Christmas tree was what it took to push Maggie forward. She loved her granddaughter enough to shove her own struggles aside – at least for a time.

Her voice sounded odd in her ears after weeks of silence. She wondered if it sounded as strange to Josie Mae.

"I've got this string done, Josie Mae. How much more do you think you'll need?"

Josie Mae looked up from the task of threading the popped corn onto the needle and down the length of thread. "Maybe one more, Granny? I just started this one, and with another from you, we should have enough to wrap around the tree several times."

She hesitated. "But you don't have to, Granny. I can finish by myself if you are too tired."

Granny brushed away the comment and reached for the spool.

Once the tree was decorated with popcorn, Josie Mae began digging around to find trinkets to hang on it. Unlike in years past, they had not made any ornaments leading up to Christmas. Maggie pushed back from her chair. "I have an idea."

She walked into the storage room and grabbed up some of the dried herbs. "We can tie bunches together with yarn. What do you think?"

Josie Mae's smile enveloped her face. "That is perfect. Exactly what a granny woman and her apprentice should hang."

Maggie winced. The title granny woman roared in her ears. Remembering she was doing this all for Josie Mae, she forced herself to look pleasant and said, "It will have to do."

As Josie Mae decorated, she said, "I'm not sure if Mama is coming this year. She likes to wait until Old Christmas to celebrate, but I guess I should cook up something, just in case. Maybe a bit of ham? Some sweet potatoes? An apple cake?"

Maggie couldn't imagine eating on such a large scale. She'd been existing on broth and thinned oatmeal for weeks. "Maybe something a little more simple? Ham hock and bean soup with some homemade bread? We have enough time to soak the beans and let it simmer. I think it sounds right good."

"Yes, it does sound good, Granny. Though I am hankering for some apple cake, if'n that's alright with you?"

Maggie nodded and Josie Mae set about putting the beans to soak. Then she disappeared into her room, coming back with a wrapped package to put under the tree. Without glancing toward Maggie, she said, "I ain't expecting nothin' in return, Granny. You've been sick. My present is you finally getting well. I don't need more than that."

Maggie sighed. She wasn't sure she was getting well,

though she had to admit being up felt a lot better than lying in bed. However, as she increased her activity, the numbness guarding her against the memories began to fade.

"I've been up for quite a while, Josie Mae. I'd like to sit quietly for a spell." At her granddaughter's crestfallen face, she interjected, "Just for a bit. Until supper?"

"Yes, yes, of course, Granny." Josie Mae hesitated, then came forward and put her arms around her grandmother. Maggie returned the gesture, fitting her arms around the child's waist into the first hug they'd shared in weeks. "Thank you, Granny. Thank you for coming back to me."

* * *

Josie Mae bustled around the kitchen, preparing the apple cake and readying the stock pot for the ham soup. Maggie, sitting in the next room, did her best to focus on the present. Her granddaughter. The slick sound of the knife pressing through the apple. The popping and hissing of the logs on the fire. The soft wool of the blanket touching her bare hands. The motion of rocking backward and forward and back again.

Despite her valiant efforts, snippets of memory intruded. The hearth empty of ashes. The tiny rabbit sitting forlornly on the pillow. Esther's feet... Maggie threw her hands over her eyes as if doing so now could shut out the picture.

She pushed herself out of the rocker and paced the length of the room and back again, her eyes landing on the walking stick propped in the corner. She reached out her hand and drew it back again, afraid to touch the stick with the memories of the dead.

After another hesitation, she snatched it from the corner and walked to her bed. Twelve notches. She rubbed her finger over them, remembering. Her husband. Her own child. Three women in childbirth and their babies. Four of Esther's stillborn children. But the record was incomplete. She hadn't added John, Maribelle, and Malcolm. Adding their names would make fifteen.

She pulled the pen knife from the drawer next to her bed and began to carve. As she did, she thought about those she lost. John. Loved his wife and children. Worked hard. Always had a smile. Laughed easily. Maribelle. Helpful. Promising future as a nurse, just like Carrie Ann. Happy yet serious. Malcolm. Bubbly. Curious. Enjoyed being outside.

Maggie didn't realize she was crying until the tears fell onto her busy fingers. These people she loved were gone and would now go with her when she gathered healing herbs. If she gathered them. She still wasn't sure what her path might be. Would she ever practice healing again? Should she? The answer was still not clear.

"Granny?"

Maggie flinched and brought her head up from her task with a jerk.

"I didn't mean to startle you. I just wanted to tell you supper was ready." Josie Mae looked from her grandmother to the stick and back again. She sat down on the bed and pulled the walking stick into her hands, letting her fingers run over the notches, stopping at the new scars in the wood.

"John. Maribelle. Malcolm," stated Maggie, her voice catching in her throat.

"I always remember those I lost. I pray you never lose someone in your care, Josie Mae, but you will. It isn't always in our power to save. I don't know why. I do know it isn't about effort or caring. It just seems to be the healing way." She didn't say the rest out loud but heard the words rumbling around in her head. "And sometimes, healers miss signs they should have seen. They do what they know to do, but it isn't good enough. Sometimes, healers fail to save those they love."

Maggie's tears fell unchecked. Josie Mae reached out her hand to wipe away the streaks left on her granny's wrinkled cheeks, unaware she, too, was crying.

Chapter 40

Carrie Ann
- December 25, 1893 -

"Merry Christmas!" called Carrie Ann as she climbed onto the porch and stomped the snow from her boots.

"Mama!" cried Josie Mae. "I wondered if you would come!"

Carrie Ann's eyes widened. "Not come? On Christmas? I certainly wasn't going to leave my daughter alone on Christmas."

Josie Mae reached on her tiptoes and planted a kiss on her mama's cheek. "But I'm not alone, Mama. Granny is here."

Carrie Ann tried not to show her irritation. "Well, of course, she's here." She pointed to the house. "But she's not really here." She pointed to her head.

"But Mama..."

Carrie Ann, unwilling to argue with her daughter on Christmas Day, cut in quickly. "Throw on your coat and help me with these things in the wagon, would you?"

Josie Mae pulled on some warm clothes and stepped toward the wagon.

"I've got presents for you. And a pie. And a few supplies. I figured you might be running low."

Carrie Ann snatched up the pie and said, "I'll just put

this inside and be back out to lend a hand."

"Mama, I have..." Josie Mae stammered, but Carrie Ann moved with quick strides into the house. She stopped, surprised, the door still hanging open, the cold air filling the room.

"Merry Christmas, Carrie Ann," Maggie said in a quiet voice.

"Mother?" Carrie Ann took another step forward, as if to get a better look. "Mother? You are... I mean... I didn't realize..."

Josie Mae staggered in under the weight of two large boxes of supplies. "Mama," she huffed, "can you push the door closed? I don't want Granny catching a chill."

Giving herself a shake, she said, "Yes, of course," and leaned against the door until it clicked shut.

Josie Mae took the pie out of her mother's hands. "Are you surprised, Mama? About Granny? I tried to tell you I wasn't here alone. See? I was right!"

Carrie Ann nodded, though the vacant look on her face had not disappeared. "I'm so... surprised. I mean, I was here a few days ago. Mama?" She now walked toward her mother and stopped just beyond reach. "Merry Christmas, Mama."

Maggie pulled her lips into a smile. "Merry Christmas to you, Carrie Ann."

"I've got one more small load. Mama, why don't you take off your coat and warm up by the fire. I've got soup and homemade bread and apple cake with Granny's famous walnut frosting for dessert. I hope you're hungry."

As Josie Mae latched the door behind her, Carrie Ann unwound her scarf and pushed the hood from her head. "I'm stunned, mother. Just last week, you wouldn't leave the bed. And now look at you. Up and dressed and celebrating Christmas. That is some miraculous turn around." Carrie Ann couldn't keep a bit of criticism from her voice.

"Yes. It is miraculous what a person will do for someone they love," her mama agreed.

Carrie Ann bristled. "Josephine isn't the only one who loves you, Mother. Or the only one who has been worried sick. And I've had to deal with all the gossip in town, as well. You can only imagine the stain this whole affair has left on the clinic."

Josie Mae came in, oblivious to the tension between the two women. "Mama! You brought presents today instead of Old Christmas. How unlike you!"

"I wanted you to feel like it was Christmas. I knew you and your grandmother always celebrated on the earlier day. I didn't realize it wasn't necessary."

Josie Mae drew her eyebrows together. "Not necessary? That's silly, Mama! You are always necessary. We're glad you are here, aren't we, Granny?" she said, then turned away without waiting for an answer.

Josie Mae stacked the presents under the tree. "I'll be right back. Then we can exchange gifts!"

She returned with a small package. "This one is for you, Mama." She reached under the tree. "And this one is for you, Granny."

"Why don't you start, Josephine?"

The girl shook her head. "No, please. Open yours first. I worked on them all year, and I'm so excited to see what you think."

The scarves were soft. Maggie's was a deep red. Carrie Ann's was a snowy white. "See the braid pattern? I learned it from Ms. Meredith. I saw her working on that stitch at the clinic. She showed me how. I practiced and practiced until I finally got it right. Do you like them?" Josie Mae's eyes glowed with excitement.

Granny opened up her arms, and Josie Mae fell in. "It is beautiful. Thank you."

Carrie Ann took her turn hugging her daughter. "Very beautiful, Josephine. I'll wear it every time I go outside."

Carrie Ann thrust two packages into Josephine's hands. "Let's see what you think of these."

Josie Mae pulled open the paper. Inside the first was a blue silk dress. The second held a matching hat. "You are becoming such a lovely young woman. I thought it was time to have at least one fashionable outfit."

Josie Mae perched the hat on her head, turning this way and that. "It's beautiful, Mama. I'll be the prettiest girl at church!"

Then, Granny handed her a small bundle.

"Granny? When did you have time to buy me a gift? I didn't..."

Granny's smile was sad. "This isn't something new, Josie Mae. It's just something I thought you might want to have. It has always meant a lot to me."

Josie Mae's fingers trembled as she pulled the strings loose. Inside was Granny's first notebook, the one filled with the things she learned during her stay near the Cherokee village when she began as a granny woman.

"I rarely use these notes anymore. I know the pages by heart. As you continue to learn from your mama and from the book Dr. McKeithen gave you, and from your own experiences, I thought what I learned from Oukonunaka might be useful."

Josie Mae ran her fingers lightly over the cover. She

reverently flipped through the pages, recognizing Granny's notes in the margins. She was so engrossed that she didn't see the rage on her mother's face.

Carrie Ann stood up, knocking her chair over in the process. "Really, Mother? Your notebook full of heathen magic? The same heathen magic that killed my father? That took your babies? That killed Esther's family?"

She glanced about the room with wild eyes, stabbing her finger at her mother as she continued. "You killed her, you know. Esther. And her child. That was your doing. They would be here today if you hadn't sent their family to an early grave. If you had called Dr. McKeithen. If you had sought help. They'd be alive. You may as well have put the rope around their necks yourself."

Maggie blanched, and the color drained from her face. Josie Mae tried to interrupt, but Carrie Ann turned on her.

"You are too young and too blind to see it. Your granny can do no wrong. Except she does wrong every time she treats someone with her so-called medicine. You never got to meet your granddaddy. Do you know why? Because the woman you call Granny didn't take him to the doctor in Asheville until it was too late. Instead, she fed him roots and herbs and sang nonsense right to his grave. I watched him die, Josephine. I was barely your age and watched him cough and choke and struggle to breathe. He turned yellow, a sour smell to his skin. In the end, I couldn't even look at him, knowing he was dying. No child should have to watch their father slowly slip away, especially when it didn't have to be that way."

Now, she turned back to Maggie. "And your babies? Maybe God wasn't so pleased with your silly little rituals and belief in the river gods or your dancing during the moon ceremonies. Maybe if you'd stayed true to your beliefs, the Christian beliefs we learn in church each Sunday, and stayed away from the heathens, I would have brothers and sisters."

She stepped closer to her mother. "You killed Papa. You killed my brothers and sisters. You killed Esther's family. And you killed Esther."

She pivoted on her heel, heading into Maggie's room, and came back out holding the walking stick in the air. "Which notch belongs to Esther, Mother? Or had you not considered you killed her? You did. Everyone in town knows it. I know it. Josephine knows it, though she won't ever admit it. But most of all, Mother, you know it."

Carrie Ann, spent of emotion, stopped yelling. The only sounds were her panting and Josie Mae's sobs.

Finally, Maggie spoke. "Go. Both of you. Go."

Chapter 41

Josie Mae
- February 23, 1894 -

Josie Mae shoved the stepstool against the far wall and climbed to the third rung, removing a white crock from the shelf. Once on the ground, she placed the jar on the counter, lifted the lid, and peered inside. Though called powder, the yellow substance inside looked to Josie Mae to be tiny grains of rice.

She closed her eyes and began reciting what she remembered. "Yellow dock root powder. Latin name Rumex crispus. Grown mostly in Africa. Sometimes known as patience herb and garden patience. Helps those with indigestion and can be used as a laxative, especially for children and during pregnancy. Good for pain and swelling of nasal passages. Can be made into a paste to help with swelling, bruising, rashes, and sores."

She opened her eyes to find her mother standing in the doorway. "Excellent, Josephine. I think you know these medicines better than I do. You are going to make a fine nurse."

Josie Mae had not realized she was holding her breath until it came out in a whoosh. She turned so her mother was to her back and couldn't read the expression on her face.

This conversation was not new. In fact, it appeared to be the only thing on her mother's mind since Josie Mae came to live in town. Josephine, the nurse. Josephine, the medical professional. What her mother really meant was she would not become Josie Mae, the granny woman.

"I'm not sure I'm going to be a nurse, Mother. I haven't made up my mind. Just because I can memorize the contents of the jars in the apothecary doesn't mean I will be a good healer. Nor does it mean I want to be one." She lifted one shoulder in a half shrug, hoping her mother would let the topic drop. But that was not to be.

"Not go to nursing school? Why, Josephine, that would be such a waste of talent! Of course, you'll go. And if it's the lack of formal schooling, you don't have anything to worry about. Dr. McKeithen has assured me his recommendation will be worth more than a diploma from a backwoods mountain school. We are going to have to catch you up on some of the sciences the city schools offer. I've ordered a few books, but with the winter..."

Josie Mae cut her off. "I'm not sure I want to be a nurse, Mother. And I wish you would call me Josie Mae. I have never been Josephine to anyone but you." She turned to her mother, eyes flashing. "I don't want Dr. McKeithen to recommend me to any school, at least not right now. And I'm not interested in catching up on science."

Before Carrie Ann could speak, Josie Mae continued. "You know what I want. I want Granny to be okay. And until she is, I don't care about anything else."

She waved her arm around the room. "I'm only here because you make me come. I'm only in town because Granny sent me away just as the big snow hit, and I haven't been able to go back to her. You can't make me be something I am not."

She turned again, replacing the jar on the shelf. As Josie Mae climbed down, she said, "I'm going home. Tomorrow, I'm going to see Granny."

Josie Mae put on her coat as she went through the door, the cold air hitting her cheeks and bare head. While she strode from the clinic, she pulled on her hat and gloves and wound the scarf around her neck. Despite the snow and the cold, she was tired of waiting. She needed to check on Granny, who had been trapped alone for weeks.

No one seemed to think it was a problem except for Josie Mae. Her mama, with her acidic words, believed Granny was fine by herself. Mama also believed Granny needed the time to think about all she had done to Esther and her family.

No one else in town, including Dr. McKeithen, realized what had been said to Granny on Christmas. They knew she had ridden out storms in the past and didn't see this one as any different. Only Josie Mae understood the anguish Granny experienced that morning at the hands of her mother and the agony those words would cause each day.

Josie Mae's cheeks reddened as she remembered her mother's accusations. "You killed Esther as surely as if you put the noose around her neck yourself."

Although Josie Mae hated what her mother said, she hated her own actions even worse. She did nothing to stop her mother's tirade. She did nothing to soothe her grandmother. When told to go, she didn't protest. She simply grabbed some of her things and left.

It didn't matter that Josie Mae returned the next day. The damage was done. Granny, though not in bed and silent, was clearly suffering. She allowed Josie Mae to stay a few hours before asking to be alone, but Granny treated her no differently than a piece of furniture, maneuvering around her and never speaking except to answer direct questions.

Then, Josie Mae did what she regretted the most. She let Granny be alone for almost two weeks. She had been hurt by Granny's indifference to her presence. "Fine. If she doesn't want me there, I won't be there. Let her be lonely." When she could not stand it one moment longer, she went back to Granny's, hopeful the older woman would have found some sort of peace.

Instead, Granny had grown more distant and less tolerant. Within minutes of Josie Mae's arrival, Granny insisted she pack her belongings and go live with her mother.

"Take what you need from your room. Whatever you want. But go. You belong with your mother. You should have always been with your mother. Please. Go."

Josie Mae protested. "Granny! That's not true! How am I ever going to be a healer without your help?"

Maggie exploded. "No! My kind of healing kills, Josie Mae. Do you hear me? Kills." She grabbed her walking stick and shook it at the child. "Do you want to end up like this? Knowing it was you who done killed the people you love, and they are now gone forever?"

She dropped her head in her hands. "No. If'n you ever loved me, Josie Mae, you'll throw away those notebooks. You'll forget everything I ever taught you. And if you really have a hankerin' to be a healer, you'll go to school and learn real medicine." She looked up, staring into Josie Mae's tear-filled eyes. "That's what you'll do if'n you love me."

No amount of pleading changed her mind. And then

the blizzard hit, keeping her in town despite her strong desire to try again.

Her mother used those weeks to insist she would be a nurse, insist she would obtain a more formal education, insist she be Josephine rather than Josie Mae. But Josie Mae was done listening. Tomorrow, she would go to Granny and straighten everything out.

Chapter 42

Carrie Ann
- February 24, 1894 -

Carrie Ann stared as her daughter's back disappeared down the trail. Notwithstanding her best efforts, Josephine remained determined to visit Granny. Although she wasn't happy, Carrie Ann knew arguing would never lead to the answer she wanted. The battle was lost, so she packed a lunch and reminded her daughter to remain on the path.

"I don't want you falling into a snowdrift. If you stay right on the road, you should be fine. There isn't any-one coming or going that way. If you were to get turned around, I wouldn't realize you were missing until dark, and it would be morning before I found you." She lifted her hand to Josephine's face. "Please be careful."

Josie Mae grimaced. "I could walk to Granny's house with my eyes closed. You don't have anything to worry about. I'll be home by nightfall." Then, as she hopped off the porch, she tossed out the words, "But I'll just be com-ing back to pack. I intend to go back tomorrow, taking all my things with me."

Carrie Ann rubbed her hands up and down her arms, trying to brush off the chill, as her daughter turned into a tiny dot on the horizon. Finally, with nothing left to follow, she stepped back inside and began bustling about the room as if tidying the space would tidy her thoughts.

Josephine's attitude had been difficult, and at first, Carrie overlooked it. Her grandmother put her through a lot with the fever and the deaths that followed. Josephine had been close to Esther's children, even making mittens and scarves for a Christmas that would never come. The child had also been thrust out of her home by the woman she saw as her second mother.

Of course, Josephine was irritable and surly. So, Carrie Ann worked to make her daughter feel comfortable and see that despite the circumstances, moving to town had many advantages. Now, as she vigorously washed the breakfast dishes, Carrie Ann began to list those advantages.

"First, Josephine would be able to develop a closer relationship with me. That, alone, should be enough. Then, there is the relationship with Dr. McKeithen, the ease of working at the clinic, the ability to get better schooling, and the proximity to other girls – and boys – her own age."

Carrie Ann shook her head, unable to fathom why her daughter pined for the cabin in the middle of the woods with a woman who didn't speak and didn't want her company. It made no sense.

Because Carrie Ann had no patience for absurd things, she found herself growing aggravated over Josephine's behavior. Even small, inconsequential statements turned into arguments. If Carrie Ann so much as mentioned being a nurse, Josephine insisted she was uninterested. The same was true about school and friends. In fact, if Carrie Ann commented on it, Josephine was against it.

Thinking about these last weeks sent Carrie Ann's thoughts whirling. "Josephine is rude. She is ungrateful.

She is immature. And it is all my fault." This final thought caused Carrie Ann to drop a dish back into the water with a splash.

How could she blame a child for being a child? Josephine was simply mimicking what she saw the other adults in her life do, and the adult she mimicked most was her grandmother.

"And the only reason she's so close with her grandmother is because it was easier to let Mama take over." Yes, she wanted an education. Yes, getting an education would have been difficult to do with a young daughter in tow. But these excuses only accounted for a few early years. What of the years since then? If she didn't like how Josephine turned out, she only had herself to blame.

She hung the towel over the stack of clean dishes and eased into the rocking chair by the fire. Dr. McKeithen didn't need her today. The clinic was slow due to the cold. However, she would have relished some busywork to keep her mind occupied. Instead, she ruminated over her daughter.

What could be done at this point? Was her personality so set that she would always be the one taking up the contrary position? Carrie Ann cocked her head to one side. "No, that's not entirely true," she thought. "Josephine gets along well with Dr. McKeithen. In fact, I've never heard her contradict him. She's never even gotten sharp with him."

Carrie Ann stopped rocking. Her daughter's poor attitude was not a general one but a specific one aimed at Carrie Ann. She wondered if it was too late to develop a relationship that didn't include sighing and raised voices. Going back in time was not possible – but was there a way forward? She watched other women in town with their daughters, laughing together, smiling over a bolt of fabric, giggling when a young man looked in their direction. Carrie Ann was not blessed to have such a closeness with her own mother, and it seemed, her own daughter, either.

She let her head rest against the back of the chair, deep in thought.

When the door flew open, Carrie Ann sat upright, realizing she must have drifted off. Because of the sunlight, the figure was backlit, making it difficult for Carrie Ann to determine who had barged in without knocking. However, before she could gather her wits, the figure ran toward her, hysterical and yelling. "Mama!" Josie Mae screamed and threw herself into Carrie Ann's arms.

"Mama! Granny. She's gone. Not home. No fire. No food. Nothing. She's gone!" cried Josie Mae.

Carrie Ann held her close. "Shhh. Shhh. I'm sure your grandmother is fine. Shhh. Shhh. Tell me what you saw."

Josie Mae's tears fell unheeded down her face. "I got to our house, Mama. But Granny is gone. The wagon is gone. And the mule. I think someone stole them and took Granny. Oh, Mama, someone took Granny!"

Carrie Ann shook her head. "Shhh, now. No one would take Granny. It's more likely she went off in the wagon, don't you think? Maybe she went on her spring trip?"

Josie Mae shook her head wildly. "Granny would never leave for the Cherokee now. It wouldn't be possible with all this snow. She'd freeze to death." Then all the blood drained from her face. "Mama? Is Granny gone like Esther? Oh, Mama!!"

Carrie Ann grabbed Josephine by the shoulders none too gently. "We won't have any talk like that, young lady.

I'm going to fetch Dr. McKeithen. He'll take us to Granny's in his sleigh. We'll figure out what is going on."

Within minutes, the doctor was at the door and bundling the women onto the seat. "Here. Cover yourselves with the blanket. We'll be moving fast, and the air will feel much colder." He turned to Carrie Ann, saying, "I brought my bag with me just in case Granny has taken ill." Then, with a look at Josie Mae, he said, "Don't you worry. We'll find Granny."

With that, they headed down the trail.

Chapter 43

Maggie
- February 24, 1894 -

Maggie had been living in the small cabin she once shared with her husband for just over one month. She spent the first several days getting the place habitable. The fireplace had been her first chore. She started a fire as soon as she arrived and quickly realized her mistake. Birds and other animals had nested in the chimney, causing the smoke to billow throughout the small room. She pulled the wood onto the hearth, stamping out the flames before they could catch the floor on fire.

Because of the heavy snowfall and the lack of warmth within the walls of the home, the roof was covered in snow and ice. There was no way to access the chimney from the outside, at least not until the snow started to melt.

So, Maggie began by lying on her back with her upper body in the fireplace and ramming a broom handle up the chimney as far as it would reach. Twigs and straw and other nesting materials rained down on her head. She repeated this process until the first few feet of the chimney were clear.

Next, she sat upright, her upper body within the chimney, and eased the broom over her head. Once again, nesting materials rained down, this time causing her to choke and gag. Tears streamed from her eyes, but she continued, easing onto her knees and finally onto her feet, totally encased in the chimney with her hands over her head while whooshing the broom from side to side.

At one point, Maggie was certain she was stuck. She seemed unable to find a way to bend back to her knees to reverse the process. She began to laugh and cry at the thought of dying in a chimney. Of course, she reasoned, it would serve her right to die in whatever fashion God saw fit.

However, the chimney was not destined to be her final resting spot. She eventually found a way to kneel, then sit, and then completely remove herself from the narrow opening.

She looked down at her dress, now covered in black, oily soot and a fine layer of feathers and twigs. Her hands were as dark. She assumed her face and hair were the same. But it didn't matter. She was now an utlinowa, alone in the world.

Once she could produce heat, she worked to keep the heat in – and the snow out. She pulled materials from the fallen portion of the barn as patches for the holes in her new home. She used her hammer and some tenpenny nails she found in a rotted sack next to the fireplace. Before the sun set on the first day, the room was warm and dry.

Maggie's days started at sunrise. She labored until there wasn't enough light to see, then ate a few bites and went to sleep by the fire, wrapped in a blanket. In the morning, she began again.

She was working on the hinges of the front door when the jingle of sleigh bells caught her attention. She blocked the light with her hand, wondering who had found her and why. As if to answer her silent question, Josie Mae began to shout. "Granny! Granny! You are okay!"

Josie Mae rushed from the sleigh and threw herself at Maggie, though the older woman kept her hands hanging limp at her sides. Josie Mae stepped back, making an awful face. "Granny, what is that smell? What is all over your face and in your hair?"

Maggie looked down, realizing she hadn't bathed since she arrived. She looked up again to find Carrie Ann crossing her arms. "Mother? What are you doing here? Why aren't you at home? What is going on?"

Maggie took a step backward, pulling Josie Mae off balance. She knew someone would discover her new residence in time, but she hadn't realized it would be so soon. She didn't have a plan and had no way to explain now that she had willingly given up her voice as part of her punishment.

She took another step back and reached for the door. If she could make it behind the door, they would be forced to leave her alone.

"Maggie?" Dr. McKeithen's concern cut into her thoughts. "Are you sick? Do you need any help?"

Sick? No, she wasn't sick. She was an utlinowa, without need of family or friends or a doctor. She shook her head, taking another step back. One more, and she'd be through the doorframe. Two more, and she'd be free.

"Mother! Stop!" Carrie Ann stepped toward her but stopped when her mother's eyes darted from side to side in terror.

"Mother," she said once more in a softer tone. "It's me, Mother. It's Carrie Ann. I'm not going to hurt you. Please, let me help you." She moved forward once again, but before she could reach out, Maggie flung herself through the door and slammed it shut, panting heavily behind the slab of wood.

Maggie listened from her hiding place as each added their opinion. Carrie Ann wanted Dr. McKeithen to break down the door. "Just go in there and demand she come home."

Dr. McKeithen suggested they give Maggie some space.

"I'm afraid she's had a breakdown, Carrie Ann. But she's not a danger to anyone, and we don't have the right to intrude. Now that we know she is here, we can keep an eye on her. Bring her food and supplies. Make sure she's doing okay. Hopefully, when she realizes we aren't going to hurt her, she'll let us come closer. Maybe with a bit of time, she'll recognize she needs our help."

Josie Mae's constant refrain of 'Granny! Granny! Granny!' tied everything together.

Then, without warning, Carrie Ann started to cry, something Maggie had not witnessed since Henry died all those years ago. "I can't leave her here like this, Daniel. Oh, Mama!"

For a while, everyone remained as they were. Maggie behind the door. Josie Mae on the porch steps crying her name. Carrie Ann on her knees in the snow, sobbing into her mittens. Dr. McKeithen mumbling words of encouragement. Eventually, the yard grew quiet. Maggie, wary of a trap, stayed perfectly still until the light began to fade. Only then did she peer out the window. They were gone.

She sat down with a thud, leaning against the wall and letting the tears fall. She was now an utlinowa, and she was utterly alone.

Chapter 44

Josie Mae
- March 6, 1894 -

Every day for the last ten days, Josie Mae went to her Granny's new home. She never stayed long. There was no need because Granny hid away as soon as Josie Mae approached.

Nonetheless, Josie Mae went, taking homemade bread or a jar of jam or a bit of leftovers from supper the night before. She would set the offerings on the porch, then sit on the steps to chat.

"Good morning, Granny. I spent the day yesterday at the clinic. Mrs. Murray had her baby last week. I got to go with Dr. McKeithen to check in on her. The baby is so round and squishy. Dr. McKeithen said she is very healthy, and it looks like Mrs. Murray's milk has come in just fine.

"Mama and I have been working on a quilt. She says it will be part of my trousseau. You know Mama. She likes to be fancy. I'm just going along with it because she seems so sad about you being out here on your own. 'Course, I'm sad, too. I miss you. I love you. And I know you love me, too."

Then, she would spread her hand on the door, hoping Granny would sense the touch before turning to leave.

Dr. McKeithen had given her use of his small sled,

which she hooked to her mama's mule. The trip from start to finish took an hour and a half. Once back in town, she would either go to the clinic or work with Mama around the house.

Mama never came with her. "No, Josephine. I am not going to participate in Mother's nonsense." She tried to be brusque about it, but Josie Mae could see the tears threatening to fall. Despite everything said between them, her mama still loved Granny and couldn't bear to see her in this state.

Dr. McKeithen, on the other hand, accompanied her twice. He stood at the door, asking Granny if she needed anything. When he got no answer, he told her he'd be back again.

Each day, Josie Mae hoped Granny would welcome her in. She remembered how quickly Granny had gone from silent and unmoving to participating in Christmas. If Granny could do it once, she could do it again.

But each day, she left disappointed. However, Josie Mae committed to being there for Granny every day. She wouldn't become angry and leave her alone the way she did after Christmas. She carried the guilt that if she had been a better granddaughter, Granny wouldn't be suffering in quite the same way.

She said as much to Mama, who scolded her. "Josephine! What balderdash! Your grandmother can't handle losing her friend, especially since she is the main reason it happened. This has nothing to do with you!"

Josie Mae stood taller and spat out one word at a time. "Granny. Did. Not. Kill. Esther." She took a deep breath to calm her anger.

"Granny worked day and night to save Esther and

her family. She got the fever trying to save them. There is nothing more she could have done." Then she pointed a finger at her mother. "There is nothing more you could have done, either. Sometimes, Mother, people die. Granny isn't the only healer who has lost a patient. Would you like me to remind you of those who've died in your care?"

Carrie Ann sputtered. "That's... that's different! The people I lost – that Dr. McKeithen and I lost – were too sick or too old. Some had accidents that were too severe. No one can be expected to save everyone."

Josie Mae gave a curt nod. "Exactly, Mother. John was too sick, as were the children. And Esther's death? That isn't Granny's fault. Esther just couldn't see a way forward all alone trying to raise a child who was likely to always be like a child. I hope you are never so alone and so despondent that hanging from a tree seems like the best option, Mother. But if you are? It won't be anyone's fault." With those words, she stormed out of the house.

Josie Mae had no patience for her mother's righteous indignation. She did not understand why Granny couldn't practice medicine in a way that made sense to her while her mother practiced in a different way. As far as Josie Mae could tell, both had the same goal – to make people well.

Working in the clinic helped her see how many of the newer meds used by Dr. McKeithen were useful and valuable. She saw people recover quickly from diseases that were not always easy to cure.

On the other hand, it didn't matter to Granny if a shipment didn't come in from New York City because she relied on what she could find in the holler. And unlike her mama, Granny had a way of calming people and making them believe they'd get well. It was the belief in healing that was often the difference between living and dying, at least in Josie Mae's opinion.

Josie Mae cleared her throat, noting the frigid air was causing pinpricks of pain. She wound the scarf tighter around her neck. "It's probably because of all the traveling I've been doing in the cold," she thought. "I just need a bit of tea with honey, but in the meantime, I think I'll buy a piece of penny candy."

With a smile on her face, Josie Mae entered the general store. Now that she was at the clinic several days a week, Dr. McKeithen gave her a small wage. Josie Mae liked having her own money to spend, especially on sweets. She eyed the jars, settling on sassafras, and handed a copper coin to Myles.

"Back for more candy, I see?" laughed Myles as he took the penny.

"It is hard for me to walk by now that I have a bit of money in my pocket!" Josie Mae began to laugh, but her smile turned to a grimace.

"What's the matter, love?" Myles put his hands on Josie Mae's shoulders.

"Oh, nothing, really," said Josie Mae, unwrapping the treat and popping it into her mouth. "My throat has a tickle from all this cold air. Nothing a little sassafras candy won't cure!"

"You sure, child? You ain't comin' down with somethin', are ya?"

"No. No. I'm sure I'm fine. It's just a tickle. I'm going to have a little honey with my tea tonight. That should do the trick."

Josie Mae waved at the man and headed back outside.

Although she sucked on the sassafras, the tickle didn't disappear. If anything, it felt worse as she swallowed. Despite not wanting to deal with her mother, she decided to head back home. A cup of hot tea would do her good.

Josie Mae was thankful her mother was not there when she arrived. She put the kettle on to boil and placed some tea into a mug.

She yanked her hat and scarf off as soon as she came indoors but left her coat on. The air still seemed chilly. She threw a couple of logs into the fire and pulled her chair up close. "Ahhh, now that feels good." She chided herself for going out into the cold when she didn't have to. If she could learn to control her temper, she wouldn't be so chilled.

The warmth of the fire and tea caused her eyelids to droop, so she pushed herself out of the chair and into her room. "I'll just take a quick nap, and then I'll fix a bit of supper." She crawled into her bed, still wearing her coat, and fell into a deep sleep.

Chapter 45

Carrie Ann
- March 7, 1894 -

Carrie Ann came home from the clinic to find Josephine asleep in her room. She closed the door, careful not to wake her, realizing just how tired the child must be to rest with her coat on. "Poor thing. She's working so hard at the clinic. I'll let her relax while I fix something to eat."

Carrie Ann cut some ham and began peeling the potatoes. She made sure to add extra, so Josephine would have enough to take to Mama the next day. Carrie Ann was worried. She couldn't make herself visit, but she could be sure her mama had food.

She dropped the potatoes into the water one by one and added a bit of salt. Then she put the pot on the stovetop. As soon as it started to boil, she went to Josie Mae's room. "Sweetheart! Wake up, sleepy head. Supper is almost ready. I just have to mash the potatoes."

Josie Mae didn't stir.

Carrie Ann moved around the room, pulling the scarf from the floor and draping it over the chair. "Come on, honey. Wake up. I could use your help setting the table." She reached out to shake Josie Mae's shoulder and pulled her hand back quickly. The child was burning up.

Carrie Ann ran to the front door, grabbing the dish

towel on the way. She filled the towel with snow and returned to Josie Mae's room.

Leaning over the bed, Carrie Ann turned Josie Mae onto her back. Her hair lay plastered to her forehead, and her cheeks shone bright red. Carrie Ann pulled Josie Mae to sitting.

"Josephine, honey. You've got a fever. Let Mama help you out of this coat." She tugged one arm from the coat and then shimmied the sleeve off the other side. "There now, that will feel better."

She emptied the snow from the towel into the wash basin and placed the cold, damp cloth on Josie Mae's head. Josie Mae turned away and feebly pushed at the towel.

"Leave it be, Josephine. Come on, now. Let Mama do her job. We need to bring this fever down, and this cold rag will help."

When Josie Mae became still, no longer fighting the cloth, Carrie Ann filled a glass with water. Sitting her daughter up once again, she put the glass to her lips. "Josephine, I need you to drink a little water. Come on now. Just a sip."

Josie Mae let the water dribble out of the corner of her mouth. She looked at Carrie Ann with glassy eyes. "Can't. Hurts. Can't."

Carrie Ann settled her daughter again, murmuring, "Don't worry. It's okay. I'll bring you some broth in a bit. Something warm is always easier to swallow."

Josie Mae opened her eyes again. "Cold. So cold." Despite the heat radiating from her body, Josie Mae began to shake. Carrie Ann wrapped her in blankets and held her while she shivered. Twenty minutes later, Josie Mae was pulling at the covers. "Hot. Please. No. Hot."

Carrie Ann repeated the process throughout the night,

each time believing the fever would surely break this time. But when the sun came up and Josie Mae still alternated between shivering and sweating, Carrie Ann decided she needed help.

"Mama's going to be right back, Josephine. I'm going to find Dr. McKeithen. I won't be gone but a minute."

Carrie Ann rushed from the house, making her way as fast as her feet would carry her to the clinic. The door, however, was still locked. She swung her head to and fro, looking up the street toward Dr. McKeithen's house, but didn't see him coming this way. As she stepped down to take a better look, a voice stopped her. "You lookin' for the doctor, Ms. Carrie Ann?"

Carrie Ann swung around. Old Man Jones was wrapped in a ratty blanket and sitting in the doorframe of the seamstress shop. Everyone in town knew him as a drunk. His wife kicked him out years ago. He spent his days wandering around the stores and his nights finding shelter in a barn, usually without the owner's permission.

"He's gone thataway." He pointed a skinny finger in the direction opposite Dr. McKeithen's house. "Said he was gonna play some checkers up at the hotel."

Carrie Ann looked one more time toward Dr. McKeithen's house.

"He ain't there. Nope. Sitting at the hotel, he is."

Carrie Ann gave him a curt nod. She had no choice but to believe him. She couldn't waste time, not when Josie Mae couldn't shake her fever.

She hollered thank you over her back as she began running in the direction of The Wray. When she reached the building on the edge of town, she was out of breath. She bent forward and held her sides before ascending the stairs.

The lobby was dimly lit compared to the morning sun, and it took a moment for Carrie Ann's eyes to adjust. Finally, she saw a cluster of men in a corner. "Dr. McKeithen? Daniel!"

Dr. McKeithen stood up and strode toward Carrie Ann. "Are you okay, Carrie Ann? What is the matter? Here, let me get you some water."

He reached for a jug on the front desk, but Carrie Ann grabbed his arm. "It's Josephine. She has a fever. She's been having the chills all night. I... I need your help."

"Of course. You head home. I'll stop by the clinic on the way to your house. I'll be right behind you." Then he turned to the men seated at the table. "Boys, you'll have to excuse me. I've got some work to tend to." He threw up his hand in a wave as he left the building with Carrie Ann two steps ahead.

"Carrie Ann?"

She turned her head but kept moving in the direction of her house.

"Josie Mae will be fine. I'll be along shortly."

Carrie Ann nodded, her mouth set in a straight line. She prayed he was right.

Chapter 46

Maggie
- March 13, 1894 -

Maggie looked up the road for the fifth time in as many minutes. Josie Mae hadn't stopped by in a week. She tried to tell herself it didn't matter.

"I'm an utlinowa. I am made to be alone. Josie Mae has finally accepted the woman she knew as Granny no longer exists. There is no reason for her to continue to visit."

Maggie craned her neck, despite her self-inflicted exile, hoping to spot the granddaughter she still loved.

Maggie didn't blame the child for giving up. She drove the long distance for what? To talk to a door.

What Maggie found interesting was her reaction to both Josie Mae's presence and the cessation of her presence. Each time the girl came, Maggie felt a tug-of-war happening in her brain.

The Granny side of her wanted to run to the girl, throw her arms around her, and drink in her clean, fresh scent. She wanted to tell her all the things that had been haunting her, ask her how she was doing in town living with her mother, but mostly to tell her she loved her.

The utlinowa side wanted to throw rocks at the child so she would never come again. Utlinowa wanted to be alone. Wanted the visits to stop. Wanted Granny to disappear as well.

Now that the visits had ceased, Utlinowa was satisfied. "Good riddance to her and her chatter. I have no need to be reminded of what once was." Granny, however, hung her head with yet another loss. She knew she could never return what Josie Mae offered, but she had hoped the child would continue. Without Josie Mae, Maggie knew Granny would eventually cease to exist.

Maggie was deep in thought and nearly missed the jangling on the trail leading down from the big house. She looked up in time to glimpse a wagon with one rider too large to be Josie Mae before she moved to hide behind her closed door.

Maggie hadn't realized how much the weather had changed in the past week. Josie Mae's last visit had been by sleigh. This visitor came by wagon. "Spring must be almost here," she thought. It was the first time she had considered the passing of time beyond the coming of nightfall after a long day.

Heavy footsteps sounded on the wooden steps leading to the door, and a man's voice rang out. "Maggie? Maggie, I don't want to intrude. I can't begin to understand your desire to be alone, but I have news. It's Josie Mae. She's sick. Very sick."

Maggie held her breath. Josie Mae was sick. The child had not given up on her. Tears of relief flooded down her cheeks.

"Maggie? Did you hear what I said? Josie Mae is sick. She's got scarlet fever. She's not responding to the medicines. Carrie Ann and I have tried everything, but the fever won't break."

Maggie's tears of relief turned hot and salty. What was she, an utlinowa, to do? "Nothing. Utlinowas do nothing but harm." She leaned her back on the door and covered her mouth with her hand. She had nothing to offer.

Daniel let out a deep breath. "Maggie. Josie Mae needs you." He paused. "That's not entirely true. I need you, too. I have nothing else to try to help your granddaughter. I've paid close attention to you, Maggie. You have..." He hesitated, stumbling over his words. "A gift... powers... something I do not possess, and no amount of education will ever give to me."

He stopped speaking, and Maggie leaned heavily on the door.

"Maggie, I'm afraid she's going to die."

Maggie sobbed silently on her side of the door. She lifted her eyes to the walking stick, which held a prominent spot over the fireplace, and mocked her with its notches. "Seventeen dead. Are you ready to add one more?" it seemed to say.

But a louder voice, one she recognized as Granny, said, "If you don't offer aid and the child dies, you will have to add one more. Can you live with yourself if you lose your granddaughter because you did nothing?"

Maggie crushed her skull between her fists, willing the voices to stop.

"You are a murderer. You will kill the one person you love most on this earth."

"You are her grandmother. You have to help if you can. You'll never forgive yourself if you don't try."

Back and forth, the words flew in Maggie's head, each one louder than the next. Her head spun with noise, and she thought she might be going mad. Then, softly but clearly, Daniel's next words stopped the spinning.

"Maggie, you are not responsible for the deaths of Esther's family. You did everything within your power to save them. But you and I both know some people do not live despite everything we can do. And Esther?" He continued, whispering now. "Esther's death is not your doing, either. She simply couldn't imagine living in this world any longer. Just the way you will feel if Josie Mae dies without you trying to save her."

Maggie held her breath. Esther had been helpless. She could do nothing for her family. In the end, she could do nothing for herself.

But Maggie had been given a gift. She could often heal when others said it was impossible. Turning her back on her gift now, when her granddaughter needed it most, was unthinkable. Daniel was right. If Josie Mae died while she wallowed in self-pity, she would never be able to forgive herself.

Maggie grasped the door handle and pulled. In a hoarse whisper, she uttered the first words she had spoken in weeks. "I can't go like this. I've got some clean things up at the big house. And my bag. My bag is there, too."

Chapter 47

Josie Mae
- March 13, 1894 -

Josie Mae knew she was dying. It had been a full week, and she still had a fever. Her entire body was covered in a rosy, red rash. But the worst part was she had begun to cough. Hers was not a slight cough to clear a tickle in the throat but a deep, wet cough rattling her chest and leaving her panting for air.

Dr. McKeithen had her propped in the bed to help her breathe. He also put a tent around her to hold in the steam from the pots of water on the floor. "I've added eucalyptus, Josie Mae. It comes all the way from Australia!" Josie Mae wrinkled her nose as the sharp, medicinal aroma seeped into her nose and throat.

"What... does... it... do?" she panted.

"That's a great question, Josie Mae. I just learned about this recently and purchased some for the apothecary. You are the first patient to give it a try. According to the paper I read, eucalyptus oil reduces the amount of phlegm your lungs produce. Plus, it loosens up the phlegm already there. It will make it easier for you to cough it up."

Josie Mae began hacking, clutching at her sides. "It... must... be... working," she said with a weak smile. Then, she pulled the makeshift tent flap aside and asked, "Am I dying?"

She scrutinized his face, looking for his eyes to glance away or his hands to flutter at his sides. Although his posture remained neutral, he stiffened ever so slightly.

"No! Don't even think that. You have scarlet fever, Josie Mae. A pretty strong case of it. I am a bit concerned you have developed pneumonia. But you are young and healthy. You have a nurse for a mama and a doctor for a friend. You don't need to worry about dying."

His denial was too emphatic, as though he was trying to convince himself as much as he was trying to convince her. "No... lying... I'm not... stupid... I'm sicker... than Esther's... family..." She put her head back, gasping for air before continuing. "And they... died."

"It's true, Josie Mae. You are sick. I'll even agree you are very sick. But I don't intend to let you die. I suggest you do the same. Now, let me add some more hot water to those pans."

In addition to the steam, Dr. McKeithen had been giving her tea with marshmallows and peppermint. And every three hours, she was given a liquid medication made in New York just for scarlet fever.

"What's in it?" she had asked. She didn't remember everything Dr. McKeithen said, but she did remember some kind of quinine and ether. Despite all the care, she wasn't getting any better. She knew her mama was worried by the appearance of deep lines between her eyes and at the corners of her mouth.

Josie Mae began to shake again. With the last of her energy, she called out to Dr. McKeithen. "I want Granny..."

* * *

When she woke, Dr. McKeithen no longer held her. Through her slit eyes, she saw him standing in the corner with folded arms. Next to him stood her mother. Who, then, was holding her while she slept?

She opened her eyes a bit wider and tilted her head back. Granny? Had she died? Was this heaven? It would make sense for Granny to be in heaven. Except Granny was not dead. She was in her tiny house.

Granny leaned close. "Shhh, now. Granny's here. I'm here. We're going to get you well."

Tears streamed from Josie Mae's eyes. "Granny. How?" She didn't have the strength to say more.

"Dr. McKeithen came for me. He told me how sick you've been. He said you needed me. He said he needed me. What's a granny woman to do when she's needed, other than come?"

Josie Mae started coughing again, this time choking on the phlegm. She gagged, eyes bulging, desperate for air.

Deftly, Granny turned the child in her arms and began to rub and pat her back in a rhythmic, circular motion. Quietly, almost beneath her breath, she chanted words familiar to Josie Mae. The sounds of the Cherokee. Finally, just as her lips turned blue, Josie Mae cleared her airway and sucked in a big gulp of air.

"That's my girl. That's my girl. Relax now. Close your eyes and rest. Let Granny help these lungs."

Josie Mae did as she was told. With her eyes closed, she listened to Granny's song and felt herself float along with the steam, bumping into the tent before drifting down toward the bed again. Over and over she floated until she fell into a deep sleep.

Josie Mae woke slowly, listening to Dr. McKeithen

explaining to Granny everything he had tried and what remedies he was currently using.

"I like the tent, Daniel. I had never considered trying to trap the air around the bed. I've always just placed a towel over a steaming bowl. This is so much more effective." After a pause, Granny said, "Have you thought about adding turpentine to the eucalyptus? It is something folks in this area have used for centuries."

Daniel's lower voice rumbled. "It's not something I've ever done. Do you have any with you, or should I send Carrie Ann to the general store?"

"I have a bit with me. Let's see how it does before we go buyin' more. Now, tell me about the tea."

"I make it with marshmallow for the kidneys and peppermint for the cough."

Josie Mae opened her eyes just enough to see the two standing near the foot of her bed. Granny nodded while digging into her bag. "I usually use a tincture of belladonna and wolf's bane for congestion, though I've never worried about the kidneys. What do you say we keep the marshmallow and add these instead of the peppermint for now?"

Dr. McKeithen took the tinctures from her hand. "I'm willing to try anything. We've got to bring this fever down – and that cough..." He shrugged in defeat. "I have no idea what else to do for the cough."

"I learned something from the Cherokee. Doesn't go over too well with folks in town, but I've seen it bring a fever down might quick when it's something like scarlet fever or a lung ailment."

Daniel leaned forward. "What is it, Maggie?"

Granny sighed. "I'm not sure Carrie Ann will approve..."

Her mama took a step toward them and came into view. "If those Indian friends of yours know something, I'm willing to try it. I don't have to like where it comes from as long as it saves Josephine's life."

Granny nodded. Josie Mae realized how difficult it must be for her mama to accept help, especially when the help was something she saw as Cherokee magic. Granny cleared her throat, then whispered, "Poison ivy."

Both Dr. McKeithen and Carrie Ann repeated it back in unison. "Poison ivy?"

Maggie began speaking right away, as if knowing she needed to help them to understand before they pushed it away as unheard of.

"We think of poison ivy as something dreadful," she said in a rush. "Something to be avoided at all costs. But the Cherokee understand most everything has a good side and a bad side. Plants, like poison ivy, were created to help humans stay in balance and keep man within his bounds. On the one hand, the poisonous juice that causes a red, blistering rash reminds us we are not lord over the plants."

Maggie held out her left hand. Then, holding out her right hand, as if creating a scale, she said, "On the other hand, the same juice can remove the poison that causes fever." She let her hands fall to her sides, stiffening her shoulders and bracing herself for the criticism sure to come.

"Many medicines we use are toxic when used incorrectly. I don't see why poison ivy should be any different," suggested Dr. McKeithen.

Carrie Ann was a bit more hesitant. "She's already got a rash. And her mouth is full of sores. This won't make it worse?"

Granny took Carrie Ann's hands. "I won't give it to her

if'n you say no. But Carrie Ann, if I were lying in the bed with a stubborn fever, I hope you'd give it to me."

Carrie Ann lowered her chin. "All of this," she waved her hand toward Josephine, the tent filled with steam, the teas, and medicines, "isn't working. Everything I learned. Everything I know. Everything in the books I suggested you read. And my baby is still sick. Who am I to say no to poison ivy?"

Chapter 48

Maggie
- March 16, 1894 -

Maggie was exhausted. She had spent the last seventy-two hours at her granddaughter's bedside listening to her cough and watching her grow weaker. Her medicine didn't seem to be any better than her daughter's. The only thing she offered the child was comfort. When Maggie was close by, Josie Mae was able to rest. So, Maggie stayed in a chair by the bed, only getting up to relieve herself and stretch her legs.

"Mama, you have to sleep. Let me take a turn."

"It's alright, Carrie Ann. I snooze some while sitting here. Josie Mae keeps calling out to me in her sleep. I want to be here if'n she needs me."

She didn't say everything on her mind, which included the fear Josie Mae would die just as soon as Maggie wasn't by her side. She knew if her grandchild died, she had to be the one holding her as she went.

Despite the difficult circumstances, she and Carrie Ann were working together, as though a temporary truce had been struck for the sake of Josie Mae. Both women loved the child, and both knew the situation was dire. More importantly, both understood that sometimes a patient, even a patient much loved, couldn't be brought back to health. Both prayed Josie Mae wasn't in this category.

Maggie cautiously asked Carrie Ann if the notebooks Josie Mae took from the cabin still existed. She worked to keep her voice neutral with no hint of accusation. Carrie Ann looked to the floor. "Yes, Mama, but not because of me. Josephine insisted. I'm ashamed to say I intended to burn them when I got the chance."

Maggie waited until her daughter looked up again. "I understand, Carrie Ann. Losing Esther and her family nearly did me in. Had Josie Mae not taken them with her, I would have burned them myself."

Carrie Ann shuffled from one foot to the other. Maggie knew her daughter well and saw the tug-of-war on her face. Should she apologize for her words, or should she tell her mother, one more time, that she should have gotten help? Maggie understood that her daughter's angst was made all the more impossible now that Josie Mae was getting the best care possible and still grew smaller and paler by the day.

Carrie Ann excused herself to find the books and stacked them by the chair. "What are you looking for, Mother?"

"I don't rightly know. I just keep hoping there is something I've missed. Something I ought to be doing to make all the difference."

Between Josie Mae's bouts of coughing and fitful sleep, Granny scoured her notes. She didn't read in any particular order, instead skimming the book on top of the pile. So much of what she wrote dealt with childbirth and diseases of the very young and very old. Occasionally, she came across fevers and coughs but didn't find anything they hadn't already tried in some form or another.

She listened to Josie Mae wheeze. She had no color except for high spots of red on her cheeks and the dark bags beneath her eyes. Her skin was sallow and hung loosely. She knew, in that moment, Josie Mae was dying.

And then, she remembered. Water. She needed to take Josie Mae to the water. The river helped her conceive when nothing else could. The river had the power to save. Surely, the river would heal her granddaughter.

She moved quickly into the kitchen, startling Carrie Ann and Daniel. "I need to take Josie Mae to the river. The river is sacred and has powers beyond our own."

"The river? Mother, you aren't making any sense. You can't mean to dunk Josephine into the frigid water?"

Maggie shook her head. "Ordinarily, the medicine man would recommend ritual cleansing, but no, I don't think it is wise to put her into the river. But Carrie Ann, I've seen the power of the water. I know what it can do. The Long Man brought you to me. Surely, he can bring your daughter back to you?"

Carrie Ann began to pace. "I wasn't happy when Daniel wanted to fetch you, but Josephine kept calling for you during her feverish dreams, so I finally relented. I held my tongue when the two of you decided to try the herbal remedies. I closed my ears to the Cherokee songs. I even agreed to use poison ivy. But this? This isn't sane."

She shook her head and slammed her fist on the table.

"No. Absolutely not. This goes against everything we believe. The Long Man. Sacred water. What about God? Don't you worry God will punish us for abandoning Him in the midst of our trials?"

The corners of Maggie's mouth turned up in a slight smile. "You remind me so much of your father, Carrie Ann." She took her hands. "He had the same worries when I began bathing in the river before you were born. But he finally agreed when he understood what the process meant to me.

"It's just a symbol of God. A remembrance of His power and grace. A realization He is in complete control. He is the healing waters, Carrie Ann. But when I participate in the 'going to water' ritual, it helps me feel His healing power. I don't see it as something contrary to what we believe, but just a different manifestation. Please, Carrie Ann. Please help me take her by the water. I need your help."

Carrie Ann shook her head. "No, Mother. This is where I draw the line. I believed you might have some herb that would work when our medicine would not. But I will not allow you to drag my daughter from her sick bed to the river to perform some magic ritual. I don't care if Papa finally gave in to you, Mother. We both know where his confidence in you eventually landed him."

Carrie Ann had more to say on the matter but turned as Josie Mae began to cough. She had pulled herself upright while they argued and had her legs over the side of the bed.

Maggie rushed to her side. "Josie Mae, honey. Shhh, now. Let's get you back into the bed." Before Maggie could place her arm beneath Josie Mae's knees, the girl gasped. "Water."

Carrie Ann moved to pour some water from a pitcher on the bedside, but Josie Mae weakly pushed it away. "No... water... Granny."

Daniel kneeled in front of Josie Mae. "Do you want Granny to take you to the water, Josie Mae? Is that what you're asking?"

She nodded with the last of her strength and slumped back onto the pillow.

Daniel stood and, with complete authority, stated, "Gather some blankets to keep her warm. I'll bring around the wagon."

Chapter 49

Josie Mae
- March 16, 1894 -

Although she sensed an urgency and movement, Josie Mae couldn't force her eyes open. Cool air fell on her cheeks. Pinched voices carried the words 'river' and 'sacred' to her ears. Her body swayed back and forth as someone combed their fingers through her hair. Light played peekaboo on her eyelids.

Granny's voice floated through the space separating them. "I need to face east – leastways, that's what Oukonunaka had me do. 'Course, we always came at dawn, but I think God will understand why we can't wait."

Granny settled onto the riverbank, and Josie Mae felt herself being lowered until she was sitting in her granny's lap. The water rushed and gurgled, singing a song with words she could not comprehend.

Josie Mae forced her eyes open, taking in the swirls and eddies. Granny, seeing that Josie Mae was awake, began to speak.

"Josie Mae, I brought you to the sacred water to ask for a complete healing of your illness. But, from what you learned on our trip last spring, healing of this kind is so very different than the medicine your mama provides or even what I do. Long Man doesn't prescribe a pill with the

"

expectation you will do as you are told. Instead, the spirit of the water expects you and the spirits of the medicines provided to work together.

"The only way to receive the healing power of the water is to expect to heal from within. So, I ask you, Josephine Mae Killian, do you believe in the power of God, which flows in these waters? Do you believe He has the power to heal?"

Josie Mae nodded, and Granny began to pray:

Grandfather, sacred one,
Teach us love, compassion, and honor.
That we may heal the earth
And heal each other.

Dr. McKeithen repeated the words, each phrase echoing in her mind. Then Granny repeated the prayer in Cherokee.

Once the last words left her lips, Granny leaned forward, cupping a bit of water into her hands, and let it fall onto Josie Mae's hands. She reached forward again, this time dripping water onto Josie Mae's forehead and cheeks.

Then Granny turned to Josie Mae again, asking her if she believed in the power of God to heal her. And when Josie Mae nodded, she prayed again, and again brought river water to her hands and face. Then again. And finally, a fourth time.

Granny held her tight and whispered Cherokee words into her hair. She didn't know what they meant, but she knew how much Granny loved her.

As Dr. McKeithen lifted her into the wagon, Granny said in a whisper, "She needs to come again at dawn. I'll need your help." Josie Mae felt Dr. McKeithen's chest rumble with his words. "I'll do whatever you ask, Maggie."

By the time Josie Mae was back in the house, she was shivering again. Granny's concern showed on her face. Josie Mae tried to smile. "I'm okay, Granny. Just hold me."

Granny crawled onto the bed and held Josie Mae tight. The tiny body quivered, followed by spasms of coughing. She said a silent prayer to God to spare the child. "If'n I've sinned by taking her to the river, God, then take me. You have the power to heal if'n it's Your will. So please, save my Josie Mae."

Early the next morning, Josie Mae woke to harsh whispers.

"No, Mother. I allowed you to take her yesterday. But not again. She's just as bad off today as she was then. Your stupid little prayers to some river god did nothing."

"Not yet. But the healing power of water is not something that happens instantaneously. The ritual repeats four times, Carrie Ann. Every morning for four days."

"That's absurd. You expect me to let you drag my dying daughter out into the weather for the next three mornings to bathe in a frigid river while you chant to some god called Long Man?"

Dr. McKeithen walked into the room and added his voice to the argument. "Carrie Ann, as her doctor, I'm prescribing she washes in the river at dawn for the next three mornings. I'm here to make sure this prescription is carried out."

"You, too, Daniel? I don't understand how Mama does it, bewitching a doctor to believe in magic. But it doesn't matter. I won't allow it."

Josie Mae, though exhausted and wheezing, pushed herself into a sitting position. "Yes, Mama, you will." She paused to catch her breath. "It is what I want." Then she cast her eyes toward Dr. McKeithen. "Help me, please."

This time, Josie Mae remained awake during the drive,

despite being too tired to sit. Dr. McKeithen drove the wagon, and Granny sat in the bed with Josie Mae's head in her lap. Although the sun had not yet risen, the sky was becoming lighter, allowing Josie Mae to distinguish the branches overhead from the darkness, and the bulky shadows of bushes from the horizon beyond.

The wagon came to a stop, and Dr. McKeithen placed his hands under her shoulders and knees. He held her close until he settled her into Granny's lap. Just as the sun came up over the edge of the river, Granny asked Josie Mae if she believed in the power of the healing water, and just like the day before, she confessed her belief.

She wasn't sure about her belief in Long Man. Or her belief in God. Or even her belief in healing powers. What she was sure about was her belief in Granny, who loved her and would do everything she could to help her.

Granny always told her healing was as much about the person being healed as the healer.

"If'n someone doesn't want to get well, they aren't likely to. I've seen someone die over something that should have never had that kind of power. But I've also seen people beat back a disease that should have sent them to the grave. Medicines help. Knowing how to use 'em helps. But none of it will do any good unless everyone involved devotes their entire energy toward healing."

Josie Mae closed her eyes, listening to every word of the prayer, the syllables soothing the pains in her chest. She imagined the water on her face and hands washing away the sickness and floating down the river. She felt Granny's arms surround her in love.

Chapter 50

Carrie Ann
- March 18, 1894 -

Carrie Ann paced in the dark kitchen. Dr. McKeithen and her mother had just taken Josephine for the third time to the river's edge. She could not understand why Daniel insisted on participating in this bizarre ritual, especially when it did no good.

Josephine still had a fever. Her cough was worsening. The rash on her chest was no less red. Josephine could barely sip broth, yet the doctor and the granny woman were insistent she make daily trips to the river.

She understood why her daughter persisted. Josephine was a child with a child's belief that her grandmother could do no wrong.

Carrie Ann once believed the same thing. But then her father died of cancer while in her mother's care. Nothing her mother had to offer – not her medicines, not her healing prayers, not her precious Long Man – saved Papa from dying. And now she would lose Josephine in much the same way.

Carrie Ann stopped pacing, as a thought that she'd been unable to chase away came into her mind yet again.

"Dr. McKeithen is a good, knowledgeable doctor. He keeps the apothecary stocked with the latest medications.

Medically, everything is different between my father's death and what is happening now with Josephine's sickness. Nonetheless, she is dying. Why?"

Carrie Ann had no answers. She quit believing in herbs and roots and chants, focusing instead on disease management and professionalism and schooling. But where had it gotten her? More importantly, what had it done for Josephine?

The sun was entirely above the horizon when the wagon pulled up. She flung open the front door, needing to see her daughter. She was so small, tucked inside a blanket in Daniel's arms. Her eyes were closed, and her face was white. For a moment, Carrie Ann thought she was dead until a rasping escaped from Josie Mae's lips.

After tucking Josie Mae into bed, Daniel took Carrie Ann's hand in his own. "I want to believe in Maggie's cure because there isn't much left to hope for. But I don't see it doing much good. If she doesn't break the fever soon..." He let the words trail off.

Carrie Ann covered her mouth and hurried to her daughter's bedside, warm broth in hand. "Mama, let me sit with her a bit. Please."

Maggie started shaking her head no but changed her mind when she looked into Carrie Ann's pleading eyes. "I'll go wash up and have a bite to eat. See if you can get some of that soup into her. I'll be back in a while."

Carrie Ann put an extra pillow behind Josie Mae's head to make it easier to swallow the warm liquid. "Josephine, it's your mama. Open your mouth, and let me spoon in a little broth."

Josie Mae's eyes fluttered open. "Mama?"

"Yes, baby. Shhh now. Here's a little something for you."

Josie Mae took a small sip and turned her head away. "Mama? Do you love me?"

"Why, Josephine, what a crazy question. Of course, I love you."

Josie Mae looked up at her mother with pleading eyes. "Believe."

Carrie Ann scrunched up her face, trying to understand her daughter. "Believe? Do you not believe me? I love you, Josephine. You matter more to me than anything. You must know that."

Josie Mae sighed. "Believe Granny."

Carrie Ann let her hand fall from her chest to her lap. Her child was asking her to do something that just wasn't possible. And yet, it was likely her final wish. Could she really deny her daughter the last thing on earth she wanted?

"Come with us... river... please." Josie Mae's eyes pleaded.

Then she started coughing again, bringing everyone to the door. Granny got underneath her granddaughter and began patting and rubbing. Despite Carrie Ann's stance on her mother's way of healing, she murmured the Cherokee song that brought so much comfort to those who were suffering. Slowly, Josie Mae relaxed until she fell asleep.

Carrie Ann excused herself, saying, "I'm going to take a little walk. I won't go far. Holler for me if..." She didn't finish the sentence. There was no need.

Her daughter's words rang in her ears. "Believe Granny." "Come with us." "Please." Could she put her misgivings aside for her daughter? Could she participate in the strange ceremony her mother gleaned from the Cherokee? What good would it do?

On the other hand, what was the harm? At this point,

Josephine was unlikely to make it to morning. Couldn't she offer her the comfort of knowing her mother was willing to do anything to make her well?

Carrie Ann rushed back to the house and to her daughter's side. She leaned close and whispered in her ear, "I cannot promise to believe, Josephine, but I promise to be there with you in the morning. You matter more to me than my disbelief."

Josie Mae's eyes opened and focused on her mother. "Thank you, Mama. Thank you."

The night was long. Josie Mae swung between feverish dreams and bouts of shivering fits, often calling for her granny or her mama. When it was time to go to the river, though she still clung to life, Josie Mae's eyes were glassy and unseeing.

For the final time, Dr. McKeithen wrapped up the child and placed her into the wagon. This time, her head rested in her mother's lap. Carrie Ann crooned to her in a singsong way. Although she didn't use Cherokee words, she realized her tune mimicked the one her mother used.

As they came to the river, Josie Mae's eyes opened. "Mama... you... came."

"Yes, Josephine. Mama is here."

Josie Mae tried to smile, but the effort was too much. "Believe... with... me."

Tears filled Carrie Ann's eyes. She wanted to grant her child her last wish, but how could she believe? Wasn't being here enough?

Maggie turned to Dr. McKeithen. "Please take Josie Mae to the riverbank. I'd like a moment with Carrie Ann."

When he had Josie Mae securely in his arms, Maggie began to speak. "There is so much about healing that isn't understood. If we had all the answers, people wouldn't die needlessly. We would know exactly what Josie Mae needed, and we would give it to her. But that's not the way it works."

She took Carrie Ann's hands in hers. "Josie Mae is dying. Only she can do anything about it now. The only thing in our power is our belief that she is capable of being healed. I believe it is possible, Carrie Ann. Do you?"

Tears streamed down Carrie Ann's face now. She shook her head from side to side. "By a river god?"

Now it was Maggie's turn to shake her head. "I'm not asking you to believe in a river god. Or Cherokee ways. Or even granny woman medicine. I'm asking you to believe in Josie Mae. Can you believe in your daughter?"

When Carrie Ann said nothing, Maggie continued. "My prayers are those used by an ancient people for thousands of years. They believe they can harness the power of their faith, together with the faith of the sick and the spirits of everything the gods put here on earth. Together, they have the power to heal. It's no different than what we believe, Carrie Ann, but with different names."

Carrie Ann tilted her head slightly, trying to grasp the meaning behind her mother's words.

"I come to the water not because I believe in water. I come because the water reminds me of my faith in God. It reminds me I have been given a gift, and He is the giver of the gift. It reminds me when many come together in faith, great things can happen. The river is nothing more than a symbol of God's amazing power to heal."

Carrie Ann swallowed. "I believe God can heal Josephine if it is His will."

Maggie pulled her daughter close. "That's all you need to believe."

Following closely behind her mother, Carrie Ann stood with Dr. McKeithen as her mother began. "Josephine Mae Killian, do you believe God has the power to heal you?" Josie Mae nodded.

Maggie looked to Carrie Ann. "Caroline Ann Killian, do you believe God has the power to heal your daughter?"

"Yes, yes I do," stated Carrie Ann clearly.

"Daniel McKeithen, do you believe God has the power to heal Josie Mae?"

"Yes. God has the power to do anything He chooses to do."

"I, Margaret Louise Tucker McCoury, also have complete faith in God to heal my granddaughter."

She spoke the words of the prayer, pausing between phrases to allow Carrie Ann and Daniel to repeat the words. Then she repeated them in Cherokee before bending down to cup the water to wash Josie Mae's hands and face.

Before she knew what she was doing, Carrie Mae bent toward the water and began cleansing her hands. "God, listen to my mother's prayers." Then she cupped water onto her face, saying, "Wash me clean of my unbelief."

After each cycle of prayers, Carrie Ann washed herself while her mother washed Josie Mae. When the ritual was completed, she stood and hugged her mother. "I'm sorry, Mama. For everything."

Maggie pulled back, looking into her daughter's eyes.

"I was so sad when Pa died. It made no sense to me that he was fine one day and sick the next. It made no sense you could heal the old woman up the road but not Pa. I had to blame something, so I blamed you. I see that now."

Carrie Ann sniffed loudly. "I've spent all these years trying to prove I would have done it better. I would have saved him. All my training would have been enough to keep my pa here with us."

Carrie Ann began to weep, making her words hard to understand. "But now? Now it is... my... Josie Mae. And everything I thought I knew... doesn't... matter. I hope you can forgive me."

"I don't need to, Carrie Ann. There is nothing to forgive."

Chapter 51

Josie Mae
- March 19, 1894 -

Josie Mae woke to the sunlight streaming in the window and the sound of light snoring in her ear. Granny held her close, as she had for the last several nights, but had fallen asleep. Josie Mae blinked rapidly, realizing she didn't have any difficulty opening her eyes. And, for the first time in days, she was hungry.

"Granny?" she whispered.

Granny started awake. "Yes, Josie Mae. I'm here. I'm here with you."

Josie Mae squeezed her arm. "I love you, Granny. And, Granny? Can I have something to eat?"

Granny put her hand to Josie Mae's face and began to laugh. "Carrie Ann! Carrie Ann!" The fear on her mother's face turned to astonishment before melting into tears.

"The fever broke. She's asking to eat!" Granny was laughing, crying, and stroking Josie Mae's face.

Daniel stepped into the room with an enormous grin. "Are we just going to touch her and cry, or are we going to fix this girl some food?" he boomed.

Carrie Ann scrambled to her feet. "I'll warm some broth. You'll need to start slow, Josie Mae. It's been many days since you ate anything solid."

Josie Mae didn't care what they brought as long as it stopped the hunger gnawing at her insides.

After a couple of spoonfuls, Josie Mae fell back, too tired to continue. "Don't you worry none about that, Josie Mae," Granny said. "It's gonna take time to get strong. Rest now. When you wake, you'll eat some more. Before you know it, you'll be good as new."

* * *

It had been a week since the fever broke. Josie Mae had trouble figuring out what really happened to her and what had just been a dream. Had Mama actually gone to the river? Had she really apologized to Granny?

Her mother came into the room with soup and fresh bread. "Here you go, Josie Mae. I've got some of Granny's tea, too. She gives it to the ladies after they give birth to regain their strength. She says it will help you, too."

The ease with which she talked about the tea gave Josie Mae the courage she needed. "Mama? I remember you going to the river. And washing your hands and face while Granny washed mine." She stopped, not sure how to ask what was on her mind. Thankfully, her mama answered without being asked.

"I went to the river, Josie Mae, because I love you. I was afraid you were going to die. In fact, I was certain of it. I wanted to give you your last wish. But..." she hesitated before going on, choosing her words. "While I was there, I began to understand something about my mama I hadn't understood before."

She sat down on the edge of Josie Mae's bed. "My mama is not a doctor. Or a nurse. Though she could be either if she chose. Instead, she is a healer. She believes when she combines her knowledge and belief with the belief of others and the power of God, marvelous things can happen."

She picked up Josie Mae's hands. "I always wondered what it was about Mama that made people follow her, listen to her, take her advice, especially when there was a real doctor right here in town. It infuriated me that Dr. McKeithen was enchanted with her and found value in what she did. It made no sense. I hated that you wanted to be just like her."

Josie Mae started to protest, but Carrie Ann held up her hand.

"But standing there by the river, I finally understood. Your granny has more than the knowledge passed from generation to generation. She has more than some remedies given to her by a Cherokee medicine man. She has the ability to tap into her beliefs and the beliefs of those around her. Somehow, she harnesses those beliefs and uses the energy to offer healing to those who seek it."

Carrie Ann smoothed Josie Mae's hair. "On the day by the river, when I had nothing left but a wisp of hope that you could be healed, I finally experienced Mama's power. She has something I don't have. It's good I became a nurse because I would make a lousy granny woman."

She laughed wryly but then grew serious as she looked at her daughter. "But you, Josie Mae, you have the gift. I hope you'll let Granny teach you how to use it."

Epilogue

Josie Mae
- April 26, 1926 -

Josie Mae pulled the door shut, making sure the lock caught. She pushed a strand of hair that escaped from a low bun and was beginning to show signs of graying behind her ear. Although Monday was not typically a short day at the clinic, she had something special planned for the rest of the week and wanted to have plenty of time.

But first, she needed to stop by and check in on Mama and Daniel. Mama quit practicing nursing the same year Josie Mae purchased the practice from Daniel. He had been kind enough to give her what he called the family rate. "Though not by blood, you are definitely my daughter," he said while squeezing Carrie Ann around the shoulders. "Isn't that right, darling?"

Josie Mae thought back to the day Daniel proposed, sending her mama into a fit of apprehension. She came to Josie Mae and sputtered, "What will the townsfolk think? What would become of the clinic? What will Mama say? And you, Josie Mae?"

Josie Mae laughed. "The townsfolk will say it is about time he asked and about time you said yes." Carrie Ann's hands fluttered about with an incredulous look, as if she had no idea anyone had been aware of the romance blossoming. "As for the clinic? What has to change? Daniel can be married and be a doctor. You can be married and be a nurse. These are not mutually exclusive activities, Mama."

Carrie Ann tried to say something about impropriety, but Josie Mae waved away the words. "And I won't speak for Granny, though I feel confident she'll approve, but I can speak for myself. I love Daniel. He is like the father I never had. And he obviously loves you, which makes me happy. I couldn't want anything more for you."

Then Josie Mae hugged her mother and whispered, "Go say yes before he changes his mind!"

That had been almost thirty years earlier, and the older couple still lived in the house Mama bought in town all those years ago. Even now, after retirement, the two stayed in town, and Josie Mae stopped by frequently to have meals or sit on the porch and talk about her day. Though they were no longer actively practicing medicine, neither could completely let go of the comings and goings in the clinic.

Josie Mae gave a rap on the door and hollered, "Knock, knock," as she opened the door. Her mama glanced at the clock. "So early, Josie Mae? Is there anything wrong?"

"No, Mama. Remember? Tomorrow is the Flower Moon. I'm headin' to Cherokee this afternoon, so I can attend the entire celebration. You are still welcome to join me."

Carrie Ann smiled. "Thank you, Josie Mae. Daniel and I did enjoy going with you a few years back, but staying up late to overeat and dance? I think we are a bit beyond that now."

Daniel laughed. "Speak for yourself, Carrie Ann. I'm not beyond anything!"

Josie Mae turned her attention to Daniel. "So, you want to come along, then?"

He smiled, then shook his head. "I'm not admitting to being too old. But I am admitting to being too tired."

"Speaking of being too tired, have you noticed any difference taking the blend of dandelion, nettles, and basil?"

She started giving Daniel Blaud's pill several months ago, but he wasn't happy with the results. Not only was he still tired, but he told her with a red face, "I'm all stopped up. I have to spend far too long in the outhouse." She had switched him to an herbal remedy she first learned from Granny and tinkered with a bit over the years.

"I think it may be helping," Daniel replied. "At least I'm not spending as much time in the privy."

"Daniel!" Carrie Ann gasped. Both Josie Mae and Daniel guffawed.

"Mama, trust me when I say I've talked about a lot worse."

Carrie Ann sniffed. "I suspect that's so, but that doesn't mean you have to do so with Daniel."

Josie Mae worked hard to keep her face neutral. This arrogant side of her had never gone away and was often a sore point between them.

"Anyway," said Daniel lightly, "I'm willing to see how this treatment works now that the other problem," he paused and looked pointedly at his wife, "has disappeared."

Josie Mae nodded. "It wouldn't hurt ya none to use it twice a day. I'm pretty convinced it's low iron. Happens a lot as..." She let the words fade away as Daniel made a face. "As we mature," she said with a laugh.

"Well, then, if I can't convince either of you to come with me, I'm going to head on home and throw my things into the car."

She turned to Daniel. "I left word if anyone needs a doctor, you are here and willin'. I do want to thank you for being available. I hate sending folks too far when you are right here in town."

Daniel nodded. "Any time, Josie Mae. Glad to help."

Josie Mae kissed her mama on the cheek and gave Daniel a hug. "See you on Saturday!"

She went out to her Model T and cranked the front until the engine rattled to life, then headed toward the homestead. She took to living in Granny's house when she passed away ten years ago. It was a bit of a distance from town, so she often spent nights with her mama and Daniel until she bought the truck.

It was a big purchase, and she had one of the first vehicles in the area. Thankfully, the wagon path to her home was well-worn and better than many of the local roads. It made getting into town, at least during the warmer weather, significantly easier.

She reminisced about her first trip to Cherokee by mule. So much had changed. First, she could reach her destination by car in half a day, though she always took along enough for an unplanned overnight stay. She had been stranded too many times with an overheated radiator or flat tire to count on making the trip without a problem.

The entire village had also changed. Although they still had a medicine man and continued to practice their beliefs, many of the Cherokee worked in towns nearby and were more like their European-descended counterparts than not. In fact, more and more, it was difficult to find those learning the language and traditional ways.

Even the ceremonies had changed, becoming something the locals from neighboring towns came to experience. Dances no longer started at dusk and lasted until dawn, instead often beginning midday to allow townsfolk the opportunity to participate in much the same way as they did during the fair held every October.

Josie Mae wasn't sure what she thought about the changes. On the one hand, she wanted others to understand the rich history of the Cherokee. She relished the idea that people came from all around to learn about those who settled in these lands long before the Europeans arrived. It would only be through such discovery that the bigotry still entrenched in these hills would disappear.

On the other, she believed these fair-like displays offered entertainment, but onlookers rarely gained much in the way of an accurate understanding. No one experiencing the dances and songs tomorrow would feel what she felt the first time she witnessed the celebration because they didn't have any idea what they were looking for. They didn't have a Granny who had prepared them for what they would see.

Despite these changes, Josie Mae continued the yearly trek as a way of honoring the woman who helped her discover her calling in life. In the past ten years, she hadn't brought back any new knowledge. Because of her job and family, as well as the local changes, she hadn't developed more than a casual acquaintance with the current medicine man. She respected him, and he respected her, though neither felt a strong connection.

Nonetheless, she believed going to the ceremony reminded her to keep her mind open to learning and to be willing to find answers in places others might neglect to look. It also reminded her to be aware of her intuition, the gift she first learned of when visiting the village for the first time over thirty years earlier.

As she fingered the friendship bracelet she donned each year at this time, she could still hear Granny's voice.

"Intuition is your gift, Josie Mae. Learn to listen carefully to the voice inside your head that whispers answers. You'll always have to be mindful because the voice will not be loud and bold, but quiet and unassuming. That is the way with gifts. They come with burdens, and your burden will be to figure out how to hush your mind so the intuition will not be drowned out by the noise of the world."

Josie Mae smiled at the memory. She worked her entire career to follow her intuition. She took the best of what her mama and Daniel had to teach her, the best of the granny woman, and the best of the King Eclectic Medical College in Kentucky, where she graduated.

But she hadn't stopped there. She read medical journals touting the latest breakthroughs and botany journals extolling the benefits of medicinal plants. And she never neglected to glean information from the local women and healers. Then, she tempered all her learning with the voice that never failed to whisper.

As she packed up her truck and headed down the winding mountain paths to Highway 69, which would lead her toward Cherokee, she held Granny close to her heart – knowing she was part of the tapestry of healing hands produced in the shadow of Green Mountain Gap.

About Atmosphere Press

Founded in 2015, Atmosphere Press was built on the principles of Honesty, Transparency, Professionalism, Kindness, and Making Your Book Awesome. As an ethical and author-friendly hybrid press, we stay true to that founding mission today.

If you're a reader, enter our giveaway for a free book here:

SCAN TO ENTER
BOOK GIVEAWAY

If you're a writer, submit your manuscript for consideration here:

SCAN TO SUBMIT
MANUSCRIPT

And always feel free to visit Atmosphere Press and our authors online at atmospherepress.com. See you there soon!

About the Author

TERI M BROWN came into this world with an imagination full of stories to tell. She now calls the North Carolina coast home, and the peaceful nature of the sea has been a great source of inspiration for her creativity.

Not letting 2020 get the best of her, Teri chose to go on an adventure that changed her outlook on life. She and her husband, Bruce, rode a tandem bicycle across the United States from Astoria, Oregon, to Washington, DC, successfully raising money for Toys for Tots. She learned she is stronger than she realized and capable of anything she sets her mind to. The ride was the impetus for publishing her first novel, *Sunflowers Beneath the Snow*. Her second novel, *An Enemy Like Me*, came out just one year after her first.

Teri is a wife, mother, grandmother, and author who loves word games, reading, bumming on the beach, taking photos, singing in the shower, hunting for bargains, ballroom dancing, playing bridge, and mentoring others.

Follow Teri by signing up for her newsletter at https://tinyurl.com/terimbrown or by scanning the QR code: